dirty little rendezvous

EMMA HART

dirty little rendezvous

Copyright © by Emma Hart 2016
First edition

All rights reserved. No part of this publication may be reproduced, distributed, or transmitted in any form or by any means, including photocopying, recording, or other electronic or mechanical methods, without the prior written permission of the publisher, except in the case of brief quotations embodied in critical reviews and certain other noncommercial uses permitted by copyright law.

Cover Photography by Sara Eirew
Cover Design and formatting by Emma Hart
Editing by Mickey Reed

The Burke Brothers:
Dirty Secret
Dirty Past
Dirty Lies
Dirty Tricks
Dirty Little Rendezvous

The Holly Woods Files:
Twisted Bond
Tangled Bond
Tethered Bond
Tied Bond
Twirled Bond (coming July 21st)
Burning Bond (coming September 1st)
Twined Bond (coming late 2016/early 2017)

By His Game series:
Blindsided
Sidelined
Intercepted

Call series:
Late Call
Final Call
His Call

Wild series:
Wild Attraction
Wild Temptation
Wild Addiction
Wild: The Complete Series

The Game series:
The Love Game
Playing for Keeps
The Right Moves
Worth the Risk

Memories series:
Never Forget
Always Remember

Standalones:
Blind Date
Stripped Bare (coming June 21st)

For Darryl – and the day you told me I should
write my own book.
You will always be my number one inspiration.

chapter one
Leila

"An idea? You want a goddamn *idea*?" I can't believe what I just heard. "Why don't you go and fuck a starving Venus flytrap? Then, when you're done, call me *never*."

I end the call and throw my phone on the floor. It bounces, flips over, and narrowly misses hitting the leg of my desk chair.

I throw myself onto my bed, bury my face in my pillow, and scream. *Men.* I'm literally this close to becoming celibate and purchasing twenty-eight cats. Why twenty-eight? I have no idea. It seems like a well-rounded number.

Yes—there it is. I'm going to buy a cat. I bet a cat wouldn't lie to me or use me simply because I'm the sister of all four parts of one of the world's biggest boy bands.

Maybe I need to update my Facebook. *No, I won't introduce you to my brothers right away. No, I don't have Simon Cowell on speed dial, because he isn't their manager. No, I can't introduce you to their manager, because I don't know them. And, no, I'm not going to make a sex tape with you just so you can ride my surname to get a record deal.*

Go on *American Idol* or something, fuckhead.

"Anny Lei Lei. Why you scream?"

I turn my head to the side and peer up. Mila is standing next to my bed, her bright-blue eyes wide and just visible beneath the thick mound of dark, curly hair that flops over her forehead. Poor girl needs a hairclip. Not that she'll keep it in, mind you.

"Because boys are very silly," I answer.

She pats my cheek with her soft hand. "Uh-huh." She purses her little lips and shakes her head when a curl falls into her eye. "Two dollars, pwease."

"Two dollars? I only cussed once."

"No. Two." She makes a gimme motion with her hand, flapping her fingers back and forth, and then puts her other hand on her hip. "Fuh and duh."

"What?"

"Damn," Sofie says from my doorway. "It's a cuss word now."

I sit up and stare at her. "Since when?"

"Since Tate got cocky and tried to bypass the Cussword Police." She nods toward Mila. "She's smarter than he is and sussed him out. So, now, we're all screwed. You can bill him after. She'll give you a receipt now if you ask."

"Is that tax deductible?" I mutter, opening the drawer of my nightstand while Mila watches me like a hawk.

Jesus. Three-year-olds are creepy little things.

"Here." I pull two dollar bills from the pile I keep stashed for this reason. Honestly, if anyone doesn't know about Mila and her odd little business, they'd probably think I moonlight as a stripper. "One, two." I show them to her.

She plucks them from my grip and grabs them so tight that they crinkle up. "Tankoo." She spins on her toes and runs out of the room.

"You're very welcome," I lie, watching as she disappears. My eyes travel to Sof's. "You know how people have a gaydar? I think your kid has a cuss-dar."

She nods in agreement. "Yes. I think she's actually richer than I am. Apart from the talking Pinkie Pie she was determined to buy, she's saved every one since Christmas."

"What's a Pinkie Pie?" I frown.

"My Little Pony?"

"Was that a pony when we were kids?"

"No, they're all new now. Like Twilight Sparkle and Princess Celestia."

I snort. "Sound like slang names for STDs."

She rolls her eyes, comes into my room, then sits on my bed. "Why are you throwing a tantrum?" She tucks her blond hair behind her ear.

"I'm not throwing a tantrum," I argue. "Can't a girl break up with a guy and scream without the whole world thinking she's falling to pieces?"

"Ah. I see. What did he do?"

"The usual." I grab my pillow and hug it. "Wanted to know when I was going to introduce him to my family."

"So...Conner, Tate, Aidan, and Kye," she summarizes, unscrewing the top of a water bottle I didn't notice she was holding. "Yeah. Now, the Venus flytrap thing makes a lot more sense."

I fight my smile. "Exactly! And, if we want to get right down to the point, I've only met the guy a handful of times, and he was nowhere near good enough in bed to be with me for long enough to meet my family."

Sofie spits water across my bedroom in a spray.

"Ew!"

"Sorry," she mutters, wiping her mouth with the back of her hand. "He was that bad, huh?"

"He is a man. He wouldn't take directions. That's not my fault."

She looks at me and blinks harshly. "I can't imagine why you're this single."

"I'm not single. I'm entering into a very dedicated relationship with a vibrator I'm going to order on next day delivery at the earliest opportunity, and I'm going to call the local shelter about a pussy."

Again with the blinking. "It's not that bad, Lei." She sips her water and puts the cap back on. She puts it down on the bed, and a tiny bit of liquid seeps out onto my sheets, so I grab the bottle and put it on my nightstand.

"Leaking," I mutter, rubbing at the small wet spot.

"Whatever. It's not that bad. Maybe you're just looking for love in the wrong place."

"Whoa, now. Who said anything about love? I just want a half-decent orgasm. It doesn't even have to rock my world. Just nudge it a little bit."

"All right, all right. Then maybe you're looking in the wrong place full stop. Clearly the guys who approach you are not the ones you should be giving the time of day."

I sigh heavily and lean forward, hugging my pillow tight. She has a point—I know that. And maybe I am being a little bit of a dirty liar when I say I'm not looking for love. I wouldn't mind if it found me, admittedly, and I am kinda peeking around for it, but I'm unlucky.

All the guys I find want me for my brothers. Like they think I'm the key to a record deal.

Please. I can't even sing "Twinkle Twinkle" in freaking tune.

"What am I supposed to do, Sof? I'm twenty-three years old, I'm living with my parents with no chance of moving out any time soon, I just got let go from my job, and my best dating prospects are lying at the bottom of a tub of Ben and Jerry's."

She chews on her lower lip and looks down. I can see her brain working as she thinks it over, but I'm not sure what ideas she's going to be able to come up with.

Hell, I'll be lucky to afford Ben and Jerry's next week without breaking into my savings, and I don't want to do that.

I guess that puts an end to my plan of a battery-operated boyfriend and a bunch of pussies to pet.

Sigh.

"Why don't you come to Europe?" she asks, looking up quickly. "With us. We go in two days, and we're going on the plane, so it's not like you need a ticket."

"And where am I going to sleep when we get there? On the sofa of one of y'all's suites?"

"In your own room. That's what they have their business accounts for. Plus, they're Dirty B. Who's gonna refuse them an extra room?" She waves her hand dismissively as a grin forms on her face. "Come on, please? Ella, Chels, and Jessie are all coming. It's just the second leg of the tour, so it's Paris and then the UK. And we're in London for two weeks of it."

Tempting. Very tempting. "I do love Paris. And London."

"Right? And you're never gonna get a better opportunity to go back than this."

"Go back where?" Tate pokes his head in my bedroom door.

"To London," Sofie answers without turning around.

"Aw, hell no. I don't want my little sister taggin' along!"

I throw my pillow across the room at his head. "Fuck off! Why are you even here? You don't live here."

He chuckles and grabs the pillow from the floor. I wasn't even close to hitting him.

"I know," he says, "but Mom promised to make chicken pot pie, and who am I to argue with my stomach?"

I glare at him. "So, you're here all evening? Great. That's just what I want when I'm recovering from a breakup."

"Leila, the last breakup you needed to recover from was when your credit card was suspended."

"One payment. I forgot one payment." Maybe three. Or four. I paid it in one go in the end.

Tate raises his eyebrows. "Whatever. But the fact remains: You're not emotionally traumatized. You don't need to recover from anythin'."

"Seriously," I say to Sofie. "He's in a relationship for a year and he think he's an expert."

"Actually, it's almost two years," he says, leaning against the doorframe. "So I'm more of an expert than you."

"*Actually, it's almost two years.*" Does he want a medal? Gold star?

I snort. "Hardly. Are you an expert on romance novels if you only read one or two books?"

"I'm not likely to ever read a book, let alone a fucking romance."

"Y'all are way off topic," Sofie butts in. "And, if you're not careful, Mila will be back when her F-bomb radar starts beeping."

I roll my eyes. I'm not the one throwing the F-bombs around. He is. Not that Tate Burke's swearing is surprising to anyone at all.

"True," I say. "We were talking about London and Paris."

"You're not coming to London and Paris with us." Tate shakes his head and throws my pillow back at me. "Sorry, Lei. I'm not babysittin' your ass."

"Why would you need to babysit me?"

"Single woman in foreign countries?"

"I backpacked Europe last year. Alone. And they're civilized countries, thank you very much. Plus, I don't talk to strangers."

"You screwed your way around the continent," he reminds me.

"Precisely. I don't talk to strangers. I screw them. Big difference." I grin.

"I don't know if I'm proud or not," he mutters, turning around. "You're still not coming!" he yells over his shoulder.

"If you were a guy, he'd be proud," Sofie says, reaching forward and grabbing her water bottle.

That's what I keep saying. If I had meat and two veg instead of a genital taco, he'd have patted me on the back and bought me a pint of beer.

Sexist bastard.

"You're going to come to Europe, aren't you?" She pauses with her water in front of her mouth.

I nod. I have no job, no boyfriend or even prospective boyfriend now, and all of my best friends are going. "Damn right I'm going to come."

"You're not fucking coming!" Tate yells.

"I can't believe you came," Tate mutters, hauling his bag out of the back of the car.

The bellboy takes it from him and hangs it on a hook on the cart. "I'll get those for you, sir," he says in a lilting French accent, stepping around my brother to get to the trunk.

"I told you I was coming," I reply, then quickly throw a "thank you" to the man who pulls my case from the back of our car before turning my attention back to Tate. "You were the only person who had a problem with it."

"That's because I don't trust you alone in a foreign city."

"I don't trust you alone in a local city." I snort, folding my arms and leaning against the car.

"Oh, y'all need to shut *up* already," Jessie snaps, tying her long, scarlet hair back. She winds the ponytail around and twists another hair tie around it so it's a loose bun. "It's been at least twelve hours since you started. Tate, she's here—deal with it. Lei, stop bitchin' at him, for the love of god, or my jet lag is gonna be responsible for my actions."

Aidan claps his hand over her mouth from behind. "Maybe your jet lag should make you shut up, sunshine."

"Or oodin' ah," she mumbles against his palm, elbowing him as he laughs.

"Give her a break, Tate," Conner says, lifting Mila out of the car. "It's just one three-week trip. Not even Leila can cause that much trouble in such a short space of time."

Well... That sounds an awful lot like a challenge I shouldn't take up.

"No." He points his finger at me. "That wasn't a dare."

I jut my bottom lip out Mila-style, and the kid in question giggles but quickly follows it up with a yawn. "I never assumed it was."

"Liar," Sofie mutters.

Why aren't our bags loaded yet? Can't we just check in? When did a work trip to Paris devolve into kicking Leila's ass outside a hotel after a long-ass flight?

I'd like to call unfairness. And a severe case of sibling-assholery-itis.

Kye and Chelsey finally get out of the car, and Kye rubs his hand through his messy, dark hair. "Are y'all still fightin'?"

Tate holds his hands up and darts to the side as Ella makes an attempt to cover his mouth with her hand. "Look, all I'm sayin' is that there's a good chance she"—he pauses to point at me—"will find someone to spend some *quality* time with, and I'm gonna have to break his neck for messin' with my little sister."

My other three brothers stop and stare at Tate. I frantically shake my head in defiance as that thought passes through their tiny little pea brains. That is a thought they do not need to think. At any point. Ever.

Nobody needs their neck breaking.

Except perhaps the four idiots standing in front of me.

"He has a point," Kye and Aidan simultaneously mutter, twin-style.

I stare at them all flatly. "What if I promise to put my vagina on lockdown? And I'm talking, like, metal bolt, lock and key, guarded by snakes and giant, penis-eating puppies?"

"That makes me a feel a little better," Tate acquiesces.

"Entrance only by marriage proposal," I add.

"What?" all four of them exclaim, horror flitting across their faces.

I grin widely. "Gotcha."

Sofie giggles, taking Mila out of Conner's arms. "Burke males: zero. Leila: one."

"Screw one," Chelsey says, slamming the trunk of the car after the final case has been removed. "The looks on their faces means she gets a point each. That was amazing."

"Anyone else think we should have dated girls who hate our sister?" Kye asks, watching as Ella, Sofie, Chelsey, and Jessie walk into the hotel lobby, Mila now trailing behind them, clutching Bunna's ears tight.

I sidle up to Kye's side and smile even wider. "Yeah. But then that would be no fun at all for me, would it?"

"Yes, it would," Tate argues. "You'd just piss them off all the time."

I purse my lips and consider this, slipping my arm through his as we enter the lobby of the fancy-schmancy hotel. "I suppose you're right. I would. Then again, there's no saying I can't piss my best friends off, either, is there?"

He cuts his eyes down to me, skepticism glimmering back at me. "When we're settled, before dinner, we're going over ground rules."

"Ground rules?" I gape, stopping just past the doors and unlinking my arm from his. "What the hell do you mean, ground rules?"

"Ground rules. It is what it says on the label, Lei. It's not Morse code."

"I'm also a twenty-three-year-old woman who doesn't need babysitting," I hiss when he walks away.

"We'll see." He throws a smirk over his shoulder, holds eye contact for a moment, then disappears.

I narrow my eyes.

Ground rules.

Fuck off, Tate.

I feel like I'm walking into a government interrogation. Not that I have any idea what that feels like, of course, but if I had to imagine, it would be like this.

Four famous, tattooed guys who work out a lot.

I refuse to say muscular or fit, because muscular, fit, or not, they're still my older brothers. Their fitness could eclipse Usain Bolt's and I'd still say no, thank you.

So. I'm going with four famous, tattooed guys who have a serious thing with intimidation are sitting around a table.

Ha. Sounds like I'm starting a joke.

What's the punchline, you say?

Well. That's the line *I'll* use to punch them in the heads.

Asshats.

I sit back in my chair, putting my hands together in front of me on the table. Honestly, I'm not sure if I'm ready for ground rules or a jail sentence. All four of them look kinda serious. And by kinda, I mean really.

Still, I take a deep breath and slowly meet their eyes, one after the other. It strikes me that I'm probably the only female on this world—except for my mom, but she doesn't count—who can look each of the boys of Dirty B. in the eye and not be intimidated in the slightest.

"You're all full of shit," I tell them. "I don't need ground rules."

Aidan holds one finger up. "One: no unchaperoned dates."

"Are you fucking kidding me?"

"Two," Kye adds, holding a finger up in the exact same manner Ads just did. "No dates with a guy we haven't met yet."

"Seriously. For real?"

Conner leans forward, this time holding three fingers up. "No dates with a guy you just met at the Louvre or any museum anywhere in Europe. Or national landmark. Or café. Or restaurant. Or randomly in the street."

"You're eleven months older than I am. Kiss my ass."

"Four," Tate growls, standing. He leans forward, his arms tensing as he slams both of his hands on the table.

I guess he's the one who worked out I don't need to use fingers to count to four any longer.

"Absolutely no hitting on anyone within five hundred yards of us, because we'll know."

"Can they hit on me?"

"No, because we won't know."

"That's the idea."

"Leila," Conner groans, slumping forward. "Come on. We love you. We've seen you get screwed around a hundred times this year alone, and it's just past Easter. Let us be protective assholes, okay?"

"Only if I can refer to you as human condoms," I retort, raising an eyebrow.

What? Essentially, that's what they are. Giant, rubber compressants and libido killers.

"Whatever," Aidan butts in, slapping his hands on the table. "Now I'm pretty sure it's dinnertime because I'm hungry as fuck, so can we please get food now?"

I glance at my phone, which has switched over to Paris time, whatever that is. "No!" I exclaim. "In fact, it's only lunch."

"Fuck off," he and Kye say together, standing.

"Seriously!" Conner snaps, shoving between them. "Freaky!"

And that's what happens when twins don't live together and get their freak out, my friends. You slip them together and they morph into one even freakier, verbal person.

"For real," I mutter, pushing off the chair myself.

Do they really think their rules are going to last long? I mean, don't get me wrong. I understand. They like to protect me. They need to, almost. Require themselves to. If you ask them, it's part of their kick-ass, alpha personalities.

But shit.

If being Leila Burke has taught me anything, it's that being alpha isn't a quality simply applied to males. Women can be alpha too, and I've had to be. While they're not living at home, off doing tours and appearances and radio shows, this little lady is fending for her own vagina.

I think the next three weeks will be a show of defiance to my brothers. And that's before they get a slap upside the head for being pigs.

They can enforce their rules. Hell—they can try. But they'll fail before they've even touched base because, unfortunately for them, I'm exactly like they are.

Strong-willed. Pigheaded. Stubborn-hearted.

And it's gonna take one hell of a man to break my walls down.

It's not like I haven't been around the block and figured my way out of the maze, after all. I know what they want.

"All right, fine," Tate gives in. "Let's get lunch. We can get a big-ass burger here right, Lei?"

I shrug and open the door. "How do I know? I haven't been here for a year. The French might not like burgers anymore. Wait, can you even order a burger in French?"

"*Un burger, s'il vous plaît*," Kye spurts out. "Close enough?"

"Nowhere near," I say.

Dear Lord. And they were worried about *me* coming to Paris? I'm the one who can speak French.

Tate's phone beeps as we wait for the elevator. "The girls already got an elevator, and Els says Jase is here already."

Jase?

I frown. "Jase?"

"Jase Masters. Our supportin' act," Aidan answers, jabbing his fingertip against the down button. "Some British guy the world is silently ravin' about."

"How can the world silently rave? Are they using headphones?" I question, stepping into the metal box and scanning the four of them.

They all shrug.

Almost at the same time.

Shit. They're weird as fuck. How did I never notice that?

I side-eye them as I push the button that'll take us to the lobby. I'm almost a little tempted to, you know, push a button and skirt right on outta here. Maybe go back to bed. Yeah—a nap sounds real dang good right about now.

"Hold it." Kye snatches me back by grabbing the back of my shirt. "You need to eat. You need to get on European time."

"I'm tired," I whine, although I know the real reason why I have the urge to get away.

Jase Masters. I feel like I know that name. I don't know why. If he's an up-and-coming talent, it makes sense that I'd know him right? My finger is on the pulse of the music world. I spend an unhealthy amount of time online.

Which is why I know that you don't so much as whisper the two words *One Direction* in the presence of my brothers.

The one—and only—time I did it, I got a crusty bread roll thrown at my head. Yeah.

The elevator doors ping open, and I run out before my brothers can. The hotel allows us a considerable amount of privacy, I noticed when we arrived earlier, and as I look at the frosted glass windows that line the lobby, I'm thankful for it.

Not for my brothers. But for Mila. They've chosen this life—she hasn't. My poor baby niece is assaulted by bright flashes on a regular basis.

Despite being the first to leave the elevator, I hang back as Tate, Kye, and Ads step ahead of me. Here, I grab Con's hand and squeeze his fingers tight in gratitude. Even without Mila, I know that my friends haven't quite adjusted, despite the time that's passed.

Con squeezes my hand right back. Then he looks at me and winks. He tugs me against his side and whispers, "Love you, Lei."

"I know," I whisper back. "You overprotective little fuckhead."

He pauses then laughs. He wraps his arm around my shoulders, a low chuckle escaping him. "Just don't want you jumping on top of the supporting guy," he mutters, amused, as we enter the restaurant.

"I'm not going to..." I catch sight of the guy sitting with my friends.

His name was familiar for a reason.

I know him.

And there's no worry about me jumping on top of the supporting guy, because I already did.

What kind of sick coincidence is this? The guy I met in London when I backpacked is the guy supporting my brothers on the final leg of their tour? Karma, you really are a bitch, and I didn't even do anything bad this time.

"What's up?" Con asks, stopping and turning back to me.

Apparently, I've stopped walking. "Nothing," I lie. "Nothing at all."

Nope. Nothing is wrong with the fact that I'm just feet away from Jase Masters. All six feet of him. Six feet that comes complete with dark-brown hair, piercing, green eyes, and a smile that could win over even the most coldhearted person.

I'm not even going to mention the dangerously tattooed arms or the body so chiseled that it could cut diamond. Especially since he looks hotter and more toned than he did when we first met.

Jesus.

I'm fucked.

Totally, completely, totally, utterly, totally fucking fucked.

chapter two

T his kid keeps staring at me.

I don't know why, and honestly, I don't want to ask in case they think I'm rude. She's cute though—not gonna lie.

It's not a freaky stare. Kinda not. She just looks really confused about who I am and why I'm here.

"Gape?" she asks, holding a purple grape out to me.

"Oh, I'm okay. Thank you," I refuse politely.

"No. You want gape." She shoves it toward my face, and the moment I open my mouth to refuse it once again, she puts it in my mouth.

"Mila," Sofie says, taking her hand. "You can't force-feed people. Only Papa. Sorry," she directs to me. "Conner's dad is a pushover and lets her do just about anything. Including feed him grapes."

"It's all right, honestly," I say once I've swallowed the grape. "If being force-fed grapes by a three-year-old is the worst part of my day, then I've had a pretty good day." I grin.

She smiles. "True. But, if you'd like to put it in perspective, stop by at bedtime."

"I'm gonna pass." I sip my ice-cold Coke.

"Finally," the girl with the bright-red hair groans. *What's her name again? Bessie?* "I bet they were doin' their dang hair. Bunch of girls."

I snort right before I swallow my drink, and the fizzy bubbles go up my nose.

"Oh shit! I'm sorry. I didn't mean to make you die," the redhead babbles. "Aw, crap," she mutters when Mila's hand shoots out. She pulls her bag from the floor, pulls her purse out, and pauses. "Uh, I don't have any dollars. The heck do I give her now?"

I frown.

"Mila's a human swear jar," the quiet girl with dark-brown hair tells me.

Ella. Tate's girlfriend. Her name I remember. She's cute.

"Tate cusses a lot, so she started charging. She's probably close to a thousand dollars at home." She smirks at me and leans over to the redhead. "This one, Jessie," she says, pulling a coin out. "This is one euro. Right?" she asks me.

I shrug. "I don't know. We use pounds, and I don't pay attention to most change because it's too flipping confusing. I can look though." I take the coins from Jessie's hand. "Yeah, here. These are one euro."

"Thanks. I think." She frowns as she plucks two of them from my hand and gives them to Mila. "There, trouble. These are like dollars, but they're shiny."

"Ooooh." Mila snatches them up with a chubby hand and peers intently at them, her dark hair falling in front of her eyes, shielding her from everyone's view. "So pitty."

She isn't wrong. Americans use way too many notes.

"Nice of you to join us," the second blonde drawls, staring at Kye. "Y'all needta stop to do your makeup or something?"

"Ground rules," he grunts. "You know Leila's crazy." He turns to me and holds a hand out. "Hey, man. Jase, right?"

"That's me." I stand up and grasp his hand. "Nice to finally meet you all."

"Hey." Tate steps in front and grabs my hand right after Kye, shaking it firmly. "Thanks for this. We love your stuff."

"No, thank you," I respond honestly. "This is a great opportunity, and I'm really thankful for the chance."

I meet Aidan and Conner, and then I turn toward the girl with dark hair and pursed lips.

She looks familiar.

Really, really familiar.

And, fuck, she's gorgeous.

"Jase," I say slowly, offering her my hand.

"Leila," she replies, sliding her tiny hand into mine. It's soft, but she grips tightly, and I narrow my eyes as she meets my gaze.

The brightest blue eyes look back at me, but there are tiny gray flecks around the edges of her irises. Barely noticeable unless you look hard enough, but they lend a hypnotic, silvery glint to her gaze.

Her cheeks flush pink, and she steps back, jerking her hand from my grip. Her long eyelashes fan against her skin when she blinks. Recognition hits me again. I know I've seen her somewhere before. Fucking know it.

"Have we met before?" The words escaped me before I could stop them.

Leila parts her pale-pink lips then closes them as her throat bobs with a swallow. She lightly shakes her head. "I don't think so. I don't remember you, and I'm pretty sure I would."

I quirk an eyebrow. That sounded like a compliment to me. "Are you sure? You seem quite familiar."

"Nope." She smacks those glossy lips together and pushes hair from her face.

"You've probably seen my picture before. I'm stalked because of these idiots." She nods toward her brothers and looks away from me. "Can we get food now? My stomach is contemplating jumping from my body and going on a murderous rampage to the nearest grocery store."

Sofie rolls her eyes. "You're so dramatic. You ain't that hungry."

"Starvin', Sof. Look at me." Leila pinches nonexistent fat on her stomach. I'm pretty sure she's only grabbing the material of her shirt. "I'm wasting away."

"Shut up and sit the f—fudgin' hell down," Tate snaps with a nifty look toward Mila.

I like his style.

Mila glares at him then points at herself before turning an accusatory finger on him.

"Hey, Mimi," he says. "It's two fingers." He demonstrates the correct motion.

"My don't care. Mama, my hungry," she says, turning to Sofie.

"Me too, Mi!" Leila exclaims, reaching for a chair. "Starving. Why is nobody feeding us?"

"Because you haven't ordered," I reply dryly, pulling the empty chair next to mine out.

Leila looks at it then up to me. "I can pull out my own chair."

"I don't remember insinuating that you couldn't."

"I'm just saying."

I shove the chair back under the table and sit down, holding my hands up. "Then, by all means, love, go ahead and get your own chair."

Someone coughs to hide a laugh as Leila purses her lips and grabs the chair. She yanks it out and drops onto it in a way that's so unladylike but so hilarious I have to bite my tongue to stop myself from laughing.

Shit me. Not only is she gorgeous, but she has attitude by the fucking bucketful. What is it about girls with attitude? Hot. As. Fuck.

"Where's the waitstaff?" she asks, grabbing a menu.

"Up your ass, which is where you shoved your manners," Aidan mutters next to her.

"I will cut your balls off with a breadstick, Aidan Burke."

"Shut up, Lei. Clearly, your jet lag is taking over."

"Look at that," Jessie says, peeking over her menu. "And you thought it'd be me being an insufferable pain in the butt."

"You're always an insufferable pain in the butt, sunshine," Aidan responds, looking at his own menu. "I just have a high tolerance for your crap now."

"I'm right behind your sister with a breadstick, rocker boy."

"Can we please stop discussing this? Mila's gonna be a dang millionaire if everyone carries on."

Mila grins, looking around the table. "A free coins, pwease," she says, holding her hand out. "Shiny coins. Pwease."

Well, at least she has manners. Really, she's rather polite for a girl who is demanding money for swearing.

Mentally, I make a note never to swear in front of the F-word nazi.

She'd cost me a lot of damn money—that much I do know.

"Good afternoon," the waiter says in a thick accent. "My name is Philippe, and I will be your server today. What can I get for you?"

Around the table, one by one, everyone orders, including me, until he gets to Leila. She peers over the top of her menu, her blue eyes sparkling with amusement.

"*Bonjour, monsieur,*" she greets him. She follows it up in fluent French. So fluent I don't understand what she just said at all.

"*Merci, madame,*" Philippe replies. "That will be out soon," he says, addressing all of us.

I look at her out of the corner of my eye. She picks up the water in front of her, a smug smile curving her lips, as the rest of our table either roll their eyes or shake their heads.

I get the feeling they're used to her antics.

"When the hell did you learn French?" Chelsey slams her menu on the table. "And you decided to let us all suffer before you decided to share you can speak it like the chicks in those 'French girl' paintings?"

"I learned it before I came here last year," Leila admits. "I wanted to learn basic phrases in Italian, Spanish, and French before I left. I figured I couldn't get by with my usual sweet Southern charm."

Last year.

I rub my hand over my mouth.

"Again, you let us all struggle by without helping?" Jessie asks, leaning forward.

"Got a point," Aidan mutters.

"Wait. You just spoke French? I thought it was Plutonian," Tate drawls.

"Shut up, Tate." Ella elbows him.

"Ploototeean!" Mila yells, giggling.

Sofie sighs. "Well done. Conner, swap seats."

"Why?" He looks at her, his water glass suspended in front of his face.

"Your brother. Your daughter." She waves her hand. "You deal with the ploototeean questions that will ensue."

I like her style. Not gonna lie. She knows what's up and how to delegate tasks.

"Y'all are mad," Leila mutters from behind her glass.

I lean over. "Is it usually like this?"

She snorts as they talk among themselves. "Oh, yeah. Last family dinner, it took Mom fifteen minutes to offer dessert. It's like feeding time at a safari park, never mind a zoo. She brings earplugs to dinner now."

"I can see why," I admit, looking around. Damn, they're loud. And it's not even the three-year-old yelling about plootatean stuff. I cut my eyes to Leila, letting them linger on the way her dark eyelashes, thinly coated with mascara, blink over her blue eyes for a moment. "So, you were in Europe last year?"

She freezes. "Yeah."

"You go to London?"

"No." She sips her water right as our drinks are brought over. She grasps the glass of white wine like it's a lifeline and takes a giant mouthful, bulging her cheeks out with the liquid for several seconds before swallowing. "No, just Rome, Madrid, Paris, and Barcelona."

"Seems odd. Most Americans I've met have been to the UK when they come to this side of the pond." Alarm bells ring in my mind.

I know her.

Fuck, I do.

I know it.

Who the fuck is she?

She sucks her lower lip into her mouth. She slowly releases it, digging her top teeth into the soft, pink flesh.

She arches her back, taking her lower lip between her teeth and biting down as my mouth travels down between her perky tits.

Fuck.

I know her because I fucked her.

Bloody hell.

Bloody fucking hell.

This is a clusterfuck of...well, fuckery. This is going to be a torturous few weeks. I know that without even thinking about it. It's like a neon sign blaring back at me.

Leila.

Burke.

Leila Burke. The girl I met in the coffee shop on the second floor of Waterstones, the book store, in Trafalgar Square. Who complained about the amount of people like she'd expected a tourist hot spot to be empty of that very thing—tourists. Who wondered why those "dang kids" kept climbing up on the stone lions. Who wondered why there were so many coins in the fountain and didn't believe me when I said that the coins were collected and given to charity.

The girl who took me back to her hotel room after having accepted my offer of dinner and fucked me senseless. Or let me fuck her senseless. I forget which way around it went, just that it was the kind of night you're not gonna forget.

Now I think about it, though, she never told me her surname. No wonder it never crossed my mind when my manager told me yesterday that we'd be accompanied by their sister.

I knew her as Leila. Just Leila.

"You're starin' at me," she mutters harshly.

"Sorry. Can't shake the feeling I know you. That's all."

"Well, you're makin' me uncomfortable."

"Because you know we know each other?" I lower my voice.

"I have no idea who you are," she hisses. "You have me confused with someone else."

I shrug a shoulder and turn away. I don't want to blow bubbles up my own arse, but I've been called a deity enough times to know that I'm not exactly...forgettable...in the bedroom. Either Leila is lying or...

Yeah, she's lying. She's blushing like hell. She remembers, all right. She's just pretending she has no idea who I am.

That's fine. If she wants to play that game, then I will too.

"Actually, I think you could be right." I reach for the pint of beer in front of me. Condensation coats the glass, so I grip it tight to lift it. "I just remembered meeting this American girl from South Carolina last year, and since I know you all live in South Carolina... Well. Coincidence, I'm sure."

"Probably," she says shortly. "It's not a small place."

"Did you just say South Carolina isn't small?" Jessie raises an eyebrow. "It's one of the smallest states. Maybe you should put down the wine, Lei."

I smirk into my beer. I'm not even hungry—I'm not even sure I want this beer. I'm not as nervous as I thought I would be, even given the surprise appearance of the girl sitting next to me.

Well, I say girl. She's nowhere near a fucking girl. She's more woman than the average man could probably handle, and given that I'm having to ignore my cock as it twitches every time I get an eyeful of her cleavage, I'm glad I'm not the average man.

Hey. No arse-bubble-blowing here, either. Just honest repetition of things I've been told.

"It's big compared to the UK," she argues.

"No, it ain't," Tate says. "The UK is freakin' small, Lei, but not that small."

"Oh my god." She puts her glass down. "Y'all have been pickin' on me since we left. So I'm shit at geography. How is that my fault?"

Mila's hand shoots out in front of me and she coughs.

"See? Now, you're costing me money," she mutters. "I'm gonna have to owe you, Mi. I don't have my purse with me."

"Here." I pull my wallet from my pocket and select one euro. I drop the shiny coin into Mila's hand. "Now, she owes me."

Leila turns her head to look at me. "What are you doin'?"

"Paying your debt. Now, you owe me." I grin teasingly.

"Oh, man," Sofie mutters.

"I owe you?" Leila blinks quickly.

"You got something in your eye?" I ask her.

"Yeah, the spot I'm fixin' to punch you at."

"Fixin' to? What the heck is fixin' to when it's at home?" *What the...*

"Getting ready to," she replies, frowning. "Y'all really don't say fixin' to?"

"Never in my life," I tell her. "Why don't you just say 'getting ready to'? Why complicate it with another phrase?"

She raises one curved eyebrow. "I'm pretty sure I've heard the expression 'dog and bone' for telephone, and 'apples and pears' for stairs. And you're confused about fixin' to?"

Shit. She's got me.

"That's old cockney slang," I say. "I'm not cockney."

"I heard the word..." Chelsey looks up. "Cockney," she finishes, glancing to Mila and making Kye snort. She elbows him.

"What's cockney?" Jessie asks.

"Accent or dialect spoken by working-class Londoners," Ella answers before I can. "But now just used to describe people who live in the East End."

"How do you know that?" Tate asks her.

"How did you know South Carolina is smaller than the UK?"

"Touché, Els. Touché."

"I don't actually care what cockney is," Leila says, bringing the conversation back and meeting my eyes. "I just want to know why you think fixin' to is strange, but calling a telephone after a pet and its favorite chew toy isn't."

I open my mouth to argue, but I've got nothing at all. I don't have a single word to explain that because I can't. She has a point, and it's well made.

"When did you hear those stupid phrases?" Aidan asks, tilting his head to the side.

"When she was in London, presumably," Sofie drawls. "I doubt she would have heard them here or in Italy."

"Oh. You've been to London?" I ask Leila smugly. "When were you there?"

She snaps her jaw shut and glares at Sofie. "Last year," she bites out, clearly hating every second.

"What's your favorite part?" I'm not letting up. This is too good—way too fucking good.

She swings her bright-blue eyes back to mine. They're blazing with annoyance, the metallic-gray flecks shining brightly at the edges. "Trafalgar Square," she says defiantly, running her tongue along the plump curve of her lower lip. "I just *love* how they collect the coins in the fountain and give them to charity. I think it's great."

My mouth twitches up on one side. The certainty in her eye contact has had her go from flat-out defiance about even recognizing me to a blatant throwing-out of the very place we met.

Damn.

It's gonna be a long, long few weeks.

chapter three

I slam the door to my room behind me and fall back against it.

Holy shit. Holy, holy, holy fucking fuckey fuckety *shit*.

This isn't good. Not that it needs to be said. It's pretty damn obvious that it's not good. It's as good as... I don't even have a comparison—it's *that* bad.

No, no, no.

The idea of having fun in Europe was that *I would never see them again*. No expectations, no risk, just fun. How was I ever supposed to know that the hot guy who'd sat in the corner of the coffee shop, tucked away upstairs in a bookstore that overlooked Trafalgar Square, and needed help with his song lyrics would eventually come to support my brothers on tour?

That's not how it was supposed to go.

Who thought coming back to Europe was a good idea? I should have listened to Tate. And those are six words I never thought I'd say.

He looks different. I don't think I noticed until our food was delivered. He has more tattoos now, and his jaw seems sharper than it did then. Or maybe that's just the stubble that's there now. That's new too. The stubble. I'm dang sure he wasn't that rugged and manly when we met before.

No, he wasn't. I'd have remembered him for sure if that was the case.

He never told me his last name. No wonder his name didn't set off more than a whisper of recognition. I remember meeting him as clear as day.

I tried and failed several times to get pictures on the square, so I decided that the bookshop looked like the perfect place to lose an hour. I was super happy to find the coffee shop upstairs, so I bought a book and planned the perfect afternoon. It was full though, and his table was one of the only ones with empty seats.

"Excuse me. Is there anyone sitting here?" I ask, motioning to a chair with my book.

The guy looks up and hits me with bright-green eyes. "Oh, no. Help yourself."

"Thanks." I smile gratefully and sit down, ignoring the butterflies in my stomach. Coffee,

books, and a hot guy? Hello, London. I like you. "What are you working on?" I ask after a moment of watching him write and then cross out what he just wrote.

"Song lyrics." He shrugs. "Nothing important. Just can't seem to get some wording right."

"Well, if you need another pair of eyes, my brother writes a lot of lyrics. I'd be happy to help."

"Actually, that'd be great." He sits up and holds one hand out, revealing the inking of a boat on his forearm. "Jase," he says, introducing himself.

"Leila." I slide my hand into his and shake, then reach for the notebook. "Let's see."

Now, I sigh, the memory filtering through my brain. Of course, the rest of the weekend was—and is—history, but that moment. I remember that moment so well. What I'd thought was a lucky coincidence turned into the ultimate touristy tour and dinner as a thank-you for having helped him with his lyrics, and we exchanged several very enthusiastic orgasms in my hotel room later that night.

Yep. Shit.

I bang my head against the door. This situation is a mess. Of course, if I had any sense, I'd tell my brothers I've changed my mind and get on the next flight home.

The truly unfortunate part? My sense got up and ran away the moment I locked eyes with Jase Masters. Sprinted right on out the fucking door like a little chickenshit.

"Leila!" Jessie demands from the other side of the door. A fist hammers against it, making me jump. "Open the damn door!"

"No. I'm mad at y'all!" I yell back, moving away from it.

"So help me, I'll break it down!"

"Sheesh. All right, all right." I open the door and stare at all four of my best friends. I drop my eyes to the floor, expecting to find Mila, but I don't. "Where's Mila? I thought the guys were having a business meeting?"

"Yeah, right," Sofie snorts as she strolls past me. "They're going to last ten minutes before they all ultimately decide they're hungry again. Ajax is already getting a car ready so they can go out."

"That doesn't answer the Mila question," I say, shutting the door behind Ella.

"Well, these three are shopping." Sofie points at Ella, Chels, and Jessie. "And, since Mila ultimately decided that naps are for sissies and I didn't get to sleep, I'm napping. Conner's taking her to find a park."

"Except we're all here, in your room, ready to beat your ass until you tell us how the hell you know that hottie downstairs." Ella grins. "And we couldn't tell *them* that."

My family has been such a bad influence on her. Really. She never would have said that two years ago.

"I have no idea who he is," I lie, grabbing the bottle of water I left on the side table earlier. "Honestly, I've never seen him in my life."

"Liar!" Sof punches the bed. "You kept blushing every time he looked at you."

I gape. "I do not blush!"

"Yeah, ya do. You turned the color of my hair when I brought up London."

Chelsey gasps, grabbing the edge of the bed. "The British singer!"

"No!" Ella slaps her hand over her mouth. "That's him?"

"I don't know what you're talking about," I say calmly.

Huh. Glad my voice can sound calm. My heart is thumping, and there's a chance my clit might be a little tingly at the thought of him. Just a little chance.

A big chance.

Dead certain, actually.

"Leila Burke, you tell me the truth right now!" Sofie demands, narrowing her eyes and brushing hair from her face.

Jesus. The full name, the demand, the harshness of the way she said *now*... The only other person she uses that voice on is Mila.

I glare at her. "You did not just mom-voice me."

"Oh, I mom-voiced you, all right."

"Don't ever mom-voice me again."

"Yeah, that's great and all," Jessie butts in, "but can we please get an admission over Mr. Hot Brit?"

"Hot Brit. Smooth." Chelsey nods appreciatively.

"We are not nicknaming Jase Hot Brit," I argue. "This is ridiculous. Y'all fuck off and leave me alone."

"He's the British singer," Ella says, looking at everyone before settling on me. "You're not usually this reserved."

"I'm not being reserved!"

"You are! Normally, you'd laugh it off, but you're holding it in so badly you're going to give yourself verbal constipation."

A frustrated cry escapes my mouth, and I throw myself face first on the bed. Luckily, this bed is comfy as hell, and the fluffy covers envelop me in a warm hug that clearly the heartless bitches I call my best friends are not going to provide me.

"Yep," Chelsey muses. "We've found the British singer."

"Do you think we'll run into the French artist who moonlights as a taxi driver?" Jessie asks, giggling. "Or is it the taxi driver who moonlights as a painter?"

"Why don't you go to the Louvre to find out and then bite me?" I snap, but the words are muffled by the bed.

"Hi on't ogo oov to you too."

I roll over onto my side and glare at her. I grab a pillow as I shuffle up the bed and lean against the headboard. "What am I going to do?"

"Find another French taxi driver?" Chelsey offers.

"Not helpful, Chels," Ella whispers.

"Shit. Sorry."

I rest my head back against the wooden board. "Okay. This situation is totally manageable, right?"

I mean, it's not the end of the world. We're all adults here. So we had sex. That's not a big deal. People who have sex see each other all the time. Granted they're usually in a relationship, but it's just sex. We didn't have an emotional heart-to-heart, and our souls haven't fused together, so I'm gonna say we're good.

"Sure. As long as you consider we'll all be traveling together for the next three weeks, across two countries," Sofie offers up.

"There'll be a lot of time when they'll need to work."

Ella grimaces. "Not as much as you want them to be working."

"You're the Dirty B. schedule organizer. Give them more work to do."

She pulls her phone out and, two seconds later, shakes her head. "Can't. Between promo visits, sound checks, meetings, practices, the necessary family and down time... Sorry, Lei."

"Well, I can avoid them. It's not like I'm a stranger to exploring strange places on my own."

"Really?" Chelsey says dryly. "You're going to avoid everybody for the next three weeks?"

"Not everybody. Just...him." Maybe I'm not quite the grown-up I thought I was. Apprentice adult seems more like it.

"You wanna hire a boyfriend?" Jessie asks. "We could do that."

See? She's always got my back.

"Jessie. No." Chelsey hits her. "Don't be dumb."

"Don't be me. Ah! I give up. I want to go home," I groan.

"No, you don't," Sof says.

"You're right. I don't."

"Can we hold on a minute?" Ella says, tugging her legs behind her on the spare bed. "We're all wondering how you're gonna cope with this...strange...situation, but nobody has considered the real problem here."

I frown, and we all share a look before focusing on her.

"We have a bigger problem than the fact that I screwed Jase Masters over a year ago and I still get turned on when I think about him?"

They all burst into giggles.

So. Didn't mean to say that out loud.

This is awkward.

"Yes," Ella forces out, and then she coughs to compose herself. "When your brothers find out, they're going to kill him."

We all sober immediately.

"Oh, hell," I whisper, then hesitate, stilling. "They can't find out!"

Oh, man. She's right. They'll lose their minds if they ever know.

And I'm gonna have to talk to him.

"Shit, no." I scratch slowly at my chin. "Someone is gonna have to grab him and warn him that the Burkes aren't fond about their sister being a real-live, thinking, breathing, sexual human being, so what may or may not have happened in London between us needs to be forgotten and our prior connection dismissed."

"Leila." Sofie shakes her head. "You're going to have to talk to him. We're not doing it for you."

"That's so unfair."

"You wanted to come with us."

"You suggested it!"

She shrugs, grinning. "And? I was joking."

"Why did nobody tell me he was going to be here?" I rest my chin on my pillow and sigh heavily.

It wouldn't have mattered, of course, but still. I can totally throw that out there. I can lament the fact that I didn't get all the details of the tour before I made an informed decision.

I'm going to blame Tate and his insistence that I couldn't come. It made me want to come more just to annoy him. Damn it, Tate.

I don't want to acknowledge the fact that we've met before. I mean, hell's fucking bells on heroin, I'm physically well acquainted with Jase Masters.

But he got hot.

So hot.

Hotter than should be legal. I shouldn't be expected to exist under these conditions. What did I ever do for Karma to hate me so?

"She looks like she's torn between talking to him or fucking him," Jessie remarks.

"Well..." I say, dragging the word out and almost considering it.

Well, dang. Now, I am considering it.

"I can't. My vagina is grounded," I correct myself, cutting that line of thought off. Nope, I don't need to think about the specifics of being under, around, over, and in front of Jase Masters.

It's sad that I'm familiar with all four places.

This is why I can't be expected to talk to him. I don't want to play this game.

"Fine," I murmur. "I'll talk to him. Tomorrow. I want to go explore right now before I pass out on this bed."

Ella sighs. "You won't talk to him tomorrow though, Lei. You'll avoid it, him, and everyone else by leaving early in the morning and returning super late."

I bite the inside of my lip. Shit. How did she know what I was thinking?

"She's right." Sofie tucks her hair behind her ear and swings her feet against the side of the bed. "You do have a penchant for avoiding awkward situations. One I share, admittedly. But still. The longer you leave this, the more awkward you know it's going to be."

"It's just going to get harder," Chelsey inputs.

"Really, really hard." Jessie fights to keep a straight face.

I hate them all, because now, I'm grinning. "You say that like it could be a bad thing."

"Bad girl." Chelsey throws a stick of gum at me.

"You brought up hardness!" I unwrap the gum and put it into my mouth before chewing. Mint explodes on my tongue.

"You're so screwed." Sofie catches the stick Chelsey passed over to her.

"She wishes," Jessie whispers, her eyes lighting up with her smile.

"Y'all are bad influences," I huff out and get off the bed, making sure to replace the pillow. "If anyone yells at me for this, I'm going to blame you guys. And I'm still not going to talk to him until tomorrow, no matter what you say."

They look at me skeptically as I resign myself to the fact that I have to talk to him tomorrow morning before breakfast. They really do have a point—it will just get worse if I don't address it.

I mean, my gut wants to address a plane ticket to South Carolina, but that won't exactly make the problem go away, because then I'd need an excuse as to why I'm leaving.

Like it or leaving it.

I guess I'm leaving it, because I'm sure as heck not liking it.

Ella: *Room 312.*
Ella: *Leila? Wake up.*
Ella: *Leila, don't make me send Mila in.*
Ella: *ROOM 312. ROOM 312. ROOM 312. ROOM 312.*
Ella: *Go and speak to him right now or I'm waking Tate to tell him you fucked Jase.*
Me: *Fuck you very much.*
Ella: *:)*

She can smile all she likes. Fuck her very much indeed. Seriously? Five text messages? Like she didn't know I was ignoring her. On second thought, though, that's exactly why she did it. She knew I'd get pissed off and respond, thus confirming I'd seen the messages...

Sigh. Her mind games are bananas. Usually, I love them, but they're distinctly frustrating when they're on you.

Note to self: Get her back.

I liked her more before Tate had fully corrupted her and rubbed a bit of his assholish personality off on her.

I slip my feet into my shoes and look in the mirror. I don't know why I'm so worried about the way I look. It's not even eight in the morning, but I've showered, dried my hair, and done my makeup. I shouldn't be this concerned when he might not even be awake yet.

Me: *Is he awake?*
Ella: *Yes. I already texted him.*

Of course she did. She knows what she's doing, that one. Sneaky little snotface. It's a good thing I love her, isn't it?

I take a step forward and then stop again. I find my own eyes in the mirror. Butterflies are having a disco in my stomach, and honestly, I want to be sick. I'm ridiculously nervous, and as much as I want to slap myself for being an idiot, I can't because my hands are trembling.

Get it together, Leila.

I'm such a dick.

Pinching the bridge of my nose with my finger and my thumb and closing my eyes alleviates some of the pressure I'm feeling. A little. Not at all, really. I'm lying through my goddamn teeth.

Teeth.

I need to brush my—no, I don't. Damn it.

My phone buzzes, and I press the home button.

Ella: *Have you left your room yet?*
Me: *Yes.*
Ella: *Liar.*

Oh my god. She's watching me. This isn't what my parents were talking about when they discussed peer pressure with me, folks. Or maybe it was. I was never much bothered about peer pressure. Probably because I'd just tell everyone where to go.

With a heavy sigh, I resign myself to the fact that I have to do this. I have to stamp the butterflies out, swallow the nerves back, shake the apprehension off, and go on and do this.

Being an adult is fucking hard, man. I'd be way more prepared for it if I had been taught how to talk to people instead of algebra.

I can legit say I've never used algebra. Ever. In my life.
And never will I, either.
Okay. No more procrastinating.
Oh, god. Why is it always easier to think than do?
Jesus Christ, Leila. You had sex with the man. If your best friend can come home and reveal her secret baby girl, you can talk to a man you fucked.
I nod at my own thought. Perspective.

I grab my room key and my phone and leave my room. True as hell, Ella is standing in the doorway to her and Tate's room, her head poking around and down the hall. I stick my middle finger up in her direction, and she laughs quietly, watching as I shut my door and head to the elevator to go down a floor.

Every sound is ominous to my flighty self. The scrape as the doors open, the beep as I press the button for floor three, and the slide as the doors close again. Even the whirring of the metal box as it propels me downward is terrifying.

Dear Karma, if I survive this, will you give me Zac Efron? As he is now, all hunky and stuff. Not High School Musical *Zac. Kthanks.*

That doesn't seem like too outlandish a request given my current predicament.

The elevator stops way too quickly, and the doors open in front of me. Kinda feels like I'm walking to my doom. I'm sure as hell not going toward a boom, I'll tell you that.

I run my fingers through my hair as I read the sign that directs me to room numbers. Left. So I go left. Smooth my hair. Keep going left. Scratch my neck. Keep moving. Shiver.

Walk past his room.

"Shit," I whisper, doing an about-face and turning back to his room.

Okay. I've got this. I know I do.

I knock on the door before I can wuss out then step back. *Deep breath, Leila. It's not that bad.*

The door opens, and Jase fills the doorway.

Shirtless Jase.

Sweats hanging low on his hips.

Tatted arms at his sides.

Broad shoulders bare.

Abs traceable by sonar showing.

Lick-me lines on display.

Nope.

Deep breath ain't gonna do it.

"Hey," he says in a husky voice, like he's just woken up. "I thought we didn't know each other."

I purse my lips and meet his eyes. Boy, is it ever hard to look at his face and not his abs.

Fuck, those abs. You could eat yogurt out of those things.

"Can we talk, please?" I ask.

"Sure." He steps to the side and opens the door for me to pass him.

I take a deep breath as he runs his hand through his hair. Darting past him, I do my best to keep my eyes everywhere but his body. This is literally so awkward. I want to stare at the intricate ink that coats his arm and the boat that hugs his other forearm, but I can't. I can't look at the hard, defined body that I'm ninety-eight percent sure is a weapon of mass destruction.

That's it.

This is how the world gets us women, should we ever rise up against the men. With hot guys who have hot accents and hot bodies. 'Cause, I swear, I'm like Dracula in sunlight where Jase Masters's body is concerned.

It's also why I didn't want to talk to him.

"What's up?" he asks, closing the door and folding his arms across his chest.

Jesus, I wish he hadn't done that. I blink harshly and force myself to drag my focus away from his bulging biceps and to his face.

Where he's wearing an amused smirk and his eyes are lit up with a knowing glint.

"You know what's up," I fire at him before I can get distracted completely. "As far as anyone outside this room is concerned, we've never met, and we recognized each other by coincidence. Maybe I saw you playing in London when I was there and forgot."

He raises a questioning eyebrow and walks around me to the table, where I notice there's a platter of fruit set out. He grabs a small, empty plate and offers it to me, shrugging when I shake my head. He piles it full of fruit and goes to sit on the edge of the sofa.

I guess I'm the only one without a suite. Figures.

"You can sit down. I only bite on request." He flashes me a grin and puts a grape into his mouth.

"I might ask."

"I'd be hard-pressed to refuse."

I roll my eyes although I was the one to stoke the fire and perch on the corner of the L-shaped couch. "I'm not here for a slow breakfast chat, Jase."

"I figured. You look like you're going to bolt as soon as I come within touching distance of you."

"Are you going to?"

"Maybe. Although it might only be to throw you out before I get tempted."

I won't ask. "To do what?" *Or maybe I will.*

He cuts his startling, green eyes toward me before shaking his head and putting the fruit plate down next to him. On a long, shuddery exhale, he says, "Please get to the point, Leila."

"Fine. My brothers don't know about our prior connection, and they can't know about it, or they're gonna rip your balls off with their toenails."

"A little more graphic of a point than I was going for, but it works." He laughs low. Huskily.

His laughter is like a warm hug.

"I don't beat around the bush. While it might be a slight exaggeration, the preparation is necessary," I tell him.

"Do you really think you can keep this a secret, love?" Jase captures my gaze with his, and the question burns in his eyes, his curiosity a genuine stoker of the fire that I know is searing inside him. "That we can pretend to be complete strangers?"

"As long as you stop calling me 'love,' I think we'll be just fine."

He shuffles forward on the sofa and bends over, resting his elbows on his knees. His tattooed arms tense, and it should be harder to keep my eyes on his, but...it isn't.

His gaze is compelling. The swirling, green mass of emotion is hypnotic, and I'm locked in on his eyes, unable to comprehend anything but them. But him.

I don't like it.

My flight instinct is roaring to life, consuming me, gripping every part of my body. I should have listened to my doubts. Should have run before. Should have gone. Should have gotten the motherfuck outta Dodge.

"Really? Just fine? You don't look fine to me, Leila, love." He didn't say it maliciously. Just matter-of-factly. "You're blushing, your lips are parted, and your chest is heaving. I don't have to be an expert to see that you're affected by me, and there's three foot of space between us."

Three foot. Why is that so goddamn charming?

"I'm hungry," I lie. "Plus it's kinda hot in here."

"You and I can't pretend we don't know each other." He gets up, walks to the entertainment unit, then opens a cupboard. It reveals a fridge inside, and he pulls out two bottles of water, no bigger than his fist. He passes me one then opens his and drinks it.

A tiny drop escapes the corner of his lips as he lowers the bottle, and I watch as it trails down his skin and gets caught in the dark-brown stubble coating his chin.

I swallow. Hard. "Sure we can," I say quietly. "It won't be hard."

"Leila..." Jase takes a deep breath and looks away.

My eyes skim over his body, but I gather my composure and stand, fiddling with the cap on my bottle of water. "It's not hard." A shiver runs down my spine as the effects from my name having rolled off his tongue hits me. "We just pretend. You're a rock star. Are you telling me you don't pretend every day of your life?"

"Oh, I do. Every day," he says in low voice, turning back to me. His eyes are even more intense than before. "I pretend I'm not tired or that I don't mind getting a cramp in my arm from signing everything from T-shirts to tits. I don't pretend that

I've forgotten one of the most memorable twenty-four hours of my life. I don't pretend that I can't remember a fucking thing about the attitude-filled Southern beauty I'll be forced to face every single day."

I draw in a sharp breath. "Well," I say, taking a step back and bumping into the sofa. "Maybe you should get to practicin' that."

His arm twitches, and he closes the distance between us in one large step. His body is right in front of mine, his lips inches from mine. As I struggle to breathe, our exhales mix and play in a tension-filled dance that tingles across my skin, from my mouth right down to my toes. I fight a shiver that threatens to cascade across my skin and reveal the truth about how my body is responding to his proximity.

He raises his hand to my jaw and cups my chin, his thumb less than a breath away from my lower lip, and I fight not to close my eyes as lust skitters through my veins.

"I went to stage school," he whispers. "But I sure as fuck failed acting."

"No kidding," I whisper right back. "You shouldn't be touching me."

"I know." He lets out another long, shuddery breath. "But we can't pretend, Leila. I can't. You might be able to lie and tell me you don't know who I am, but you do. Don't insult me and pretend I'm nothing more than a stranger."

I bite my lower lip, drawing it between my teeth. Jase's eyes drop, focusing in on my mouth. He watches as I gently release my lip then touches his thumb to it. Green eyes flicker up to mine, and that's the last thing I see as he dips his head and my lips are taken by his.

chapter four
Jase

The tastes of mint and coffee mix together richly on her lips as I cover them with my own.

This is a bad idea.

She is a bad idea.

And an even worse idea is her sliding her hands around my neck, dropping the water bottle so it hits the floor and explodes over the carpet.

The worst idea is my circling her body with my arms and pulling her against me.

I'm a fucking idiot, I know. I'm a fool and a total dick, but damn, I'm fucked if I want to pull away from her.

She's right. We do need to pretend that we don't know each other. I don't want to jeopardize my place supporting Dirty B. on the final leg of the tour, but keeping my hands off her is going to harder than I imagined.

I didn't imagine she'd be here though. I didn't ever consider that, when I walked out of her hotel room some year ago, it would ever be possible that I'd see her again.

I thought she'd live to be nothing more than a glorious memory, full of happiness.

Leila gasps as I break the kiss, but I don't let her go. She trails one hand down so her nails gently drag across my bare skin, almost tickling me, causing me to bite a happy shudder back as the sensation goes straight to my cock.

"Bad idea," she whispers before inhaling sharply. "Very, very bad idea."

"I know." My voice is just as breathless as hers. Fuck, I didn't know I missed that kiss. I didn't know you could miss something you'd barely experienced, but I'm finding out right now you can, and I do. "Still think we can hide it?"

She licks her lips in response.

Fuck, it's tempting to kiss her again.

"Yes." She pauses before extracting herself from my arms and darting around me. She bends over to pick up the water bottle she dropped when I kissed her, and I still, staring at her arse. Her light-blue jeans hug it tight, stretching over her curved backside.

"Are you starin' at my ass?"

Bloody hell, that accent is hot. "Beautiful, if you're gonna bend over in front of me, you bet your arse I'm gonna stare at it."

She snaps up to standing, and I deliberately adjust my trousers over my erection. I didn't need it, as it's not uncomfortable, but she saw it, so she's gotten the message.

I'm turned the heck on and all I've done is kiss the girl. Once.

Leila shoves the almost-empty water bottle at me. "Do you have a paper towel or anything I can use to clean this mess up?"

Instantly, my eyes drop to her mouth and linger there for a long second.

"Dang it, Jase!"

I guess that, by mess, she doesn't mean the way her lips are wet and swollen.

I laugh. "It's just water, but there are towels in the bathroom. Right there." I point to the door I can just about see from here. "Get me one too."

She disappears for two seconds while she grabs some, and then she comes back out. She glances up at me with a playful glint in her eye then throws the towel at me before I can react. It hits me in the face, and I grab it as it falls.

She laughs quietly and kneels to mop up the water. I get down to the floor with her and help her clean the mess up. I don't know why she's so fussed—it's just water, and it's not even a lot.

Although, from this angle...I have a really, really great view down her shirt, so I'll be damned if I'm gonna tell her to stop cleaning.

Shit. She's turning me into a creep.

Already.

I'm fucked.

Leila stills, her arm still outstretched, her towel in the middle of the wet patch on the carpet, and lifts her head. Our eyes meet, and she smacks her lips together.

"You're starin' down my shirt, aren't you?"

"If I say yes, does that make me a pervert, considering I was just enjoying the view of your bum?"

She takes a deep breath then shuts her mouth, looking to the ceiling, clearly contemplating my question. "No... But only because I like the way you called my ass a 'bum.'"

"You don't call it a bum?"

"Butt."

"But what?"

"No, butt." She laughs. "We call asses butts."

"So do we. Sometimes." I sit back on my heels and stare at her, one of my eyebrows twitching upward. "It's beginning to occur to me that Americans speak rather oddly."

"Rather oddly." She grins, sitting back herself. "I'm just gonna start askin' you to say random things, okay? Like...garage."

"Garage?" Now, I frown.

And hear it.

She says gah-rarge. I say garridge.

The hair on my arms stands on end as her giggle fills the room. She looks down, covering her mouth with her hand, and her hair falls in a dark curtain across her face.

"What's so funny?"

She peers up, dropping her hand, and sinks her teeth into her lower lip as she beams a smile at me. "I just love your accent. That's all. It's pretty much the best thing ever. Gah-ridge," she attempts.

"That's the worst attempt at a British accent I've ever heard in my life," I tell her, shaking my head and taking the towel from her. I stand then hold my hand out to help her up.

She glances at my outstretched palm for half a second before she wraps her fingers around mine and I tug her up to standing.

We hold the touch for a little too long.

She coughs and steps back, running her hand through her hair so it falls in a haphazard mess around her shoulders. Messy and rough... Just-fucked hair.

"We, er." She rubs the side of her neck as she lets her hand fall back to her side. "I've gotta go," she eventually ekes out. "I promised Mila muffins for breakfast, and then I'm going to be a horrible tourist."

I smile. Ah, yes. That hatred of tourists.

"Where are you going today?" I ask.

She shrugs, her lips turned up at the edges, and backs toward the door. "Wherever I feel like."

"Wherever you feel like?"

"Paris isn't a city you plan. It's a city you...experience." With that, she allows me one last look at her pretty smile and leaves me.

Experience.

Huh.

⁂

I've never been to Paris in my life.

France, even. It's strange when you think about how close it is to London. Maybe an hour or so on a plane, yet I've never done it.

Leila's words before she left my room have been swirling in my mind all day. We have two days until the first concert, and with this morning's early rehearsal out of the way, I'm starving and need something to eat. Staying in the hotel would be the simple option, mostly because I'm certain we're being spied on by fans outside, but I can't help but think that Leila's right.

Planning is too easy. There's no fun in it, really. After all, the next few weeks are planned right down to the wire, except for the precious hours that are for ourselves.

Why should I waste time planning when I can experience?

I slip my shoes on, and after shoving my wallet into my pocket, I leave my room. Something seems a little strange about planning to explore Paris alone, but I'm up for the challenge.

As long as I can find food first. You don't see Indiana Jones busting shit open on an empty stomach.

The elevator doors ping open in the lobby, and I double-check the time to make sure I'm not just imagining that it's lunchtime. There's a chance my stomach has taken my mind over before and I've eaten a full lunch at ten in the morning.

I think it's a male thing. Definitely a male thing.

"Going somewhere?"

I pause in the middle of the lobby at the sound of her voice and then turn. Leila's sitting on one of the sofas, her face in a book. She's not even looking at me.

"I'm going to...experience," I say, trying not to laugh.

"Are you going to experience lunch by any chance?"

"How did you know?"

"Because my intestines are trying to escape my stomach's ravenous hunger clutches—that's why." She puts a bookmark between the pages and closes her book. "There's a great place not too far from here. Right on the corner, best food ever. I went there when I was here before."

"Are you asking me out for lunch?" I raise my eyebrows.

"Of course not," she replies calmly, tucking her book into her bag and standing. She looks up at me with those blue eyes, but they're dancing with mischief, the gray flecks only enhancing the playfulness. "I'm not allowed to hit on anyone. It's in the ground rules. I'm simply being polite. Not to mention I had a feeling you'd go and experience Paris on my advice, and there are so many things wrong with a man doing anything without knowing where he's going."

"So, you can go and experience Paris without a map, but the second a man does it, it's not okay?"

"Not so much 'not okay.' More to the point that you're more likely to get lost than I am. Being male."

"There's an insult in there somewhere, I'm sure." I grab the door and hold it open for her.

"Thank you." She flashes me one of those cheeky smiles and passes through to outside. She slips her sunglasses down off their perch on the top of her head so they cover her eyes and sighs happily when the sun hits her skin.

I fall into step beside her. "I thought you were going to experience Paris this morning."

"Well, I was. But then I went back to my room and took a nap."

I look at her out of the corner of my eye. "That was quite the change of the plans."

"Jet lag." She shrugs a shoulder. "I didn't sleep until really late last night, and then I woke up early."

"It's harder coming forward, right? I remember when I went to Disney as a kid. It wasn't too bad going to Florida, but when we came back, it was quite hard to adjust."

"Yeah. I found it relatively easy when I came to Europe last time. I'm not really sure why." She tucks her hair behind her ear, tilting her face up toward the sun. "I forgot how pretty Europe is. There's just somethin' real charming about it."

"Really? You think so?"

"Well, yeah." She looks at me—I think. I can't tell through the dark lenses of her glasses. "Look at the buildings here. All the cute flower boxes. They're so bright and colorful, and they lend a kind of...magic...to the old buildings. I think I could walk for hours through the random streets here, doing nothing but stare."

"How romantic of you," I tease her.

"Hey. You should try it sometime."

"Will I 'find myself' along the way?"

"I don't know. Are you lost?"

"By your standards, yes. I'm male."

She laughs, her head falling back a little. "You joke, Jase, but I learned more about myself in the three months I was in Europe than I have in my entire life."

"Why? Because you could do what you wanted?"

"I'm not sure. Oh, here's the place!" She grabs my arm and tugs me toward the restaurant on the corner.

Cute really is the only way to describe it. Cute red canopy, cute wooden tables with cute decorations... Yeah. Cute. Exactly the kind of restaurant one could potentially find themselves at.

Assuming one is lost, of course.

Mentally, I'm good.

Physically? Not a fucking clue, and we've only been walking for ten minutes. Maybe she has a point about the direction thing.

"*Bonjour, monsieur,*" she greets the guy at the door. "*Avez-vous une place pour deux personnes?*"

"*Oui, mademoiselle.*" He smiles and grasps two menus. "*A l'intérieur ou à l'extérieur?"*

Leila turns back to me, still holding my arm. "Inside or outside?"

I guess that's what he just asked. I look around. We're in a relatively quiet place, and I don't see anyone with a camera who might be overly interested in me...

"Wherever you want to sit."

"*L'extérieur, s'il vous plaît.*" She smiles at him, glances at me, and then, as if she's realized she's still touching me, drops my arm like I'm on fire.

We both follow the host to a table tucked against the window, and I pull Leila's chair out for her before she can grab it herself. She gives me a pursed-lipped, amused smile, her eyebrows creeping above her sunglasses, and sits down.

"*Merci, monsieur.*" She keeps her focus on me as she takes the menu from the host.

Jesus fucking Christ. An American with her Southern drawl should not be able to pull the French language off that well. Especially not with perfect pronunciation.

Amazing. She can speak French, but she can't say *garage* correctly.

The mind boggles.

"You appear to have an issue, Jase," she says without looking up from the menu. "And it's a severe case of staringitis."

"Then get ugly," I mutter. Petulant, I know, but it's the only cure I can think of right now.

She tilts her head forward and peers at me over the top rim of her glasses. "Or get manners."

I grab the menu and whip it in front of my face. "Should've experienced Paris alone."

She laughs but doesn't say anything in response.

I turn my attention to the menu, happy it's in English, because now, all I can think about is looking at her. Given that, some four hours ago, our conversation was about how we're not supposed to know each other, I'm thinking that everything that's happened since is completely contradictory.

Granted, I kissed her, but I didn't mean to.

I slipped and fell onto her mouth, and that's the official line if anyone asks.

Nobody will ask, of course, because we just met at dinner last night so there's no reason to ask.

Jesus. Now, I'm paranoid.

The host comes back over to take our order. She, of course, answers in fluent French, but I happily point to what I want on the menu and order that way. We're shaded by the canopy over our heads, but Leila still has her glasses on.

"Why do you still have your glasses on?" I ask her as our drinks are brought to us.

"I've had lunch enough times with my brothers. The media know they're here, and if what I hear about you is true, I'm going to be in the papers tomorrow as your mystery date." She picks her glass of white wine up and sips.

"If what you 'hear about' me?"

Her forehead furrows. "So, you're not some big and fancy up and coming superstar?"

"Well...I don't know. I mean, I guess. Could be." I shrug.

I always find it awkward to talk about the success I've had. I think it's because I'm all too aware that I could wake up tomorrow and it could all be gone, and that thought is quite terrifying. I wouldn't refer to myself as big, fancy, or a superstar. Up and coming? Perhaps. That just makes sense. But the rest? No.

"Hm." She looks away, down the street, and doesn't say anything further.

I hide my confusion behind my glass of Coke. I have no idea what she meant by *hm*. I don't want to know what she meant by it. I shouldn't want to know what she meant by it.

So, why am I bothered?

I don't know that, either.

One thing I do know: Leila Burke is unlike anyone I've ever met.

And I'm not sure it's that much of a good thing.

chapter five
Leila

"My feet are fallin' off!"

Jase laughs. "What do you expect me to do? Haul your arse over my shoulder and carry you back to the hotel?"

I sigh at the thought. "That would be amazing."

"Or we could just get a taxi."

"Or we could Uber. That would be cheaper. Right?" I look across the bench at him.

He shakes his head, smiling. "The funniest part about all this is, this morning, you were all for experiencing, and now, you want to get an Uber back to the hotel."

"Well, you're not going to carry me, are you? And I've never gotten an Uber in Paris, so therefore, I'm experiencin' it."

"You have an answer for everything, don't you, love?"

"Is that a rhetorical question, or did you want an answer?"

I hate it when he calls me *love*.

Actually, I'm lying.

I don't hate it at all. But I do strongly dislike it. Not because of the rich way it rolls off his tongue, or the way his lips twitch whenever he says it, or how it tingles across my skin and makes me want to wrap myself around him like a koala bear, but because—

No, no. It's... *Oh, sigh*. It's because it sounds so damn good that I want to climb him like a tree whenever he says it. Whoever created the British accent has a lot to answer for.

I think the funniest thing about my feet hurting is that we haven't walked far. We haven't even been gone that long. Maybe three hours, including lunch, and that in itself was almost an hour.

I'm aware of the fact that I'm going to have some serious explaining to do when I get back to the hotel, because I've already gotten three texts from Tate demanding to know—

My phone buzzes in my hand, so let's make that four texts.

"You're popular," Jase remarks, glancing at my phone.

"Is it popular if the person who keeps texting you is your overprotective big brother?" I ask, swiping the screen to open it. Yep, sure as hell, it's Tate.

Tate: *Where are u? Why are u ignoring me?*

He's so needy.

Me: **you*

Jase coughs. "Did you just correct his grammar via text?"

Vy-ah. He just said vy-ah. Not vee-a. *Oh. My. God. Down, clitoris. Down.*

"Yes," I say. "This isn't nineteen ninety nine. He doesn't need to push buttons eleventy billion times to write the word 'you' anymore."

Tate: *YOU are fucking pissing me off.*
Me: *Ten points for Slytherin.*

I giggle and lock my phone. Jase snorts next to me and leans back on the bench, stretching his legs out. The clouds that have been playing with the sun for the last fifteen minutes finally win the fight and slowly move in front of it, dimming its brightness and dulling the shadows that have been cast by its position behind the majestic Eiffel Tower.

"That is kinda mean," Jase reasons when Tate messages me yet again, this time with a simple *Fuck you*, and I put my phone on silent.

"No, it's not. Not really." I tuck it into my purse and push my sunglasses on top of my head. "He's annoying me. I have a rape alarm in my purse. I'm pretty safe."

"What if someone mugs you then attacks you?"

"Then I scream like fuck, kick them in the balls, and run."

Jase winces, his hand moving to his crotch. "I'm not going to question you further on that."

"Good. I'd hate to get graphic."

He raises an eyebrow as he looks at me. His eyes are so expressive. I know that people say they're the doorway to a person's soul, but personally, I think Jase Masters's soul has taken up residence in his eyes. He shows everything in them.

It's real alarming that I'm already figuring this out. I shouldn't be figuring this out or thinking about his soul. Not after such little time together. Like, you know, twenty-four freaking hours.

"You'd hate to get graphic," he says flatly. "That contradicts everything I know about you."

"You don't know anything about me."

"True. I shouldn't know anything, either. I'm actually rather fond of all my body parts, so I'd hate for your brothers to feel the need to remove any of them."

I laugh and drop my head back. I close my eyes as the clouds part and the sun peeks out between them, bathing my face in a gentle warmth. "Don't worry. We're not breakin' any of their ground rules."

"Wait—you're not kidding about the ground rules? That's a thing?"

"Oh, yeah." I turn my face toward his and shield my eyes from the sun with my hand. I squint to see him clearly. "They're serious about the big-bad-protective-brother act. All four of them. Never mind that those pains in the ass would have defied all those rules if they were the guy after the girl." In fact, I'm ninety percent sure they did. Aidan sure as heck did, and Kye... Well, he was simply persistent with Chelsey.

Tate and Ella and Conner and Sofie were different situations. They had twists like things out of a romance novel. Aidan and Kye, like the twins they are, were both annoying.

It's funny, isn't it? They've set me rules they'd break themselves.

All because I'm a girl.

Assholes.

"Probably. But that is their job: to be protective. My brother is twenty-eight and treats me like I'm twelve," Jase says after a minute, looking down at me, shielding his face from the sun the way I am. "I ignore it."

"But you have one. I have four. Have you ever tried to ignore four really, really irritating people?"

"I'm a hot British singer. What do you think?"

My lips twist to the side. "And there I thought you were being all humble over lunch. It was an act, wasn't it?"

"No... Hot British singer is a fact. I'm British, I sing, and I'm boiling right now."

I sit up straight and turn my body to him. "That's not the kind of hot you meant and you know it."

He rests his bicep across the back of the bench and leans his head on his hand. His inked skin stretches against the relatively tight, white fabric of his T-shirt, and I look at it ten too many times before forcing myself to meet his eyes.

"Prove it," he dares me.

I prod his arm. "Proof. You wouldn't have tensed that if you didn't mean handsome-hot."

"You think I'm handsome-hot?"

"Boy, this conversation escalated real quick." I spin and look away.

Right into the sun. Ouch. Blinded. Ouch.

I yank my glasses down to cover my eyes. "Did we decide on that Uber yet?"

I make to stand, but he grabs my hand and tugs me back down onto the bench. I gasp when my butt hits the hard wooden seat, but he only laughs that deep, rumbling, husky laugh of his. Goose bumps erupt across my skin, covering my arms in tiny little spots, and I take a deep breath.

Somehow, I smile.

"Do you think I'm handsome-hot?" Jase asks again, his green eyes blazing at mine.

I shake my head. "I'm not allowed to answer that," I whisper. "Ground rules."

Yes, my body whispers. *You're handsome-hot as fucking hell, man. Now, shut up.*

"I don't have rules," he says quietly, his face moving closer to mine. "In fact, I'm well acquainted with more than a touch of rule-breaking."

I swallow hard. I can feel his exhales as they ghost across my lips. Oh, god. Not again. Not already. There can't be another kiss already. I don't know if my... well, my vagina...can take it.

My restraint might not. It's amazing how one little trigger can make a million memories come flooding back. And it's never a gentle trickle, is it? Oh, no. When the memory flood comes, it makes sure it comes with the power of a tsunami and the destructive power of a thousand armies stampeding through your own personal sanctuary.

I'm not ready for anyone to be the army that stampedes my sanctuary. Least of all Jase.

"I still can't answer that. I plead the Fifth," I finally whisper, forcing the words past my dry throat.

He trails two fingertips up my bare arm, coasting them across my shoulder, breaking contact for the strap of my tank top. He carries on despite the shiver that wracks my body, right on up my neck, past my pulse, and then he cups the back of my neck.

The power of restraint evaporates as he pulls me closer to him.

I'm in the most romantic city in the world. Feet from one of the most amazing structures mankind has ever built. And I'm about to kiss a righteous, slightly arrogant, smug British guy I know nothing about.

Oddly...it's totally right.

"Beautiful, I'm British. We don't have the Fifth in the UK," he breathes across my mouth.

He's so close that my eyes shut, but I force them open again, only because I want to see how green his eyes really are when the sun glances over them.

"The British are idiots," I mumble, unable to form any further words—or any that are more coherent than those.

"Truth. If only because I can taste your lips and I haven't touched them yet."

"I think that makes you real—"

He cuts me off by doing exactly what he just mentioned—touching my lips with his. It's the exact same as this morning, just fresher, almost. Realer. They're heated from the sun, chilled from the wine we had at the bar around the corner not thirty minutes ago, and...softer.

Softer—yeah.

Hesitant yet somehow forceful.

Unsure yet oddly certain.

Mesmerizing. Consuming.

I grasp his shirt in my hand, wrapping my fingers in the soft material, as he moves closer to me and his other arm snakes around my body. He pulls me against him, and I slide along the wooden seat, my heart thundering in my chest.

I've been here for twenty-four hours.

I don't want to stop.

I don't want to change this.

I don't know what's happening.

I can't feel my toes because they're curled so hard. I can't feel my fingers because they're gripping him so tight. I can't feel my lips because I'm kissing him so firmly.

I can't feel my heart's beats.

It's beating too solidly, too firmly, too quickly, too erratically, for me to get a handle on it. My stomach is flipping and my lungs tightening and I swear to god, I'm consumed.

Jase.

Twenty-four hours.

A guy I've met once before last night.

And I'm consumed.

I'm scared.

I pull back from him, just our mouths, for just a second, before he pulls me right back in. I'm compelled to continue kissing him, and I wish I weren't, but it's as though a year never passed and I'm right back in London with the boy from the coffee shop.

I feel the way I did then. Racing heart when he kisses me, tingling skin when he touches me, butterflying stomach when he looks at me...

Except this is no coffee shop.

This isn't London.

A year has passed.

And he's not just a guy trying to figure out lyrics.

Not anymore.

He's a potential international superstar, loved by possibly millions, obsessed over by far more. His lyrics could be written for him. His music produced for him. His schedule organized for him.

And I'm just a girl living in the shadows of her famous brothers, happy for a quiet life by the beach, where the loudest scream is that of the ocean crashing against the rocks that dare break the perfection of the sand.

We're so, so different.

I pull back once again, this time with finality. I slip my hand between us before he can speak or come closer and touch two of my fingers to his lips. My lips softly curve, and I reach down and remove his hand from my back. His hand trails across my side as I do, and he doesn't fight it.

I draw in a deep breath and move back a few inches. Close enough to touch. But not enough for temptation.

Maybe.

"We... We can't do this, Jase," I say quietly. My words are punctuated by birdsong and sunlight and other peoples' laughter—by happiness. "We met *once*. We met for a second time twenty-four damn hours ago. This is insane, okay? I shouldn't have asked you to join me for lunch. I sure as hell shouldn't have gone for a freakin' walk with you." I run my fingers through my hair and stand, grabbing the handle of my purse. "I remember this park well. Take a left and you'll find a cab to take you back to hotel. I'll see you there later."

I turn and walk away like I didn't just completely blow him off.

What else am I supposed to do?

I'm under no disillusions about our...friendship.

We fucked.

Once.

Kissed more than.

It doesn't mean shit.

"You did *what* with Hot Brit?" Chelsey exclaims, climbing onto the bed and crossing her legs beneath her. She reaches right over and grabs her plastic cup of wine from the nightstand.

"I didn't do anything with *Jase*," I huff defiantly, putting extra emphasis on his name. I'm not going to call him Hot Brit. His being hot is why I want to drown myself in my weight in wine.

"You just said you kissed him," Jessie points out, grinning. "That's doing something."

"No, I said *he* kissed *me*. There's a real big difference right there."

"Whatever. You still kissed him back."

"Only because he kissed me first."

Chelsey snorts. "Right. Because you wouldn't have done it, right?"

"No. I wouldn't have," I say honestly. I think it's honest anyway—who knows? I don't know what I would or wouldn't have done.

Why are they asking me so many questions?

I don't want to answer all of these questions. Now, I think I really can plead the Fifth because there's no stupid Brit telling me he doesn't accept it.

"I plead the Fifth!" I cry, scrambling for my wine before either of them can say anything else. I gulp down a huge mouthful of the alcohol.

This is me, pleading the Fifth—with alcohol.

Probably not the greatest idea this girl's ever had.

"You're such a party pooper," Jessie mutters. "What are you gonna do? And no, avoiding him isn't the answer."

"I wasn't going to say that." Fuck it. "I'm simply going to plan my days around their schedule so there's no chance of running into my brothers or him."

"That's avoidance."

"No, it's coincidence."

She rolls her eyes. "And when we fly to London?"

"I'll be sick in the restroom."

Chelsey raises an eyebrow. "Really? You're gonna spend the whole flight there cooped up in a tin can bathroom?"

"It's only an hour," I remind her.

"Really?" Jessie asks. "An hour? That's it? Oh, well, you can read a book or something. That should be deterrent enough."

I'm thinking there's an insult in there... Either that or I've made it perfectly clear that no one should ever, ever interrupt me while I'm reading.

That's not an insult, y'all. That's a freakin' goddamn compliment.

Go me.

"Really? You're dating my brother, the guy who kept bugging you even though your relationship was fake, learned how to speak the language of flowers, didn't listen to you when you told him where to fuck off to, and gave you a second first date, and you think I'll be left alone by a guy when I'm reading?"

She shrugs and flicks her scarlet hair over her shoulder. "Maybe Jase isn't... You know. Like Aidan. Like those guys in the books you read."

"Are you telling me I read about guys who are like my brother?" I'm mildly traumatized right now.

"Well, you know. The alpha, macho, 'me man, you woman' guys. Those guys. You read about them, right?"

"No. Obviously I enjoy reading about guys who do nothing but sit quietly while the other guy gets the girl instead of going and getting her himself."

"Then, yes," Chelsey chirps happily. "You read about guys like your brothers!"

I look down into my plastic cup. Nope. This is not gonna be enough wine for this conversation.

With that thought in mind, I lean over and grab the phone, hitting the number for room service. "Hi! I'd like two bottles of Chardonnay, *s'il vous plaît*."

"*Oui, Madame.*"

"*Merci beaucoup.*" I put the phone down and look at my friends. "What? One bottles does three cups. The bottles should be bigger. And if we're going to continue down this vein..."

"She's right," Jessie says, staring at the empty bottle on the side. "Wine bottles should be bigger."

Of course I'm right. I have to be right about something today. Lord knows I got the rest of it freakin' wrong.

"It's not a coincidence the wine was mentioned when your brothers were," Chels points out. "But I've read the books you read. Kye is pretty close to that."

"La la la la!" I yell over her words. "I don't want to know this!"

She and Jessie burst into laughter, and I finish what's left of the wine in my cup. Oh, man. This is getting out of control.

I do not, under any circumstances, want to read my books and picture my brothers as the book boyfriend.

Ew. So much ew.

"Look," Jessie says through her final giggles. "All I'm saying is that maybe Jase isn't a throw-you-down, overpower-you, fuck-you-until-you-can't-breathe kinda guy like the ones in your books. Maybe he's the sit-on-the-sidelines-until-she-comes-to-him guy. You might not have anything to worry about."

I frown and look down as there's a knock at the door. Chels gets up to answer it, and my mind drifts back to London.

The way how, after I'd helped him with his lyrics, Jase insisted on buying me dinner to thank me and wouldn't take no for an answer.

The way he grabbed my hand after, winked, and dragged me to the London Eye because I'd told him that it was the only thing I really wanted to do at night.

The way he took me back to my hotel and not raised an eyebrow when I tugged him into the elevator after me.

The way he took my room key from my hand, swiped it, and shoved the door open. Pushed me inside, dropped the key to the floor, and shut the door by pushing me against it to kiss me breathless.

The way he controlled it, every last second, every touch, every kiss, every sensation.

No, Jase Masters is not a sit-on-the-sidelines guy.

He's most definitely a throw-you-down, make-you-beg, overpower-you, and fuck-you-until-you-not-only-can't-breathe-but-can-only-scream kinda guy.

That's why he's dangerous.

Because I know, if he wanted to do that, my body would react to him in a way that's so convincing that telling him no would be a waste of my breath. Because, eventually, I would say yes.

Maybe I don't need to avoid him after all. Maybe it can be achieved by simply never being alone with him.

"You wanna be alone with your thoughts there, girl?" Jessie sniggers, holding a full cup of wine in front of my face.

I take it. Gratefully. "No. Just thinking that Jase is definitely like the guys in my books."

Again, she and Chelsey burst into a fit of giggles. Except, this time, it's uncontrollable.

Maybe wine bottles are big enough after all.

For them, at least, I think, eyeing the open bottle.

I'm gonna need a lot, lot more.

chapter six

"Agape." Mila leans over in her seat and pushes the green grape against my cheek.

I half frown at her as I pluck it from her tiny hand. "Thanks?"

"Welcomes." She sits up straight and goes back to feeding herself instead of me, apparently happy with herself for her achievement.

"Hey." Conner takes the seat next to Mila. "Thanks for watchin' her for a minute."

"It's all right. We shared a grape." I stare at the grape I'm still holding. "Or she tried to choke me on it. Jury is still out on that one."

He laughs. "Yeah, we can't get her outta that habit. So, are you ready for tonight?"

Day three in Paris, show one of two.

"Yeah, I think so." I nod, setting the grape down on the tablecloth behind my plate. "What time is the sound check?"

"Uh... You'd have to ask Ella. I just show up when I'm told to, to be honest. Blame it on someone else." He jerks his head toward Mila, a smile breaking across his face. "Not sure how much longer I'm gonna be able to get away with that one."

"I'll text her." I pull my phone from my pocket and, picking my cup of tea up with one hand, message Ella to find out what time we need to be at the AccorHotels Arena.

Ella: *1pm.*

She's so efficient it's a little terrifying. I've never met anyone who could keep so many people so organized.

I need someone like her for myself. I'm as organized as a starfish in the desert.

"One o'clock," I tell Conner.

He gives me a thumbs-up. "Cool, man. I've gotta take Mila to the pool, so I'll see you here before we leave?"

"Sounds good." I smile. "Have fun, Mila."

"My love smimmin'." She grins and climbs off the chair. Then she weaves her way through the tables of the restaurant. "C'mon, Daddy!"

"All right, all right. Wait there." Conner half smiles and darts between the tables himself to catch up to her.

As soon as he does, she bounces off again, giggling.

Bloody hell. It's exhausting just watching her.

I sip my tea and watch people as they move through the lobby. I don't know what it is about people-watching. It's incredibly boring, but at the same time, it's the most interesting thing I believe a person can do. From the businessman rapidly speaking into the phone plastered to his ear, to the mother struggling to grasp her child's hand, to the beautiful, young...

Leila, scurrying across the lobby.

It's the first time I've seen her since we kissed by the tower. I know I shouldn't do this, but I get up, leaving my cup still half full, and follow her.

"Leila!"

She shows no signs of hearing me, even when I shout her name again, so I catch the door before it closes and walk down the steps and onto the street. I can't see her anywhere—her dark-brown hair isn't exactly a unique color. Jessie? Sure. You'd see that girl a mile off. But Leila... No. She blends in, assumes her surroundings...

Disappears.

I sigh, force a smile at the doorman, then go back inside the hotel. I just want to apologize. She was right what she said, that it was wrong. I shouldn't have kissed her the first time, and I sure as hell shouldn't have the second. She laid what she wanted out that morning, and I disrespected it, and her, by kissing her.

And, Jesus, I'm not that kinda guy. I'm not a guy who ignores whatever he's told, but she's so...tempting. She makes me want to do it, and I don't know what it is.

I guess I lose my mind a little when she's around.

I push the button for the elevator to go back to my room.

I can't lose my mind. It doesn't matter how crazy or beautiful she is. Or even how crazy beautiful she is. I'm getting the greatest opportunity of my career right now. Supporting Dirty B. on their tour is the single best experience I'm going to get as I fight for my own place in this industry.

I can't blow it because I want to fuck their sister again.

This isn't Hollywood—I can't screw my way to the top. I need talent, real talent, and I have it. I've worked hard for it. Now, I have to work harder.

The UK isn't enough.

I want the world.

I want to hear my music on the radio in Australia and see it on the charts in America. See it on iTunes in Spain and China and India and Russia. I want messages from fans in South Africa and Hong Kong and Argentina. Mostly, though, it's more than that.

I want to change someone's life.

I want my words to alter their perspective on their life.

I want to make a difference to someone.

I can't do that if I'm not focused. Nobody ever achieved their dreams by accident. It doesn't happen by chance. You have to put the work in to get there and to stay there. I don't want just one hit. I don't want to go back to scrawling lyrics on the back of receipts on the Tube. I've worked hard enough for this over the last few years. I've busted my balls so hard it's a wonder they're still in one piece.

Leila Burke cannot distract me from my goal.

It's really that fucking simple. I can't let my head continue to be turned by that Southern beauty who wants nothing to do with me.

We're the product of coincidence and circumstance, driven together by nothing more or less than pure chance.

But I'm totally aware that chance is exactly what I have right now. One chance to achieve my dreams. One chance to be more than the indie guy on the charts. One chance to be more than Jase Masters, indie superstar with a bright future.

It's my chance to just be Jase Masters.

Dirty B. are my chance. They called me. They brought me here. They knew what they were offering—what they are offering. They wouldn't have called my manager if they hadn't thought my supporting them wouldn't be beneficial for both them and me.

To think that the only way I've repaid them is by kissing their sister.

Fuck, I'm an idiot.

I click my door shut behind me and perch on the edge of my bed. If I look up, I can see the top of the tower, but mostly, it's just the charm of the city. Damn flowerpots on the sills and pretty curtains. Flower boxes on the balconies everyone here seems to have, although I'm sure they're closer to railed ledges than they are actual balconies.

Seriously... One person is all you can fit on those things. If you're lucky.

No, it's time to focus now. Leila seems intent on avoiding and ignoring me, and I'm good with that. If that's what she wants to do, I'm gonna respect that.

I need to get my head back in the game—and the music.

I slide down to the floor and over to where my guitar case is. I grip the zip and tug it along the length of the case, the quiet noise filling the silent air of my room. It's a strangely comforting sound, unzipping something, especially when you know the thing you're about to get out is where a part of your soul lies.

I carefully pull the guitar out and carry it across the room to the chair opposite my bed. Upon sitting down, I rest the instrument on my legs and run my thumb across the strings.

Instantly, calm floods my body.

The vibrations of the strings as they let their melodic tune loose dance up and down my arms, begging for more. I move onto my toes so my knee is elevated and close my eyes. My fingers guide me through the song, through the music, and I mouth the words.

I need to save my voice for tonight, but this is enough.

Music is always enough.

The cheers are deafening. I have no idea how I sing through them or how I don't throw the fuck up across the stage. I've sung live before, one or twice in front of a few thousand people, but not like this.

Dirty B. sold out. Every seat is filled. Every bit of standing room is taken. You could try to get another person in, but you'd fail miserably.

And I've never experienced anything like this. Never experienced a rush like the one that's whirling through my bloodstream right now. Never been hit by adrenaline quite this hard.

This is it. This is why I do this. For something—a feeling, a rush—that I had no idea existed before right this moment.

It's addictive.

I want it again already and it isn't even over yet.

Somehow, I sing through it. I play through it. I focus through the deafening pound of my heart as it thunders in my ears, through the churning of my stomach as the nerves coil tighter, through the shake of my hands as the adrenaline controls my every movement.

Through the unbelievable, unreal reception these thousands of crazed women and girls give a guy they've probably never heard of before.

And then, when it's done, in a haze, I thank them and calmly leave the stage.

Like I'm not freaking the fuck out right now.

Like I'm not about to throw up.

Aidan winks at me, grinning knowingly, and he and his brothers head to the stage for their set.

If I thought my cheer was loud... Fuck me. I think the roof just flew off this place.

Ella winces, pressing her ear. "Yeah, can't hear you!" she yells. Not that it matters—she probably can't be heard by the other person, either.

"Here," a guy says, holding his hands out. He points to my guitar then the case, when I frown.

"Thanks," I mouth, knowing there's no point speaking.

I don't think I can, if I'm honest.

Probably not.

Mostly because I'm still awed from that reception. It was an excitement for the band about to go on, for sure, but I know, deep down, part of it was for me.

I exhale slowly and lean against the wall, letting it sink in. Breathing through an insanity like nothing I've ever known before.

I want to do it again.

Right now.

If only I weren't feeling so goddamn bloody tired.

Ella touches my arm and leans against my side. "Go back," she says loudly into my ear. "There's a car waiting for you outside. You don't have to stay."

"I don't mind—"

"No. Go. You look tired."

I look down at her with a grateful smile. Yeah, I wanna stay. I wanna experience what they do, feel how crazy it could be one day, but going back to the hotel does sound really good right about now.

"Thanks," I tell her as she reaches up and removes the microphone equipment from my ear. I hand her the box from the back of my jeans, gathering all the wires, and she puts them on the table behind me.

"Go rest," she orders, her eyes smiling. "You did really good."

"Thanks."

She hugs me quickly before she puts her finger to her ear and holds her hand up in goodbye. I take that as my call, and Ajax, the band's head security guy, appears seemingly out of nowhere.

"Let's go, Jase!" he yells, grabbing the back of my shirt.

I have no idea what the hurry is, but the guy's fucking huge, so I'm doing as he says.

He lets me go once we've left the main stage area. "This concert was live-streamed," he says as the noise from Dirty B.'s playing diminishes the farther away we get. "Judging by the Internet, we have two minutes to get your ass out of here before the fangirls turn up real early." He winks at me. "Cover your eyes, kid."

Kid? I'm no ki—fuck me.

Flashes assault us the second the back door opens, and Ajax's arm comes flying out at me.

"Carlos!" he shouts into his radio. "Out the back. Now."

I stay close to Ajax as photographers move in.

Two minutes was an overestimation.

Someone comes up behind me, and I jump, but I recognize the guy as Carlos, the security guy Ajax just called. He grabs my shoulders, and with Ajax clearing the way, they steer me toward the waiting car. Ajax steps to the side for me to get in, and Carlos follows me.

"They'll be waiting at the hotel," Ajax says, leaning in. "Carlos will get you inside."

I nod, working pretty much on autopilot. The back windows are tinted, and I go from high to low quicker than I have in my life.

The endorphin rush on stage is something else.

So is the insane rush from the media.

The ultimate high to the ultimate low.

No wonder people fade out of the public eye.

I've never experienced anything like that, either.

This wasn't in the plan when I decided to listen to a certain woman's advice and experience Paris.

I was thinking pastries and beer. Not...stalkers with cameras.

"Can they get in? To the hotel?" I ask Carlos.

He shakes his head. "No. Sometimes, they try to sneak in under the guise of guests, but anyone found in there is thrown out and arrested for breach of privacy. We have the hotel security team working with us, and the police are always nearby."

"They're like bloody royalty," I mutter, looking out the window. Night is falling with the arrival of spring.

Carlos laughs. "Welcome to the industry, Mr. Masters. You just married into the fame family."

"I'm gonna need to sleep on the proposal."

He laughs again but doesn't respond until we reach the hotel. It's a long, quiet twenty minutes or so, but it gives me time to reflect on the craziness I just experienced. I wasn't prepared for it, but then again, I'm still slowly adjusting to this new life I'm carving out for myself.

I guess I don't expect anything, even if I want it.

"Here we go," the driver announces, pulling up outside the hotel.

"Goin' to your room?" Carlos asks, his hand on the door.

"The bar," I mutter. I need a beer after tonight. And to people watch. Ultimate relaxation combination.

"I got the door." He acknowledges me with a smile and a nod before getting out. He walks around the car and opens my door.

I get out, and almost as soon as I've straightened up, someone takes my photo. The first flash is a trigger for others, and I'm almost blinded by the brightness, but I follow Carlos to the door. The doorman opens it up, and the moment I step through, it's like I'm entering an entirely different world.

Even if people are still trying to get my photo outside the doors. God bless fucking frosted glass, I tell you.

"Thanks," I say to Carlos, shaking his hand. "I'd offer to buy you a beer, but..."

His radio crackles as if on cue, and he leaves without another word.

Quiet, that one.

I guess the security guard thing doesn't work if you're all chatty and shit.

I turn toward the direction of the hotel bar. It's not busy, but it's not quiet, either. Still, no one here recognizes me, whereas if I were to step outside now...

I take a deep, relaxing breath and step up to the bar. A groan escapes the person next to me, and I glance down at them.

Brown hair. Red dress. Legs for miles.

"If I go now, can I pretend I didn't see you?" Leila drawls, slapping her hand down onto her book.

"You can try, love." My lips quirk up.

Ah, coincidence. You pesky bitch.

She waves her hand and gets the bartender's attention. When he looks over, she lifts a tiny glass from in front of her and shows it to him. He nods, grabs a bottle, heads over, and fills her shot glass.

I open my mouth to order a drink, but he's already gone and tending to someone else by the time I have decided what I want.

Leila snorts and downs the shot.

"You seem stressed," I remark when she slams it back down on the bar.

"Do I?" She laughs, sliding her glass forward again. "Was it the tequila that gave it away?"

"Something like that." I sit on the stool next to her and attempt to get the bartender's attention. "Is it only pretty girls who get served around here or what?"

Her blue eyes edge their way to meet mine, and her lips tug up. She leans forward on the bar, holding two fingers up, and within two seconds, the guy is coming over to her.

That's a yes.

"How do you do that?"

"I smile," she says sarcastically, still looking at me. "You want one? *Deux, s'il vous plaît,*" she orders before I can answer.

Fuck. I'm going to stand by my thought that no one with a drawl like hers should be able to speak another language so fluently, but fuck, it's hot.

I ignore the way my cock twitches when she picks her glass up and wraps her lips around the rim of it. She pauses, the glass pressed against her mouth, and looks at mine.

All right, then.

This is a stupid, stupid idea.

I pick the glass up, tilt it toward her, then throw it back. The alcohol burns my throat as I swallow it down, and I shudder.

Leila laughs. "Can't take the heat, Brit Boy?"

"The heat of what? Some cheeky American forcing me to drink tequila?"

"Cheeky? Is that like sassy?"

"Close enough," I answer. "A little birdie told me you're avoiding me. You're doing a wonderful job."

She rolls her eyes. "I'm not avoidin' you. I'm merely... Yeah, no, you're right. I'm avoidin' you."

"The bar's a great place to do that."

"Well, I'm hungover, and I was trying to read." She looks down at her book and picks it up. "But then the guys were too much like my brothers, and I don't want to think of them like that."

I'm not going to ask. I don't want to know what she means by that.

"And, now, I need another drink," she mutters, putting the book down and getting the bartender's attention yet again.

Seriously. Is it the tits? Is that how you get a bloody drink here?

He fills both of our glasses. Leila picks hers up, but she doesn't drink it straightaway. Instead, she peers at the clear liquid inside before turning to me.

"I'm supposed to be ignoring you. We made a deal. Those bitches."

"You're losing me here."

She waves her empty hand. "Never mind. I'm talkin' to myself."

chapter seven
Leila

I tip back the shot, shudder as I swallow, and put the glass down.

Fuck. Fuck. Fuck. Flying fucking fuck.

That word is so relieving. I'm going to make a note that, every time I'm stressed, I'm going to throw *fuck* around like it's confetti at a wedding.

The bar.

Idiot.

Why did I come to the bar? All the places I could have gone—a whole dang city—and I chose the bar. Of the hotel we're staying at. How much of an idiot do I have to be to have done this?

A prize dick. Blue ribbon. Gold medal. World champion.

Maybe that's enough alcohol.

I blame Chelsey and Jessie. All the wine last night left me with a killer hangover today that no amount of sunshine or aspirin could shake, so I knew my only option was a little more alcohol. Hair of the dog and all that.

Except, now, I think I'm at hair of the dog, fur of the kitten, and fluff of the bunny. Probably feather of the bird too.

Workin' my way around the petting zoo.

"How'd the concert go?" I ask him. Why did I ask that? I don't care. Well, I do. I just don't care for conversation with him.

Maybe I need a babysitter after all.

"Amazing." He's not looking at me, but I can see the sparks that light in his eyes. He means it. He loved it.

"Well, then. Welcome to Crazytown. Population between eight and twenty million. Depends if you're photographed with a girl or not." I wave my glass at the bartender.

I'm pretty sure he's only serving me so quickly because he knows my brothers are rich and he likes my boobs.

"Bitter," Jase mutters, leaning forward on the bar and grasping his glass between his finger and thumb.

"Honest," I counter. "That's it now. You've been introduced to the Dirty B. fandom. They're screamin' teenager on top of screamin' teenager. They're literally crazy. A psychologist's dream."

He frowns at me then pushes my glass away from me. "No more alcohol for you."

I laugh, sweeping my hair around my neck. "Please. I'm from the South. I bleed wine and whiskey. A little tequila is orange juice to me."

"Bit more than just a little there."

"Not really. And here I thought the British were known for holding their alcohol."

"Yeah—cheap beer and pitchers of cocktails. Not...shots of tequila."

"Cheap beer? Y'all drink cheap beer? No wonder you're all pictured tumbling out of clubs."

"We are?"

I raise my eyebrows. "I watch the reality shows on MTV. The ones where y'all sound like you're drunk even when you're sober."

He looks confused for a moment before he grimaces. "Yeah, no. They're really not a great representation of British culture, Leila, love."

A shiver runs down my spine. *Leila, love.* Why do I love that so much?

No. I don't. *Bad Leila. You don't like the silly British man with his adorable fucking nickname and sexy as shit accent. You don't like Hot Brit.*

Hot Brit.

Yep. That's enough tequila for me.

Right after this one. Maybe this will knock sense into me.

I gasp as my belly warms from the shot. Then I stare at the bottles lining the wall. Nope—no more sense.

I actually think fresh air is the cure for this. "Hey, there's a roof garden here, right?"

"Yes," Jase says, dragging his bright-green gaze to find mine. "But perhaps we should avoid your being anywhere particularly high up right now."

I bite the inside of my lower lip, bringing it into my mouth slightly, then giggle. Oh, bless his heart. He thinks I'm drunk.

"Honey, I'm nowhere near as drunk as you think I am."

"Are you sure?" Hesitance flashes in his eyes. "Because, if you dance off the edge of the roof, I don't want to have to explain that to your brothers."

I rest my hand against his upper arm. Oh. Muscle.

Hello, muscle.

Goodbye, self-control.

He has the best arms. For real—it's literal arm porn, except I'm touching it, and I'm not sure there's anything better than touching a hunk of solid, tattooed bicep.

Jesus Christ. I'm a little turned on right now.

No. More. Tequila.

I drop my hand from his arm. "I solemnly swear not to walk off the edge of the roof in my slightly drunken state." I grin.

He gives me a hard look.

"Honestly, I just want some fresh air, and if we go out there"—I cock my thumb toward the doors—"you're gonna get mobbed and I'm gonna be the mystery girl. Except they know who I am, so I won't really be the mystery girl."

He stares at me for a long moment. His eyes run over my face, touching every bit of it. He lingers on my lips, and my tongue darts out to wet them.

My heart thuds harshly, suddenly, uncontrollably, like a tornado touching down.

"Okay," he relents, finally lifting his shot glass and downing it.

My lips threaten to pull into a smile as he twitches on his swallow.

"Let's go. But you stay in the middle of the roof. Got it? On the floor."

"Yes, sir," I mutter sassily, spinning on the stool and jumping to my feet. I snatch my book up, using a receipt for a bookmark, and hug it to my chest. "Are you coming?"

His eyes flash with lust at my wording.

Maybe tequila is bad for him, too.

He grunts but doesn't say anything in direct response to my question as he gets up. I tighten my hold on my book, hugging it so tight that it's practically getting embedded in my skin. I want to focus on the way my fingers brush the pages instead of the way my heart is still beating like crazy.

This is a bad idea.

But I like bad ideas.

The elevator pings open, and we step inside. Jase pushes the button for the roof floor, and I inhale deeply as the doors slide shut. My eyes sweep upward to the little window above the doors that shows the floors. One by one, the number changes, going up, never stopping, never pausing, until it reaches *Roof*.

I swallow hard as the doors open to a small bar area. Immediately, we're stared at by a handsome man standing behind a bar.

He pauses in cleaning his glass. "*Clé de la chambre?*"

"He wants your key. To check your room," I whisper.

Shit. I didn't realize this was exclusive up here. There's no key on the elevator...

Jase fumbles in his pocket, pulls out a wallet, then produces his key. He hands it to the bartender, who takes it with a skeptical eye and runs it through a machine behind the bar.

"Ah. *Monsieur* Masters. *Excusez-moi.*" He smiles graciously and hands Jase his key back. "*Et Mademoiselle...*"

"Burke." I smile.

"Ah! *Mademoiselle* Burke." His eyes shine in recognition. "*Qu'est-ce que je vous sers?*"

I look to Jase. "Are we getting anything?"

He raises an eyebrow.

"Chardonnay, *s'il vous plaît*," I order, looking to the barman.

What? The eyebrow-raise was a challenge, and I'm going to accept. I'm not sure the wine will do much to restore self-control or calm my heart, but it'll give me something to do with my hands other than touch his arms.

"I'll have a beer, please," Jase asks.

"Really? You can't even say 'please' in French?" I tease him.

"*S'il vous plaît*," he says to the bartender as an afterthought, shooting me a dark look.

I laugh quietly, looking down as our drinks are prepared. I take my glass once it's in front of me. The barman hands Jase his pint of beer and tells him that he'll charge it to the room. Jase looks appropriately confused and turns back to me.

"What did he say?"

I can't help but want to mess with him. So I do. "He said you're an uncivilized shit."

Jase stops cold and glares down at me. "Seriously?"

"No." I giggle. "He's chargin' it to your room, so, cheers." I clink my glass against his and push the doors open into prettiest space I've ever seen, and that's saying something here in Paris.

There are flowers everywhere, planted in gorgeous, rustic wooden boxes, surrounding little tables and benches and soft sofas that fit perfectly in the vintage-type theme. Canopies stretch over the seating areas, but some of them are rolled back, revealing the dusky sky above. There are only two other people up here, and the little fairy lights strung from the canopy bars add a pretty ambiance to an already charming space.

Screw my room. I'm gonna sleep up here.

The sun has almost completely set despite its being nine o'clock, but the sky is bathed in a gorgeous golden hue. It's on fire from left to right, from horizon to where it meets the falling nighttime sky.

It's perfect.

"Nice," Jase says appreciatively from next to me.

"Nice? Really? Nice is all you've got? For this?" I put my glass down on a small, wooden table next to a sofa at the opposite end of the roof to the other people. "Look—it's one of the most beautiful sights in the world and all you have is nice. Real descriptive."

"And you said you were gonna stay in the middle of the roof, but there you are, gripping the railings."

I glance over my shoulder as the couple by the doors goes inside. "Don't worry. I'm not going to throw myself over the edge."

"It's more falling I'm concerned about."

"Men. You worry about everythin', don't you? If it's not ground rules with my brothers, it's your telling me to be careful." I leave the edge anyway. "I'm not ten—I've survived long enough to know how to be careful."

"Surprisingly. I'm starting to believe you're just terribly lucky."

"That's adorable. Say it again."

"Say what?"

I sit on the edge of the sofa, keeping my back straight. "Terribly lucky."

Jase's eyebrows shoot up. "I'm just a personal entertainment system to you, aren't I?"

"Yeah, but you're a hot one too. Oops." I clap my hand over my mouth and feel my cheeks flame bright red. Shit, shit, shit!

Way to go, Leila. Way to fucking go.

"I take it back. Can we get some more tequila?" Jase laughs.

The husky tone tantalizingly crawls across my skin, and suddenly, staring across the rooftops of Paris isn't the best thing to have happened today.

It's hearing his laugh.

And that's...scary.

"No more tequila. Definitely not any more tequila." I pick my wine glass up before swiftly deciding that *wine* falls under *tequila* right now and putting it back down untouched. I only just sat down, but now, I'm back up, and I'm walking to the edge of the roof.

I wrap my fingers around the cold metal railing and close my eyes, taking a deep breath.

"You have a thing about the edge, huh?" Jase asks quietly, his hand brushing mine as he comes up and stands next to me, gripping the railing, too.

I open my eyes and look out over the adorable rooftops. "It's prettier here than there."

"Depends what angle you're looking at it from." His gaze burns into the side of my face.

"You're like a walkin', talkin' romance novel, aren't you?"

"I think you're prettier than the view," he says quietly. Honestly. "You also have a lot more attitude than the people down there, granted, but I quite like that about you."

"You like my attitude?" I turn to him, and it's my mistake. His eyes are so bright, so compelling, that my gaze locks on to his in a heartbeat. "And it's actually just my personality. I'm a pain in the ass."

He laughs again, leaning forward without breaking eye contact. "You call it pain in the ass—I call it hot. I like a girl who challenges me. Even if she does try to avoid me more often than she talks to me."

Because I'm doing so great at avoiding him, aren't I? "Don't take it personally. I'm avoiding my brothers too. And my friends, as of tonight, actually."

"And you wonder why everyone tells you what to do."

"Yeah, actually, I do." I tuck my hair behind my ear. "Because I'm the youngest, I get…babied, I guess is the best way to put it. Ground rules from my brothers about being here and what I can and can't do, yet at home, do they give a shit? No. They're all too busy with their own lives, and that's okay, but when I come join you on your dang trip, don't parent me."

"Tell me how you really feel, love."

I glare at him. "Maybe I want to lean over the railing and feel the breeze whip my hair around my face. That's who I am."

"If you do that right now, you may give me a heart attack." He stills. "Don't you dare."

I grin and lean forward.

"Leila."

I kick up with my feet.

Jase snatches my arm, tugging me back from the railing and onto my feet.

I laugh. "Do you really think I would fa—"

He cups my face with his hands and pulls me against him. I'm so stunned by the harsh way his lips touch mine that I gasp, and he runs his tongue across my lower lip.

Like the weak fool I am, I relax against his body and let him kiss me.

He does, deeply, setting my whole body on fire. Spark after spark is ignited by the intimate way he kisses me—hard yet soft, teasingly yet satisfyingly. His touch zaps across my skin, leaving goose bumps, and every single sensation that filters through me floods down through my body and pools between my legs until I feel nothing but the overwhelming ache of desire.

My clit throbs, and I move closer to him, grip his shirt tighter, kiss *him* harder. It's like a compulsion… It's hypnotic, and the more his lips sweep across mine, the more I need to feel him. The more I crave him, and it's only a kiss—nothing more, nothing less. Yet there's nothing more intimate than the way my heart is pounding against my chest and my stomach is erupting in nervous, delighted little butterflies.

Nothing better than his fingers sliding down my sides and gripping my hips, pulling me flat against his solid body, before one of his hands glides up my spine to cup the back of my head.

Nothing better than those same fingers winding in my hair as mine fist his shirt so tight that I'm afraid I'll rip it.

Nothing better than the thundering of every possible feeling through my bloodstream.

Need. Desire. Lust. Passion.

They're the worst.

The best.

I don't know if I love them or hate them.

"You're making me crazy," Jase whispers against my mouth.

I know the feeling. "I think maybe I should go to back to my room," I whisper back, my tongue flicking across my lower lip.

He takes a deep breath and nods. "I think you should."

"Alone," I add.

"Alone." His agreement was tight, and his voice cracked halfway through the word. He releases me, and he feels as reluctant as I do to let go.

I'm in trouble.

He's in trouble.

We're both in serious trouble.

I step back from him, taking a deep breath, and grab my book from the sofa. I don't even remember when I put the thing down. We leave the wine and the beer untouched on the table, and Jase leads me off the roof and through the door. He nods to the bartender, while I keep my head down, focused on putting one foot in front of the other.

My body is alive right now.

Every nerve ending is tingling with anticipation, and no matter how many times I tell them what to do, they keep it up until I can't concentrate on anything but their distinct trembling.

Rein it in, Leila.

I know what this feeling is. And I'm not even talking about the way I can feel his hands burning into my skin through my shirt. I'm talking about temptation. The need to follow through regardless of the consequences.

The jumping in, tackling the situation, regardless of the consequences.

It's the story of my life.

I've already done it with Jase. *Before.* When there were no consequences.

When the worst that could happen was goodbye.

The elevator feels too small, too tight, too restraining. I take several deep breaths, but ultimately, they all escape me, and eventually, I huff them out. This is taking so long. Why? Why is it so long? It doesn't need to be.

Please, shit. Get me away from him.

I want to go into my room, curl into my bed, and lament my self-control.

Then again, I want to screw him until I forget my own name, too, so what do I know?

The elevator finally pings open on my floor, and I step out without a word. God, my bed. I need my bed so badly. Yes to hotel pillows. I never thought I'd say it, but yes! Give me all the hotel pillows.

As long as they're firm. Nobody likes the soft pillows, hotel managers. Y'all get with the program now.

"I'm just making sure you get back to your room." He holds his hands up in front of him, palms to me. "Honestly. I'm going to be a total gentleman from here on out."

"Hmm." I turn around and fumble for my room key in my pocket. My fingers find plastic, and I slide it out Then I peer at the back to make sure I put it in the slot the right way. The last thing I want to do is play the in-out-shake-it-all-about keycard game with Jase standing right behind me.

A shiver runs down my spine at my own thought. In-out-shake-it-all-about? I might not be interested in it with a key, but...

"This you?" Jase's question yanks me out of my thoughts.

I look at the door I've apparently stopped in front of. "Yep."

"Okay. Night, Leila."

"Night." I unlock my door and grip the handle tight. "Hey, Jase?" I look up and down the hall through my eyelashes.

"Yeah?"

My tongue runs over my bottom lip. "You could come in. If you wanted."

He exhales loudly, running his hand through his hair. "Leila... You've been drinking. Whether you say you're drunk or not, this is your tequila talking."

"What if it isn't?"

"How do I know you're not just saying it?"

"Never mind." My stomach sinks. "I can take a hint."

"A hint? I'm a man, love. I don't give or take hints." He walks toward me. "But I also respect you and I'm not going to go into your room and fuck you because numerous shots of tequila are telling you it's a good idea."

"Don't worry." My cheeks burn with humiliation. I'm blaming this on the tequila. He's so insistent it is, so fuck you, tequila. Fuck you.

"Leila." He grabs my arm before I can disappear fully inside.

I slowly turn my face back to him. The bright hall lights collide with the darkness of my room, casting shadows across the angular planes of his face. His eyes blaze at me, a bright yet stormy green that shows his inner battle.

"Don't think I'm not coming in with you because I don't want to fuck you." He takes a deep breath and lets it out quietly.

I swallow.

"I want to fuck you again. I want to follow you into this room and fuck you so hard everyone on this floor will know what we're doing."

"So do it," I whisper. "I'm not drunk, Jase. I know exactly what I'm asking."

"You're supposed to be avoiding me." He leans in so his mouth hovers just above mine. "Remember?"

"It didn't work out." My mouth gets dry as his breath fans across my lips.

"So, pursuing me is your new plan?"

"Well." I pause to swallow again, although there's nothing but the hesitant lump in my throat that won't go down. "I figure it's the more enjoyable option."

His lips twitch up on one side, and he laughs quietly. "Leila, love..."

I grab the front of his shirt, gripping it tight, and pull him down to me at the same time that I push up onto my toes. Our lips collide somewhere between us, and

he freezes. His fingers twitch around my arm, but he lets go.
I get it.
I step back from him, my heart thudding and pushing the previous twinge of humiliation around my body until it latches on to every cell and swamps me. My cheeks burn, and I can't look up at him, so I move back into my room, throwing my book in the direction of the bed.

He grabs me.

Shoves me inside.

Pushes me back against the door so it slams shut.

And kisses me.

Desire blurs my embarrassment as Jase's mouth descends onto mine and he kisses me as though he's starving. I wind my hands into his hair as he runs one of his up my thigh. His fingers ease under my dress, coming dangerously close to the top of my leg, and I gasp as he lifts it and hooks it over his hip.

Fuck me, he's hard.

His cock presses between my legs, against my throbbing clit, and the pressure from his jeans sends a bolt of uncontrollable desire firing through my bloodstream.

He groans, swiping his tongue across the seam of my mouth, and I open for him, sending my tongue to meet his. They battle when he kisses me deeply and grips my ass harder, lifting me up the door a little. My hips buck against him, and he nips my bottom lip when I whimper.

Then he brings one hand between my legs and runs his thumb over the soft cotton of my panties.

Right over my clit.

Right along my pussy.

Now, my gasp is loud, and I break the kiss to control my breathing. Jase smiles against my jaw as he kisses it. His mouth leaves trails of hot kisses along it and my neck, his tongue swirling on my pulse point, his teeth grazing down my skin to my shoulder.

And, the whole time, his fingers are working their way beneath my underwear.

The moment his rough thumb brushes my clit, his lips find mine again, and he swallows my moan.

He slowly eases one finger inside me, his thumb rubbing my clit. I tilt my hips toward him as I melt into a pool of hot need, and my hips move, and I need more—everything. I need everything right now. Another finger joins the first, his tongue exploring my mouth, and Jase fucks me with his hand so thoroughly that, before long, I'm riding it, and I don't know if he's giving me pleasure or if I'm giving it to myself.

I just know I'm losing control.

Spiraling down.

Down.

Down.
And then climbing up.
Up.
Up.
And it hits, a giant smack, and his kiss swallows my cries as my clit throbs intensely. The orgasm is unreal, and my whole body shakes as reality washes down over us.

"Jase," I whisper scratchily after a moment.

He touches two fingers to my lips, the other hand trailing across the top of my thigh. "Listen to me," he whispers right back, his voice thick and husky with desire. "I'm not an arsehole, Leila. I'm not going to fuck you and then leave you, because no matter what you say, I'm sure your decision making has been helped by the shots you've downed. No—listen," he demands quietly when I open my mouth against the tips of his fingers. "Tomorrow morning, if you wake up not regretting the fact you just came hard as fuck with my fingers inside you, then I'll be in the lobby at ten." He leans in so his lips brush my earlobe. "Babe, if you decide tomorrow that you want my mouth all over you and my cock inside you, then here's the deal. You spend the day showing me every inch of this gorgeous city, and then I'll spend the night showing you every inch of me."

I close my eyes. Not that it matters. He can't see me and I can't see him. The only light is a tiny glimpse of it sneaking through the gap in the closed curtains, but I feel as though I can think clearer with my eyes closed.

Like I'm hiding.

Like...like I'm not nodding in agreement right now because my brain has beaten my vagina down.

It's probably a good thing.

Because this guy standing in front of me could do anything he wants. He could throw me on the bed right now and fuck me, believe me when I say the tequila has no persuasive techniques, but he hasn't. More than that, he outright refuses to.

Jesus. He's a good guy.

"Okay." I clear my throat and open my eyes. Somehow, they find his. "But you need to leave now because I can feel how hard you are and it isn't helping."

He kisses me firmly before releasing me, and I touch my thumb to my lower lip, moving out of the way of the door. Jase grabs the handle and pulls it open, flooding the space with light.

His cheeks are a little pink, his hair mussed from my fingers, but it's his eyes that portray what could have happened.

Restraint. Lust. Need. Desire. Control—at its breaking point but still control.

"Ten. Tomorrow morning," he repeats, running his eyes across my body like he didn't just touch it.

"I won't forget," I reassure him, taking hold of the handle when he lets it go. I lean against the edge of the door and watch him, pulling my lower lip into my mouth, as he goes to the elevator. I flick on the light, slam the door, then peer at him through the curtains.

I feel like a stalker.

But there's something about having a guy that sweet and that hot, with *that* fine-ass accent, walk away from you with his cock super hard—and not because he doesn't want you.

Because he wants you so badly that he'll only take you when he knows you'll remember.

Jesus, I think, pulling my dress over my head and throwing it to the floor. I kick the old panties off, flicking them on top of the dress, and use the bathroom. Once I'm cleaned up and wearing clean underwear, I substitute my bra for an oversized JT concert shirt, switch the light off, and climb beneath the covers of my bed.

Lord.

Dear tequila, please don't let me forget this tomorrow morning.

chapter eight
Jase

F uck if she isn't the prettiest thing when she comes.

She didn't think I could see her, but I could. She didn't think I could see the way her cheeks flushed and her eyes lit up when she surrendered, but I did.

And, now, I can't shake it. I can't get rid of the image of her coming on my hand or the sounds of her orgasm as she let it take her over.

I've bloody well cursed myself.

How the hell I walked out of her room last night without fucking her the way I wanted to is a mystery. The moment she came apart in my arms, I almost broke. Almost killed the resolve I'd already chipped away at.

Now, I have no idea if she'll take me up on this. We're only here in Paris for another two days before we go to London, and I haven't seen nearly as much as I'd like to. And who better is there to be your tour guide than the girl who believes experiencing trumps planning?

Nobody. Exactly.

I just hope she'll do it—meet me. Hell, I'm not even down there yet and I'm bitching at myself like a bloody child.

I rub my hand over my face and step out of the elevator. Thinking about Leila Burke naked isn't going to do me any favors—and I should know because my cock is twitching at the thought about the thought.

"Tate, do you have any idea how ridiculous you are?" I hear Leila say as soon as I turn the corner close to the restaurant.

"Not ridiculous," Tate shoots back. "Lookin' out for you."

"I'm not breakin' the ground rules, okay? You know Jase. We didn't just meet at a museum, landmark, café, restaurant, or on the sidewalk."

Nope. That was just last year.

"You're missin' two," Tate replies.

"I'm not hitting on him and he ain't on me," she fires at him. "And, if I stress this any harder, I'm gonna burst a vein or ten, but this ain't no date," she says resolutely.

"Sofie came back to see Mila when she got unsettled and saw Jase leave your room last night. I don't believe you."

Fuck.

"Hey," I say, walking up to their table. "I was in her room for a reason. Sorry," I add when Tate turns. "I just caught the end of your chat."

"So, why were you in her room?" Tate asks, turning and resting his arm along the back of his chair.

Leila chews on a piece of bacon, her eyes wide and begging me not to tell him.

"She was sitting at the bar alone when I got back last night, so I checked on her. Turns out she can out-tequila half the world's population, but walking in a straight line after that event is somewhat optional." I glance at her, smirking. "So I took her back to her room, tucked her into bed with her clothes on, and left her. I wanted to make sure she returned safely."

"Damn it," Tate mutters. "Thanks, man. I knew we missed a point in the rules."

"Oh. My. God," Leila says around a mouthful of food, ignoring Tate's dark look. "I'm not a child, Tate. I don't need rules. If I'd tried to jump his bones last night, then yeah, I'd be in real agreement with y'all."

Maybe she does need rules. I cough to hide my laugh at that comment, and now, she's the one shooting dark looks, but one's at me.

"It's true. She didn't try to chat me up once. I'm pretty bloody offended, actually."

"I knew I liked you. Talented and confident. I've got a lot of time for that." Tate grins. "You remind me of me."

"Oh, fuck me," Leila mutters before grabbing a glass of juice and swigging from it.

"Hey." Tate stands and clips her around the back of the head. "No fucking. And try not to break this one with your asshole personality, yeah? We need him. And, still, no sex."

Leila stares at him flatly. Then she raises her hand to her temple and salutes him. "Sir, yes, sir. Should I report in at twelve hundred hours so y'all don't think I ran off with a French guy?"

"That'd be great, Lei. Thanks." Tate winks at me. "That's the asshole personality."

"Ah, I learned from the best." She smiles at him and grabs her purse. Her fingers tighten around my shirt, tugging me after her, before I can say a word. "Let's go before someone needs to get my ass some damn bail money."

I laugh as she drags me right outside before letting me go. "He calls it arsehole personality—I call it pretty damn hot."

"Poh-tay-to, poh-tah-to." She shrugs and squints with the sun. "Where are we going?"

I wave my arm absently. "You're showing me around, love. Not the other way around."

A slow grins breaks out across her face, making her features seem even brighter. "Let's go." She skips down the pavement, clutching her small, bright-red purse to her body.

My eyes drop down to her arse. The tiny, light-blue shorts she's wearing are ripped, and I don't know if she realizes it, but I can tell that—if she's wearing any—her knickers are really fucking small.

Nah. She realizes it, for sure.

"Jase," she calls over her shoulder, looking back at me as she rests an impatient hand on her hip. "What are you waiting for? The apocalypse isn't going to use my butt as its starting point."

Well, shit. She just called me the fuck out, didn't she?

"If the apocalypse ever comes, I'm pretty bloody sure they've got your arse pinpointed as a 'do not destroy' area."

"Aw, that's sweet." She hits me. "Idiot."

"You called me out. I don't do well on the spot."

She looks up at me, that goddamn fucking gorgeous grin on her face again. "You do *very* well on the spot. Take it from someone whose spot you've done—and done well."

I wrap my arm around her shoulders and pull her into my side, lowering my mouth to her ear. "Baby, you have no fucking idea just how well I can do on the spot. I haven't spent nearly enough time with yours for you to appreciate my tongue."

She shivers but turns toward me, grabbing my shirt, and stops us both from walking. She steps back against the wall as a kid on a scooter zooms past us. When they've gone, she glances down the street at the hotel then stares at my mouth.

"Well, then," she says, dragging her eyes up to mine. "If you think you can handle my full day of exploring, your tongue and my spot can rendezvous in your hotel room at approximately ten o'clock tonight."

A piece of hair is stuck on her eyelashes, so I push it away. As my hand falls, my thumb ghosts across the softness of her bottom lip, tugging it down.

"I can handle your day exploring, love," I say in a low voice, keeping my gaze locked on hers. "The question is whether you can handle me... And my tongue."

"Let's see, shall we?" She pulls her glasses down so they cover her eyes, breaking eye contact, and dances away. "Are you coming?"

I raise an eyebrow. "Are you talking about now or later?"

"Both."

Honestly, I have nothing to say back to that, so I laugh and walk quickly to catch up with her. Again. Why does she keep moving faster than I do?

"Hey, did you eat this morning?" She tucks her hair behind her ear and peers at me sideways.

"Nope. I slept in."

"How do you feel about pastries?"

"Is there a wrong way to feel about pastries?"

"Um, yes, and it's 'I don't like them.'"

"Luckily for me, I like them. Why?"

"Because we're in France." Her eyes light up with laughter. "And it's the only place in the world you can eat, like, four different pastries for your breakfast and nobody will say a freakin' word."

She's so excited about that. Shit, she's hot and cute. I'm screwed.

"Then why are we standing in the middle of the street?" I ask. "Let's get pastries."

"You're an enabler, Jase Masters. I like it."

"Sssh." I cover her mouth with my hand. "You can't say my name out loud. You might summon them."

She bats my hand away and frowns. "Who? Satan's legions?"

"Scarily accurate description, but no. The media. The photographers are already stalking your brothers—I'm still at the stage where they can't always decide if it's me or not, but I think they're kinda leaning toward recognition on sight."

"So let's get this straight," Leila says, pushing the door to a bakery open. "You suggested this day, knowing we could be followed just about everywhere, and didn't think to mention it before?"

"In all fairness, I thought you'd know that."

"Why? Because I make it a habit to go out with rock stars?"

"I'm not really a rock star."

"Yeah, and I'm not really a bit of a slut," she mutters, moving her hair around her neck so it hides her face from me. *"Bonjour!"* She greets the girl behind the counter, cutting me off from whatever it was I planned to say.

I don't know what I planned to say. What the fuck do I say? I swallow as she reels an order off in perfect French. Then she nods, smiles, and goes to the register. I don't move as I stare at the array of pastries, cakes, and biscuits in front of me.

"Hey." Leila looks at me. "I already ordered for you. I don't wanna be embarrassed by your pitiful attempts at speaking French."

The girl behind the counter brings her several small paper bags filled with various things I don't know—except croissant. I got croissant. She carefully slips them all inside a bigger bag, glances at me, then leans toward Leila. She says something in French.

Leila grins, looking at me, and reels her own line off before pulling her purse from her bag.

"I can get this," I offer, reaching into my pocket for my wallet.

"Too late." She hands thirty euros over, making my lips thin. *"Merci beaucoup,"* she says when the girl hands her a few euros in change back. "Let's go!"

She leaves the bakery swiftly, and I scramble to follow her out.

"What did she say to you in there?" I ask her once we're a few feet away from the bakery.

"She asked if you were Jase Masters because you look like him." She looks at me out of the corner of her eye.

My steps falter, but I right them and take the pastry bag from her so she doesn't have to carry it. "What did you say?"

"I told her I wished because he's hot, but you just look like him. And your accent is fake." She grins, but it doesn't have the same brightness as earlier, I notice.

I know it's because of the media thing.

Strange. A girl so used to it because of her brothers is bothered by it.

"Thanks." I smile back at her, but that's all I say. I don't know how to handle this girl—one minute she's all sweetness and light, the next she's not liking me too much.

She pushes hair from her cheek and turns her face toward the sun. "Good timing earlier," she says quietly, pausing at a road.

The traffic stops and we, and a bunch of other people, cross it.

"With Tate," she clarifies. "I didn't know what to say to him."

Ah. "I said the first thing that came to mind," I admit, gripping the paper bag tight.

She takes me around the corner to a small park.

"It seemed the thing that would annoy him the least," I say.

"Well, you saved my ass. Yours too, actually." She drops her purse onto the ground and sits down next to it.

I guess we're stopping.

I sit down next to her and hand her the bag. "He'd go nuts?"

"Go nuts? Oh, crazy. That one I remember." She tears the big bag open in two and lays it out like a mini blanket between us. One by one, she opens each smaller bag until there are various pastries and sugar-filled goodies covering it. "But yes. Tate would go crazy if he knew we...know each other."

"Are you ever going to tell him?" I reach for a croissant.

She drags her eyes up from her own pastry and meets my gaze. "No."

My eyebrows shoot up. "So you'll demand I fuck you, get offended when I refuse, then, when I offer it back up the next day, agree... But you won't be honest with your brothers."

"It's not a big deal." She rips a piece of croissant away. "I don't want to have your babies and ride off into the sunset in a Cadillac, Jase. I want to screw your brains out. My brothers definitely don't need to know that."

"Is that all I am to you?"

"A potential sex toy? Pretty much."

"It's a really good thing I don't want your babies either, isn't it?" I ask, grinning. "It's so much easier when we're on the same page."

She lifts the ripped piece of pastry up in a mock toast before shoving it into her mouth. I swear she was eating breakfast when I got down to the restaurant. She must have the appetite of a hundred teenage boys.

"Stop staring at me," she mutters, wiping her fingers on a napkin.

Huh. We have napkins. I didn't notice that. "Sorry. I'm just amazed you're still eating."

She shrugs a shoulder. "I like food. I like the gym. It's a love affair that works out."

"Do you really hate the paparazzi that much?" The question spilled from me before I could stop it.

Shit though—I wanna know. She froze up the moment I mentioned it before, and now, I want to know why.

She shrugs again and pops another piece of torn croissant into her mouth. I wait as she chews it, refusing to make eye contact with me.

"Hate is a strong word," she finally says after swallowing the pastry. "I don't hate them. I just have a very strong dislike for them because of the damage they knowingly inflict on people. They pretend to think that what they're doing is so innocent, but really...it's not, and they don't know. They know they hurt people, sometimes beyond repair, and they don't care. They're bastards."

I feel like I'm missing something huge. "What did they do to you to make you feel that way?"

"Nothing. Not directly, at least." She puts what's left of her croissant down and, this time, meets my eyes and holds my gaze, hesitance teasing hers. "My brothers deal with this all the time. When Sofie came home and we found out about Mila, she and Conner were hounded by the media because his 'secret baby' was a scandal. Ella avoided cameras at all costs when she went on as their PA because she was hiding from her abusive shitfuckhead of a fiancé, and I'm pretty sure just *one* photo made it possible for him to find her. Jessie lived the life of a fake girlfriend for the media for Aidan to clean up his image and suffered like hell from their fans for it—even to the point that her car was egged and flour-bombed. She took a stupid amount of abuse online and in person for that. And Chels... Well, she's always hated them because her dad—you know Lukas Young, right? Well, that's her dad, so she had major aversions before Kye even wore her down."

Lukas Young is Chelsey's dad? Fuck me. I didn't know that. But, from that point alone, I'm starting to understand.

She looks down, grabbing a bright-pink macaroon. "They're my best friends. I grew up with all of them except for Ella, but she just...got us. So yeah, Jase. Yeah, I have a severe fuckin' dislike of the media because I've watched for the last eighteen or so months as they've made the lives of the people I love a livin' hell. I love them all, and I've seen firsthand how badly the paparazzi can hurt people."

Her accent gets stronger the angrier she gets. Right now, she's a damsel in distress right out of a Western movie, but if she says *bless your heart*, I'm gonna die on the bloody spot.

"That's why I'm straight up with you when I say, if we follow through what you proposed last night, that's all it is. A secret rendezvous every other night. Avoidance of anythin' public other than 'Dirty B.'s sweet sister spends time with up and comin' star Jase Masters.' That's all it can be, because I'll be damned if they're gonna dictate my life the way they do my family's. I'm not their dang pawn and I never will be."

She means it too.

Well, shitting hell. The sassy, attitude-filled Southern girl has a big-arse heart there somewhere.

"I respect that a lot," I tell her honestly, grabbing a green macaroon. "They're not great to be around, honestly, and I guess that's why I'm trying to keep my privacy as long as possible." My mind flashes back to when I left the concert and the insanity that followed me then. "When I left the arena the other night, they pounced on me, and I'm pretty sure half of them had no idea who I am. Now, maybe, sure. But then? Nah. I was just the guy who supported Dirty B."

"It's a tough part. Sometimes, Con can't even take Mila to the park without being photographed. It's not fair to her, but there's nothing he can do. Sometimes he lets asks them to leave before he calls the police. He'd do anything to protect that sweet baby girl." She breaks the macaroon in half before putting it down. "It doesn't always work, though. He could take a security team of fifty to the swings and still have them get their shot. It's just one of those things. I just don't want that life. I'm a little too…" She pauses, clicking her tongue.

"Free," I say for her.

"I…" She looks up, her lips twitching to the side. "Exactly."

It's true. She is free. She can do what she likes without worrying about repercussions or what the whole world will think about it.

I probably don't have much longer for that. If I have any time at all.

"I envy you."

"Really?" She tilts her head to the side. "But you chose this, Jase. It's not like the lack of privacy would be a surprise."

"I know. But that doesn't mean I can't be a little jealous."

"It makes your jealousy a little stupid."

Hard to argue with that. "Do you really not want it? At all?"

She blinks her blue eyes at me from beneath her long, dark lashes. "Don't you think that, if I wanted it, I'd already have it?"

"True." I break my macaroon in two then offer her half of it.

She glances down at her own, which is split on the paper, but takes mine anyway.

Our fingers brush as she does, and a tiny smile curves her lips.

A flash catches my attention out of the corner of my eye.

"You know..." Leila says softly, staring at the treat in her hand. "You're not so bad. As long as you're kissing me or not talking."

"Great. Remember that." I quickly bundle everything up into their respective paper bags—at least I hope they're going back in the right ones—and shove them all in her bag.

"What the—"

"Where can we hide?" I stand up.

Her eyes widen in understanding, and she takes the hand I offer her. I grab her bag before she can, but she keeps a tight grip on my hand, grins, and tugs at me.

"I know where. Let's go."

chapter nine
Leila

My lungs burn from the exertion of the run across Paris. It's not exactly something I ever thought I'd have to do, but man, it was kinda fun.

Don't tell Jase that.

Also don't tell him that I flipped one of those photo-snapping bitches off.

Eat that, stalking donkey fuckers.

"The Louvre. Nice," Jase praises, pushing his hair back from his face and finally handing me my purse as he looks around the hall. "I always wanted to see the Mona Lisa."

I twist my lips to one side and peer at him through my hair before tucking it behind my ear. "Really? You're at least six feet tall, you could rock the cover of GQ better than anyone I've ever met, your arms are like adult coloring books, and you're a damn good singer. You expect me to believe you've always wanted to see the Mona Lisa?"

"You think I could rock the cover of GQ?" He raises an eyebrow. "Bloody hell. These compliments are good for my ego."

"I think you have selective hearin'." I walk into the first section of the museum. "I don't believe you."

"Why not? I let your three-year-old niece feed me grapes."

I laugh. "Please. Nobody lets Mila feed them grapes. We're force-fed. You should see how many fish she's murdered because they were 'hungy.'"

"How many?"

I stop walking for a moment and tick them off on my fingers. "Binky, Patch, Spots, Goldie, Lellow, Wed, Gangan, Pop, Shark, Rock, and, finally, Nemo. Dory is still alive, but that's probably only because Dad bought him two days before we left."

Jase nods slowly. "I see your point. But how does one tiny person kill so many fish? And why do you keep buying them?"

"I bought Nemo because I wanted him. It killed me when he died." Okay, so that's an exaggeration. "But we don't. Dad does because he's got the resolve of an ice cube in boiling water. But the point is—it's not cute. You're force-fed. Try again."

He laughs, his shoulders trembling. "I've never had any interest in this place in my entire life. But, now...I'm terribly interested in it."

I grin. *Terribly.* I get real, big-ass butterflies when he says that. *Damn that accent.* Actually, no. Don't damn it. Fuck it. I could get on board with that.

"Hey." I elbow him. "You wanted me to bring you on a tour of the city. The Louvre is part of it. You can't come to Paris and not visit here."

"I don't know. I've seen the crown jewels and I'm not sure much else could top those."

"We're not talking about personal items here, Jase."

He laughs, nudging me right back. "I mean the real ones. In the Tower of London."

"Oh." I nibble slightly on my bottom lip. "I never got a chance to go there."

He stops. A look of literal horror flits over his face. "You went to London and you didn't see them?"

"No. I got distracted by some guy writing a song in a coffee shop, but he never took me there." I peer at him out of the corner of my eye.

He turns toward me. The smile that tugs his lips upward is slow and sexy, and a lustful glint darkens his gaze. "I'm fairly sure that guy got pretty distracted somewhere around chorus number two, and the fact he made it in and out of a taxi without kissing her was quite the feat."

My cheeks flush as a warm tingle spreads through my body. People believe in love at first sight, but I'm a full supporter of lust at first sight. What happened when we met was definitely lust at first sight.

Apparently, that hasn't changed in a year.

"You should get a gold medal. I'm pretty irresistible," I manage to force out. My heart is beating a little quicker at the memory of him kissing me for the first time.

Totally random. Right in the middle of the bridge that crosses over the Thames by Big Ben.

He just...stopped...in the middle of the sidewalk, grabbed me, and kissed me.

"It's the smart mouth," Jase says. "I can't resist a smart mouth."

"'A smart mouth?' So, someone could walk over here right now and sass your pants off and you'd make out with them?"

"Oooh. That was very possessive for a girl who just laid out that we're nothing but sex only thirty minutes ago."

"Are you screwin' with me, Masters?"

He smirks. "No. Just observing, love."

I purse my lips. "I'm not your love."

"Definitely possessive."

"How did you get to that conclusion? And I'm not possessive. I'm not a caveman, thank you very much." I huff and fold my arms across my chest.

Wanna ruin a trip to a museum? Take an arrogant British bastard with you.

"I've called you 'love' a hundred times in the past few days and you've not complained once. Right after I call you possessive for getting your back up over a flippant comment, you're 'not' my love."

"I don't think I like you anymore." My cheeks burn.

Jesus. He's right. I did sound a little possessive, didn't I? Fucking hell...

"For the record, no," he says with amusement.

"No, what?"

"You have the memory of Play-Doh squished back into the tub, don't you?"

"Seriously. Not likin' you, Brit Boy." I whack his hand with mine.

He grins. "Not a smart mouth. Just *your* smart mouth. You have the personality to pull it off." He grabs my hand and slides his fingers through mine.

"Are you calling me a..." I pause when an elderly couple shuffles past us, their wrinkled hands clasped together. Aw. "Bitch?" I whisper.

"I was going to, but then you whispered so you didn't offend them," he says in a low voice. "So, no."

"Good answer." I half smirk and look up.

Oh, man.

His face is right there. Right next to mine. And his eyes are gazing right into mine, bright and compelling, and I take in a deep breath. My hand burns where his is touching mine, and mine is so much smaller than his. When I glance down, the ink that decorates the back of his hand, teases his knuckles, is so dark compared to my paler skin.

"Do you think they're gone yet? The photographers?" I clear my throat.

"Maybe. Maybe not." He steps closer to me. "But, if we go check, I'll have to let go of you."

I nod quickly.

"I'd rather go see the Mona Lisa and not give a fuck," he whispers so close to me that his hot breath skates across my mouth.

"Okay. Let's go see it. And not give a fuck."

He smiles, and I don't regret it at all.

"You've spent all day with him." Sofie puts her hands on her hips. "I've been fielding questions since ten this morning. They're like dogs with bones. Or teen boys with teen girls." She frowns, glancing down at the floor. "Anyway, my point is, what are you doin'?"

"Why do I have to be doing anything? Why can't I just be hanging out with him?"

"Because you had"—she looks at Mila, who is happily coloring on the floor—"sex," she whispers. "With him."

"No. I didn't, did I?" I retort smartly. "Why doesn't that mean we can hang out? Remember, they don't know that. And if they do..."

She rolls her eyes and sits on the sofa. "No. You know I wouldn't do that to you. I'm just... worried."

"About what? I have protection."

"Leila!"

"What? The ground rules didn't mention s-e-x with someone I've s-e-x-e-d before."

She drops her head forward, smacking her palm against her forehead. "You're gonna be the death of me."

"I know. That's my job as your best friend. To kill you slowly with my idiocy."

"At least you admit you're an idiot."

I grin.

"What did you guys do today?" She bites the corner of her thumb. "Y'all behaved, right?"

I resist the urge to roll my eyes. Just about. "Yes, we behaved. If you can count running away from photographers and me flipping them off behaving."

She pauses and obviously thinks about it for a moment. "Yeah, I'm countin' it. That's a good day for you."

Yeah... She's kinda right.

"You just hung out though? You expect me to believe that?"

"Yeah. We hid in the Louvre, gave no fucks about the Mona Lisa, led photographers on a chase around the Eiffel Tower, and caught a cab to Notre Dame, where we had fifteen minutes of peace before Jase was recognized by a bunch of teenage girls who went to the concert last night."

That definitely wasn't my favorite bit of the day. I overbought on pastries this morning, so we ended up having lunch too, and we did Notre Dame after having stopped for a drink. We were naïve in thinking we'd gotten away with some peace... Especially when I was asked in very broken English if my brothers were around.

No. I don't go in public with my brothers. It's embarrassing, and I'd like to get in and out of a store without being accosted for photographs and autographs and experiencing crying, screaming girls.

If I want to experience that, I'll watch reality TV.

Let's just say I'm glad we got around the Louvre without any problems and agreed that holding hands in really public public wasn't a good idea.

It cut our exploration of the city short. Mostly because I think Jase could tell I wasn't enjoying it anymore. I tried... Really, I did. As we walked along the path right on the Seine, beneath Lovelock Bridge, I tried to enjoy the abstract, charming art that adorned the walls, but it fell flat.

Everything has since.

I guess I gave in to the normality of being with him too much because I'm not starstruck by him.

He's just a guy to me. Just a guy doing what he loves.

I know enough of them, after all, to see that he's no different.

"Do you ever get annoyed when you're out with Con?" I cut through Mila's quiet mumbling to herself and look over at Sofie. "By the fans and stuff?"

She gives me a sly look before nodding. "Sometimes. Especially when Mi's with us. Remember last summer when we went to Destin Beach? And the guys were constantly swarmed although it was supposed to be a family vacation? It bugs me more when they don't respect me."

"Oh, beach!" Mila looks up. "My lub the beach."

"I know, baby." Sofie smiles.

"Cussels are the best."

"Cussels sure are. What are you colorin', short stuff?" I ask her, leaning forward.

She grabs the book and shows it to me. It's a mess of pink and black scribbles, but clearly Minnie Mouse.

"Great job! I love it."

She grins widely. "Tankoo, Anny LeiLei."

"You're real welcome." I can't help but grin back at her. God, that child's smile is infectious. When she's turned back to her coloring, I focus on Sofie again. "How do you cope?"

"Are you askin' 'cause you wanna get laid or 'cause you actually care?"

"I plead the Fifth."

"You're doin' that a real lot this week," she drawls.

"I can make your life a livin' hell, you know that, right?"

"Yeah, but I have the three-year-old who likes to bounce on beds at six in the morning." She shoots me a shit-eating grin that says she wins. "Seriously, Lei. I don't know this guy. Is he hot? Hell yeah. I can appreciate a hot guy. Especially with that accent." Her smile drops to a sassy smirk. "But I don't know him."

"Neither do I," I admit, realizing that it's true. "But do I need to know him to...lie down with him?"

I never thought talking sex with my best friend would be so...innuendo loaded. I'm usually a straight-out-there kinda girl.

Sofie frowns, her lips twitching up on one side. "You didn't last time."

"Shut up." I lean back and hug my knee to my chest. "Lord, Sof. What if I'm being stupid?"

"Then you're more like Tate than you thought?"

"Girl, be serious!"

"Mila, do Mommy a favor," Sofie says to the curly-haired kid.

She looks up, interested.

"Go find Mommy's phone in the suitcase in the bedroom. Please? I'll pay you a whole euro."

"'Kay!" Mila cries excitedly, scrambling up. "Oh, lid." She puts the lid back on her pen before running into the bedroom.

"Listen to me, Leila," Sofie says quickly, turning fully toward me. Her blond hair falls in front of her light-blue eyes. She lowers her voice to a whisper. "You're fucked no matter what, okay? You look at him like he's chocolate sprinkles on ice cream. You wanna sleep with him? Go ahead, but one of your brothers will find out eventually."

"Not necessarily..." I say, trying to figure out every way to keep it from them. "They'll only find out if someone tells them."

"They're already suspicious. You never willingly spend time with a guy unless you're dating them."

"We're friends."

"You're contemplating having sex with the guy. That's more than friends, however you look at it."

"All right. He's my friend who turns me on and whose brains I want to screw right out of his body."

She stares at me flatly. "You're so unbelievably eloquent, aren't you?"

I shrug. "No point beating around the bush when the point is in its roots, is there?"

"Mama," Mila says, coming back with a frown marring her cute little face. "My tan't find it."

Sofie pulls it out from under the cushion next to her. "Oh, look at that! Silly mama."

"Silly mama," she repeats quietly, yawning and lying back down next to her coloring book.

"Liar," I mutter.

"Idiot," she mutters back. "Just be careful, yeah? I'm going to deny all knowledge if you get caught."

"Get caught? Way to make it sound like I'm going to see my English professor or something. It's not forbidden, Sof." I stand, grab my phone, and check the time. "All right. I'm going to get dinner."

"And then have a quiet night in."

I open the door and grin. "Hey—the ground rules mentioned hitting on and dating. Not...quiet nights in."

"Who's having a quiet night in?" Conner stares at me.

"Jesus fu—dge!" I jump, slapping my hand against my chest. "The hell is wrong with you?"

"A helluva lot less than is wrong with you," he replies without missing a beat. He narrows his eyes. "Who's havin' a quiet night in?"

"I am. I'm going to read in the bath, watch some Netflix, and get room service. Is that a crime, Detective?"

"I love you, Lei, but I'm not averse to beatin' the truth outta you."

"Actually," I say, straightening up, preparing the lie on my tongue. "I just asked your fiancée if she'd like to go out tonight, but she said she's tired, and the others all have plans, so I am havin' a quiet night in."

"What are you going to watch?"

"*How to Get Away With Murder.*"

He stops.

I grin.

"You mentioned ground rules," he says suspiciously.

"She was hit on at the bar last night and he gave her his number," Sofie says, leaning forward. "She told him no."

Conner slides his eyes to her. "All right."

Ha! Gullible loser. He'd believe her if she insisted Santa was real. In a book, that's cute. In real life... Ugh. Maybe it's just because he's my brother.

"Try not to drown yourself." He pats my arm and pushes past me, into the room.

I elbow him and wave to Sofie. "Bye, Mi. Go sleep soon, yeah?"

"Bye, Anny LeiLei!" she shouts without looking up from her coloring book.

Anyone else, I'd roll my eyes. But for her? It's a smile and a nod.

I make it down the hall to my room in less than a minute despite my slow walk. Sofie's words about my brothers' finding out if I sleep with Jase are screaming at me. She's right. I know they'll probably find out, and I know they'll kill him and not me because that's what brothers do.

So, why do I still want to do it?

Is it because, if they punched him for sleeping with me—which is a very real possibility—I'd step in front of him and take it?

I quickly shake my head to clear that thought. How ridiculous is that?

Shit though.

I can't believe I just had that thought. Wow... Maybe sleeping with him again isn't a good idea after all. After all, it's nothing my vibrator can't do, right?

Except snuggle. Vibrators don't snuggle.

Hold the fucking phone.

Snuggle? Fucking *snuggle*? No. You don't snuggle on booty calls, which is essentially what this is. A booty call. Plain and simple.

Nowhere in the Booty Call Manual is "snuggling" mentioned. Or cuddling, hugging, or any other variation of the word.

And the only spooning that is allowed is when you're being fucked from behind, just for clarification.

I pace the length of my room. It's not real effective—it's kind of small. But still. Pace. Up and down. Back and forth. Here and there. Wall to door. Bed to bath.

I'm giving myself a headache here, actually. Quite a bad one.

Ugh.

I'm overthinking this. I hate being female—I'd dissect an ant if I put too much thought into its place in a backyard. Let's be fair.

It doesn't actually matter that I get a little heart-skippy whenever I see Jase. I have the same reaction to shirtless pictures of Zac Efron and Jamie Dornan on TMZ. But my clitoris gets excited and demands attraction, and my heart complies.

If I tell myself that, that makes it right, right? If I say it out loud, it practically solidifies it.

How did I get from thinking about my brothers finding out about me having sex to considering my reactions to Jase?

Yep.

I should have gotten on a plane the first time I saw him. Should have faked sick, gone back to my room without laying more than my eyes on him, and gotten on a plane.

I take a deep breath in a desperate attempt to flood my body with some calming oxygen.

Am I spending too much time trying to convince myself it's just sex? Is that my problem? Should I simply admit to myself that I enjoy Jase's company and maybe a snuggle or two wouldn't go amiss?

It's not like it'll ever be more than enjoyment and sex. He lives in London. I live in South Carolina. Thousands and thousands of miles apart. A completely unrealistic distance and stupid travel time.

When I put it this way... Yes, I enjoy his company. I'd like a snuggle. Maybe. But we can be friends and have great sex.

I check my bra and my panties to make sure they match—praise the god of lingerie, they do—and leave my room before I lose my mind.

We said ten.

It's not even eight.

I'm hungry.

I'm tired.

I'm confused.

I feel like a teenage girl about to go on her first date.

I don't know what I'm doing. Oh, god. Does my admission to myself that I like his company make this sex more than just sex despite my insistence that it is, indeed, just sex?

I turn around when I get to the elevator.

Yep. Maybe it does.

I slap my forehead.

No, it doesn't. I've dated guys and not always enjoyed their company unless their mouths were shut and we were in bed. So...

I get into the elevator before I change my mind again.

Just sex.

Just sex.

Just sex.

I repeat the words like a mantra, even going as far as to whisper them to myself in this steel box. I feel a little better for it, if I'm honest with myself. At least I'm trying to be honest with myself—I don't know if I am.

Maybe I just need to fuck him and get it over with. Clearly, what-if isn't giving my sanity a break.

I knock on his door three times, so hard that my knuckles ache a little.

Jase opens the door, his wet hair dripping onto his bare torso. "Hey. You're early."

"Yeah... Is it a problem?" I raise one eyebrow.

He laughs. "No, I'm just in a meeting. That's all. You can come in."

"You're in a meeting? Shirtless?"

"It was unexpected," he says dryly. "And, for the record, I've been trying to put a shirt on."

"And failed how?" I ask, following him into his suite. "Little Disney woodland creatures come to stitch it into something better for the ball?"

He smiles lopsidedly, his eyes glittering with laughter. "You're sarcastic this evening."

"Running from photographers will do that to a girl." My tone is dry.

His smile widens, and he grabs a T-shirt and pulls it over his head. "I'll be two minutes, okay?"

"Jase," a woman's voice says. "If we're done here, I won't keep you. Oh—hello."

My eyes snap up. She's a few years older than I am, her blouse and her skirt well pressed... Blond hair. Blue eyes. British accent. Gorgeous. Obviously. Isn't everyone in this industry?

"Hi. Leila." I hold my hand out.

"Leila Burke?" she asks, taking my hand.

I nod.

"Oh! It's nice to meet you. I'm Madison Bentley. I'm Jase's manager's assistant."

"Pleasure." I smile. Try to. *Some meeting if he's shirtless.*

"Anyway, if you both have plans, I'll leave you to it." She smiles, picking up a black purse from the sofa. "Jase, I'll call you in the morning to confirm the final details for the meet-and-greets. Lawrence wants me on a plane by ten, so please make sure you're available around eight."

"Got it." He nods, clicking the switch on a kettle on the side cabinet.

"All right, then." Madison shoots a beaming smile between us. "Leila, great to meet you. I'm sure we'll see each other again in London."

Wonderful. "Can't wait." I watch her as she leaves and shuts the door behind her. Jase's eyes are hot on me, so I snap my head around.

"What?" I ask.

"You're cute when you're jealous."

"Jealous? You're mistaking it for surprise, Brit Boy. Y'all need lessons in reading emotions." I drop myself onto the sofa.

"Yeah. Right. I forgot you women like to scratch each other's eyeballs out when you get surprised." He puts extra inflection on the word *surprised*. "Want a cuppa?"

"Do I want a what now?"

"A cuppa."

"That doesn't answer my question."

He holds a teabag up. "A cup of tea."

I stare at the little triangular bag for a moment before answering, "No. I don't drink tea."

His dark eyebrows draw together in confusion. "You don't... How can't you drink tea?"

"I don't like tea."

Oh man, he looks like he's about to combust.

"You don't like tea," he says.

"I don't like tea."

"You don't like tea," he repeats slowly. So slowly... Like I just told him that his mom just died or something. "I'm not sure how I feel about that."

"Probably as horrified as I am about your inability to understand 'fixin' to.'"

He shakes his head and makes his tea. His spoon clinks against the sides of his mug. "We're going to have to revisit this. It's a game changer."

Because I don't like tea? Boy, the British sure are serious about it, huh? I thought it was just a stereotype.

"What would happen if a British person didn't like tea?"

He pauses before turning his green eyes on me. "We burn them at the stake," he answers, deadly serious.

"Seems fair." I grin and kick my shoes off. "So, Madison seems nice."

Lazily, Jase smiles and scratches the side of his nose. "She is."

"Nice enough for shirtless meetings."

"You're insistent for someone who isn't jealous..."

I hold my hands up. "Just an observation."

"Insistent observation."

"Do you regularly have shirtless business meetings?"

"No. But, given that I'd just gotten out of the shower when she showed up, unannounced... Shirtless beat out wearing nothing but a tiny hotel towel."

Damn. I should have shown up earlier. Before she did.

Shit. Maybe I am jealous. But only that she got to see him in a towel and I didn't. If his hair is still wet, then his body would have been too.

My stomach clenches, and I tighten my jaw. Damn.

Jase pushes off the wall he was leaning against and crosses the room toward me. He leans over me, resting his hands on the back of the sofa, one on either side of my head. My eyes are drawn momentarily to the definition lines that decorate his upper arm. The hourglass inking that wraps around his left arm is intricate, delicately woven with many other words and symbols, but they disappear under the arm of the light-gray shirt he's wearing.

He clears his throat. "I thought you weren't jealous."

"Did she see you in a towel? Because then I might be."

He doesn't say anything.

Damn it.

"Okay, now, I'm jealous."

He smirks. "Want me to get undressed and put a towel on for you?"

"No. That's overkill. Just text me next time you're in the shower and I'll hightail it down here, get my fill, then leave you in peace." I meet his eyes.

They seem brighter for the gray shirt, and there's a tiny drop of water just about to fall onto his eyelashes. I reach up and wipe it away before it has a chance to, and the backs of my fingers brush against the rough stubble lining his jaw.

I draw in a short breath when Jase grabs my hand. His rough palm wraps around my lower arm, the callused pad of his thumb ghosting across the super-sensitive skin of my wrist. A shiver runs through me when he presses lightly on my pulse point.

Then, unexpectedly, he lifts my wrist to his mouth and kisses it.

It's the softest kiss I've ever felt.

"She's twenty-five years old and has tried it on with every guy Lawrence has signed for the past two years. She has her own failed singing career and is desperately trying to get any single man between the ages of twenty-four and thirty-five to fall in love with her so she can continue to live in the lifestyle she became accustomed to before her second album crashed," he says softly, his lips still at my wrist, his eyes on me. "I humor her. She does nothing for me."

"I never insinuated she did." I lick my lips. "I just...assumed."

"Why? Because she's blond?" His eyebrows creep upward beneath his wet hair, which is still dripping random water onto his face. One cold drop falls onto my arm. "Tall? Slim? Quiet? Agreeable? British like me?"

I feel my gaze harden as annoyance flickers through my body unbidden.

"Don't worry." He leans in, and if I didn't know better, I'd say he was silently laughing his ass off. "I prefer sassy, Southern girls with a wild soul." He winks, grins, and gets up.

I purse my lips as the annoyance fizzles out only to be replaced with a thrilling shot of happiness. I shouldn't be happy about it—not really. But, damn it all, I am. *Too happy.*

"I'm not wild," I protest.

"Leila, love, twenty-four hours ago, I watched you playfully almost throw yourself off a roof because you wanted to."

"I didn't want to throw myself off a roof," I argue, following him with my eyes. "I swung on the railing."

"Like a two-year-old trying to get into the park."

"I like the wind in my hair."

"I like the wind in your hair too." He shoots me a tiny smile. "But not enough to push you off a roof."

"You're never going to let me live this down, are you?"

"Not on your bloody life, babe." That tiny smile changes into a full-blown grin, and the hair on the back of my neck stands on end.

Jesus. One smile shouldn't elicit such a strong response.

And I'm not talking about the hair—I'm talking about the two-step my heart's taken up. It's beating twice, skipping one, beating twice, skipping one. Shit though. I want to run my thumb along the smiling curve of his lips.

I force my gaze away from him, toward the TV. Seeing the blank screen, I search for controller without saying a word. It has to be here somewhere. Has to be near. Where I can grab it. Without moving.

"Stop starin' at me." I snap my head around to Jase. "You think I can't tell, but I can."

"Can tell what?" He looks amused now. Not even sexy amused. Just plain old annoying amused. Punch-you-in-the-face amused.

"That you're starin' at me!"

"Actually, I'm not staring at you."

"Then, what? The wall?"

"I'm thinking about doing what you came here for. Fucking you until you can't breathe."

I double-take. For a girl who's so blunt, I'm sure not used to it from others. But still...

"Really?" I ask, raising one eyebrow.

"Really," he says, sipping on his mug of tea.

Jesus, a sip has never been so sexy.

"Then you're on the wrong side of the dang room, Brit Boy."

His eyes are fixed on mine as he lowers the mug. The clink as he sets it on the side is soft but, at the same time, threatening. It's his gaze though. The seriously playful glint clouded by desire is what really sends shivers rippling over my skin.

"Sounds like a challenge." His voice is quiet.

"It is," I assure him.

He's on me like a flash. I don't know how he moved so quickly, but he did, and before either of us can say another word, he's leaning over me on the sofa, his hands in my hair, his lips on mine. His kiss is hot and desperate, burning with the same lust that's flowing through my veins.

I grab the soft fabric of his shirt and tug him down on top of me. His hand slides down my body and grips my thigh tight, his fingers burning where he touches my bare skin. He hooks my thigh over his hip and pushes himself against me. His cock gets harder with every kiss we share, and he jerks when I flick my tongue at his bottom lip.

He tugs my head back by my hair, and his mouth travels from mine, down my jaw, to my neck. He keeps his grip on my thigh as he explores my neck by way of tiny kisses. "Are you sure?" he mumbles between each hot touch. "This. Be sure."

I gasp when he drags his teeth across my pulse point. "I'm sure." How can I not be? My body is on fire. I don't give a shit about consequences. I give a shit about right now and why he's still wearing his goddamn shirt.

Thankfully, it seems like my reassurance is all he needed, because he's kissing me again. My mind is swimming with foggy lust, and I'm working on autopilot, letting my body respond to him in the best way it knows how to. And it does—my heart beats faster, my lungs burn as breathing gets harder, and my clit aches so badly that my hips buck against him, desperate for more.

Jase quickly releases me, only to grab my hands and tug me up. He drags me through the suite and into the next room, to the bedroom.

I'm bouncing off the bed before I can say a word.

He tears his shirt over his head and jumps on top of me, his legs going between mine. My legs wrap around his waist, pulling him against me, at the same time that my hands slide up his back.

Our mouths meet, our tongues fighting through until our kiss is deep and frantic. My nipples harden and rub against my bra, and I whimper into his mouth when he presses his cock against my pussy.

Too many clothes. Way too many clothes here.

Together, we scramble to remove my shirt, and my fingers dive into his hair once it's off and his mouth is traveling down my neck. His breath is hot as it fans across my skin, and he wastes no time reaching behind my back and unclasping my bra in one swift movement. He pulls the straps down my arms and throws it to the side before palming one of my breasts.

His mouth finds the other, and his tongue flicks over my sensitive nipple. Each little touch shoots pleasure right down to my pussy, and my back arches, desperate for more.

"Jase." His name escapes me in a scratchy whisper as I suck a breath in.

"Fuck," he croaks out, darting down my body so quickly that my legs fall away from him. He finds the waistband of my shorts and tugs hard without warning.

As he pulls them down, he takes my panties with them.

I breathe in once again, making my chest heave, as he throws my remaining clothes to the side, leaving me totally exposed to him. My cheeks flame when he looks up at me with hot, green eyes and smirks. Instinctively, my legs clench together, but he laughs huskily and opens them.

He's so much stronger than I am, and as he holds my legs open, I glance down. His rough, stubbly jaw is scratching against my thigh, and he finds my gaze. I shiver, fighting my rapid breathing, as his face moves ever closer to my wet pussy.

He wraps his hands around my thighs, his fingertips digging into my skin. His tattooed arms against my pale legs are a complete contrast but equally so fucking hot, and my pussy clenches hard.

His face is right in front of my pussy. His mouth right there. His eyes...

His eyes lock with mine as his tongue strokes right along my wet pussy. Then he pauses to put pressure on my clit.

"Shit!" I throw my arm over my eyes, unable to watch him as pure pleasure floods my veins.

He chuckles against me, closing his mouth over my clit. The gentle vibrations from his laughter heighten the delight he brings as he licks and sucks the tender spot. He flattens his tongue, circling it, and firmly presses down.

It should hurt.

I feel nothing but blind desire for more.

For him.

My hips lift of their own accord, which presses my clit harder against his tongue, begging for more of his teasing. I feel his smile as he massages the tops of my thigh, slowly moving his hands around to my ass. He cups it firmly and then lifts, easing his tongue right inside me.

I buck against him, effectively fucking his tongue. Moans escape me, sweat trickles down my neck, and my whole body arches toward him as pleasure beats out embarrassment and I grip at the sheets as if he's going to make me fly away.

"Ask me," he demands in a raspy breath against the top of my thigh. Its harsh and hot, and it tingles across my clit.

"Please, Jase." I grip the sheet tighter as another breath flits across me.

Another deep chuckle before he returns his mouth to me and, with a few expert strokes of his tongue, tips me over the edge. Heat floods through my body as my hips grind and I ride the orgasm out until I'm a hot mess lying on the bed.

Jase stands, wiping his mouth, and removes his pants. His boxers follow, and as he reaches to the nightstand, I focus the best I can on his body.

Fuck.

His body.

Fuck.

It's toned, shadowed ridges dipping between each muscle in all the right places. Each one flexes as he moves, and as my gaze drops another inch, following the lick-me lines that curve into a V down over his hips, I find his cock. It's standing up, rock hard, the veins visible as they trail up and down his shaft.

I shakily sit up, still trembling from my orgasm, and wrap my hand around his cock. He jerks, his cock twitching against my palm. I move my hand up and down his length, kissing across his stomach. His skin is hot under my mouth as I explore his toned body, circle my thumb over the head of his cock, and use a drop of precum as lubricant.

I briefly bite my tongue, glancing down at the glistening tip, before pushing him back and taking him into my mouth.

He did this—I can too.

"Jesus, Leila," he rasps, running one hand through my hair.

I work the end of his cock with my mouth before leaning back only to grab his hardness and run the tip of my tongue from the base to the tip. Each movement is teasing, and I can't help but smile when his grip on my hair becomes rougher. I take him in my mouth, and—

He jerks back, releasing my hair, only to grab me by the waist and throw me back on the bed. He picks up a foil square and tears it open with his teeth before pulling the condom out and positioning it at the end of his cock.

I watch as he eases the rubber along himself.

Jesus.

That's hot.

When it's on, he leans over me, kissing me, and grips my ass.

Only to flip us over so he's under me and my pussy is firmly resting against his cock. I draw in a deep breath as I reach between us, lifting my hips, and position him at my opening. I meet his eyes as I lower myself onto him, feeling my pussy stretch around him. It hugs his hard cock tight as I take as much as I can, watching his entire body tense as he drops his eyes to watch me.

I watch him watch me as I lift up.

Watch him watch me take his cock deep inside me.

I have never been so turned on in my life.

His fingertips dig into my ass as he encourages me to move faster, but the moment I find my rhythm, he bends his knees up, pushing me down over him, and wraps his arms around my body. One hand slinks into my hair as he captures my mouth, thrusting so his cock is buried deep inside me.

"Fucking hell," he whispers, his grasp on me tightening. "So fucking hot watching you take my cock."

I moan as my clit rubs against the rough patch of hair sitting above his cock. Jase bucks his hips, thrusting up inside me, keeping me pinned against him. His kisses range from deep tongue strokes to playful nibbles that ignite sparks. The whole time, he's moving inside me, deeper, harder, but not quicker.

His kisses swallow my moans, muffling them until it's too much and I can't do it anymore.

I need more air.

More.

I bury my face in his neck as the pleasure becomes too much. From his touch to his kiss to his grip to his thrusts...

"Jase," I gasp against his chest. "Oh, god..."

He rubs his hand over my ass cheek before sharply slapping it. It pushes me closer to the edge, and as my hips try to move, he shakes his head, letting out a raspy, "No," before holding me frozen against him and pounding his cock into me with an unrelenting force that draws my orgasm from me.

Uncontrollable..

I fall apart in his arms, crying my release into his mouth as he keeps the pace up before finally, minutes later, he groans my name, his voice cracking, and stills.

I collapse fully on top of him, and he sweeps my hair around my neck, away from his face. His fingertips trail across the base of my neck, ghosting my shoulder blades, and I shiver. I close my eyes for a moment, turning my face toward the strong curve of his neck.

I feel nothing but content.

Completely...free.

chapter ten

F ucking hell.

Just... Fucking hell. Bloody fucking hell, even.

My body is tight and tense despite the hard hit of my orgasm, and I know why. It's because of the girl lying on top of me, curled against me, with my dick still buried eight inches inside her tight, wet pussy.

She's so warm, even if her skin is slicked with sweat. She fits perfectly against me, her legs wrapped around mine, one of her arms under my head, her face buried in the crook of my neck. Her lips brush my collarbone every time she exhales, heating my skin to what feels like a hundred thousand degrees.

I don't know what to do with this feeling.

I didn't know feelings could change so quickly—from nothing but sex to nothing but not wanting to let go. I don't want to let her go. I want to lie here beneath her, my arms around her, and bask in the moment. Breathe in this peaceful feeling of her breath tickling my skin and her soft body against mine.

In the silence of us.

"Jase," Leila whispers, slowly shifting her body. "I'm cold."

Shit. I put the air conditioning on after my shower. "Shit. Sorry." I clasp her waist and ease her up, letting her roll to the side the second my cock is out of her. I sit up and roll the condom off, refusing to lament the loss of her warmth around me. "Here." I drop the condom in the bin and hand her a fluffy robe from the chair. I think it's the one I threw on when Madison knocked at the door earlier.

Despite what Leila thinks, the woman didn't see me in a towel, but it was fun to see her get possessive again. She has a fiery little jealous streak that ignites like a match.

Leila catches the robe with a whispered, "Thank you," and wraps herself up in it. She sits back on the end of the bed and plays with the end of the robe before getting up and mumbling about using the bathroom.

I frown, watching her disappear into it when she slams the door. There's a slight air of awkwardness now, and it's not just because I'm standing stark naked in the middle of the room with my cock still half hard like it's deciding whether or not it should be saluting her arse.

I rub my hand down my face and grab my boxers from the floor. I put them on, followed by my jeans, and sit on the edge of the bed. The jeans are unbuttoned, but it doesn't matter as I lean forward and rest my chin on my thumb. I rub the side of my forefinger across my chin, just beneath my lower lip, and stare at the bathroom door.

How long does she need in there?

If we weren't a few floors up and she was wearing something other than a robe—and there was a window—I'd guess she was making a break for it.

I'd bet my left ball she's regretting what we just did.

I drop my face forward and press the heels of my hands into my eyes. Shit. She can't regret what we just did—I don't want her to. What does it even fucking mean?

I'm damn sure no woman has ever regretted that before.

Of course, though, if someone will, it will be Leila Burke.

The sound of the lock clicking clinks through the air, and I look up in time to see her emerge from the bathroom. Her messy hair is swept over one side of her neck, and on that same side, the soft robe is falling down off her shoulder, revealing a stretch of tanned skin.

"Can I be honest?" she says softly, pushing some hair behind her ear. "I've never done a...booty call...before."

I still, my hands resting between my legs. She's deadly serious. I can see it in the way she won't meet my eyes. She's staring at the floor, uncertain, roughly tugging at the robe that won't stay up on her shoulder.

A booty call.

That's what she thinks this is.

Is it? It was. But it doesn't have to be anymore.

I get up and walk to her, buttoning my jeans so they don't fall down. Leila looks different—someone completely different to the girl I saw stumble into my room and get all feisty-jealous not an hour ago. Someone who looked as though she wanted to pick another woman's ovaries out with the nail of her pinkie finger.

Now, she looks...vulnerable.

I don't like it.

It hurts my heart, this out-of-character vulnerability.

No, it more than hurts my heart.

It whispers to my soul.

Grips it.

Tightly.

I gently take her face in my hands, cupping her cheeks, and tilt her head back. She fights it, but her eyes eventually find mine, and I stare into their stunning, blue depths until I'm drowning in the sea of her gaze.

Until I'm struggling to breathe in the air of her.

I do the only thing that makes fucking sense to me.

I kiss her. Softly. The barest touch of my lips to hers. Until she leans in, a minty coating on her lips, making me smile.

"Why are you laughing?" she whispers.

"Smiling," I whisper back, correcting her. "I'm smiling, love. Not laughing."

"I don't see a difference from where I'm standin'," she snaps, pulling back from me.

I tug her back before she's out of reach and lock my hands at the base of her back. She pushes at my chest, but my strength outdoes hers, so she relaxes, giving in to my strong hold on her.

"You going to listen to me, Leila?" I ask quietly, looking down at her.

A flash of defiance illuminates her gaze for a moment, but she nods anyway.

"This isn't a booty call, babe. Or, at least, doesn't have to be." I watch her as I speak.

Her eyes are already narrowing.

"We can be...friends with benefits. Because, let me tell you, this won't be the only time this will happen. There's no way I'm going to make it another two weeks without being inside you again."

"What if I only want a one-time thing?"

"You just screamed my name so loudly I'm pretty sure London heard you. Do you expect me to believe that?"

She sucks her lower lip into her mouth and tugs on it with her teeth. "You know I'm not supposed to be doing this, right? If we got caught..." She pushes at me, and this time, I let her go. She runs her hand through her hair, looking up at the ceiling. "Jase, if they found out, they could kick you off this tour." She drops her arm and meets my eyes. "I don't know you. I barely know anything about you, but I know how badly you want this. Maybe this was just an itch we couldn't scratch, and now, it's done and we're good again."

"Do you really feel that way, or are you trying to use your brothers as an excuse?"

The soft dressing gown falls off her shoulder again, and I grab it. I softly pull it back up to cover her skin.

She sighs heavily. "Jase...I don't know," she says softly. "I...I want to, but we'd have to keep it secret, and you—"

"Hey." I cup her face with my hands. "You let me worry about me."

She rests her hands over mine. "I just don't want you to face losin' everythin' over somethin' as trivial as sex."

I wouldn't be. I'd be losing it over you. And maybe it'd be worth it.

Internally, I shake that thought off and lean into her, brushing my lips over hers.

"Really? You call that trivial?"

Leila laughs quietly, letting her hands fall to my jeans. She loops her fingers into the belt hoops, and a small smile touches upon her lips. The worry is still hinting in the depths of her eyes, but it's being outshone by her usual playful, wild glimmer.

"I'd say yes," she says, "but I'm kind of hungry and I'm afraid you'll make me do it again before I can eat."

I pause for a moment. "I've never been turned down for food before."

"It could be worse. You could be turned down for masturbation."

Fair point. "All right. I'll feed you...but then I'm going to convince you that this definitely needs to continue."

"Can I fight the argument?"

"Sure. Just make sure you're naked and my cock is inside when you do, yeah?"

The tiny smile widens into the smile that is so very Leila—cheeks flushed, eyes bright, infectious, lopsided twist of her lips. "I approve of those terms." She steps toward me and tilts her face up to mine. Her lips barely touch mine, but she lingers there, and my fingers twitch at the sides of her face.

I slide my hands down to cup her neck, my thumbs brushing her jaw, and kiss her harder. She smiles against me before pulling back.

"Jase. Food," she demands. "I didn't eat yet."

"Well, Jesus, woman. You could have said," I grumble, letting her go. I look for the room service menu and find it on the table, next to my laptop. "Here. Find something you want and then I'll order it."

"Sure. But I'm paying—"

"Leila?"

"What?"

"Shut up."

My alarm clock blares at me, and I roll over, blindingly hitting it. I miss on every attempt, so I force myself to open my eyes to find the button. I press it three times, but it doesn't register it.

"Fucking hell." I sit up and rub my eyes, and it stops. "What the—" I stop when it starts again, and shit, that's not the alarm clock.

It's my bloody phone.

I get up and stumble sleepily into the main room, where I left my phone before Leila left last night. Now, I can hear the buzzing, and I pick it up.

"Hello?" I answer blearily.

"Jase?" Ella's voice comes through the line. "Did I wake you?"

I close my eyes and sit down. "Nope. I'm always up at... What time is it?"

"Six ten," she laughs, but it's slightly hollow. "I'm sorry, but Sofie and I need to talk to you."

"That sounds ominous."

"Can we come to your room?"

"I... Sure. Yeah. Let me put some clothes on."

"TMI right there," she mutters. "Okay. We'll be right down."

The call goes dead, and Jesus Christ, if they're coming to talk to me about Leila at six in the morning, I'm screwed as hell.

I've barely pulled my T-shirt over my head and checked for any traces of Leila's having been here when there's a quiet knock at my door. I tug the shirt down over my stomach with one hand as I open the door.

"Morning." I yawn.

"Late night?" Sofie grins knowingly.

I glare at her. What does she know?

Ella looks between us, confused, but understanding soon replaces it. "Oh. Oh! Ohhh." She covers her mouth with her hand. "Well, that explains a lot."

They're not here because they know about Leila. "Can you ladies come in here before you announce my private business to the entire floor?"

"Sure, sure," Ella shuffles past me.

"Not us you gotta worry about," Sofie mutters.

"What does that mean?"

"Sof!" Ella flicks her hand in her direction. "Be quiet."

"I'm really confused here, girls." I close the door and look at them both. "It's six in the morning and you're both here. And apparently not because you know Leila was here last night."

"I knew." Sofie holds her hand up. "She was flailing over coming here like a seal in heat until I told her to just do it. You're welcome."

I shoot her a thumbs-up. "Thanks."

"Don't worry. Your secret is safe with us. We won't tell anyone."

"Good to know."

"Geez, Sof. Shush!" Ella playfully scolds her. "Hey, you have coffee, right?" she asks me.

"Sure. The machine's right there. Help yourself."

"Thanks." She puts her purse down and goes to the machine. "Tate's still asleep, and if I'd tried to start this before I came here, he'd have woken up and I would have been the subject of a late-night talk show, and I wanted to talk to you before we get them together."

For what?

"Anyway," she continues over the sound of the machine spitting coffee out. "Sit down, because you're not going to like this."

Sofie shakes her head, her lips pulled into a grim line.

"Are you lot always this vague?" I ask, sitting next to Sofie on the sofa. "The world will reach its end before you spit it out."

Ella rolls her eyes, turning the machine off and facing me. "I have Google alerts set up for everybody. I start my day with a barrage of them. Then I spend an hour or so during the day going through them and doing damage control if it's necessary. Thankfully, it isn't usually, but sometimes, something comes up that needs to be addressed."

"Do you have one on me?" I ask, although I already know the answer to this. Why would she be here if she weren't?

"Yes." She sips from her coffee then puts the mug down. She comes over, pulls a tablet from her bag, and swipes. "I was headed down to the gym when I had a feeling I needed to check them. I did, and this is what I found." With one last swipe, she hands me the device.

MY NIGHT WITH JASE MASTERS!

"Sounds like the title of a porn movie," I mutter.

"Wouldn't be the first time we've had one of those alerts. Keep reading," Sofie encourages me.

I shoot her a confused glance, but ultimately, the desire to read more wins out and I turn back to the tablet.

Model Stella Porter, 21, a shop assistant from West London, purchased tickets to the Dirty B. concert in Paris when she failed to get any for their London shows. She said she was just as excited to see their supporting artist, Jase Masters, who happens to be the UK's hottest up-and-coming young male solo artist. She said she was lucky enough to secure VIP tickets that would take her backstage to meet Dirty B. and Jase Masters, and that the latter took a shine to her...

Here, she tells us how it happened.

I put the tablet down and pinch the bridge of my nose. What the fuck is wrong with people? "That's the biggest load of bollocks I've ever read in my life."

"Bollocks." Sofie grins. "I like that word. Why don't we have fun words like that?" she asks Ella.

"Sof! Focus!" Ella snaps her fingers in her face then turns to me. "Yeah. Bollocks. You're right. That is fun," she whispers to Sofie as she sits down. "Sorry. I'm paying attention now. It is shit, because we all know you left early with Carlos. There are also pictures of you leaving the arena before the guys did."

"And you were looking after tipsy Leila," Sofie inputs. "So we all know it's fake."

"But here's the thing: Stella Porter did have a VIP ticket for the backstage meet."

"I don't do the meets," I say slowly as this sinks in. "It didn't seem like it made much sense, and now I have a couple of appearances in London, it still doesn't."

"Right. But the media don't know this, and the media love a scandal. For them, this is golden. A dirty story on the new boy?" Ella raises her eyebrows. "They're going to take this and run with it. You're going to struggle leaving the hotel without security because they will mob you. I can call Jennifer and have her show up early. She can have a statement put out refuting the article and Stella's claims."

"I... Yeah...sure." I rub my hand over my face. "Why do I get the sudden feeling this means I've 'made it'?"

Sofie quirks an eyebrow, smirking. "Because you have."

I take a deep breath. "Seems slightly anticlimactic."

"Always is." Ella looks up from her phone. "Okay, I just texted Jennifer. She should be awake because it's concert day and the day before we go to London. Oh, and I texted Leila."

I snap my eyes toward her. "Why?"

"Because Leila Burke is a tickin' time bomb, and she'll see one thing before she reads the details and good luck getting her to talk to you after that." Sofie grimaces. "Been there. Avoid it."

Ella's phone rings, and she grins. "Wait for it." She answers and hits the speaker button. "Hello?"

"What the fuck are you texting me at this time of the morning for? You just woke me up," Leila's gravelly, sleep-filled voice echoes through the room. "I will cut you if it isn't because Zac Efron just showed up to declare his undyin' love for me."

Zac Efron? Really? That's her celebrity crush? I had her pegged for a Hemsworth girl. Guess I'm wrong.

"No Zac. Sorry. But you need to come down to Jase's room."

Silence for a second.

"Why are you in Jase's room?" she asks.

"For the juicy details of your secret rendezvous," Sofie answers.

"Am I on speaker? You bitches!"

I laugh into my hand.

"I'm gonna kill you both," Leila continues. "Why do I need to come down?"

"Because, if you don't, I'm gonna call Tate and wake him up and tell him I need him in the hall," Sofie answers. "Then I'm gonna bring Jase up to your room and sit back and enjoy the show."

"Whore," she snaps back. "I have no idea how I put up with you people."

The line cuts dead, and Sofie collapses back in a small fit of giggles.

"She's on her way." Ella grins. "Give her two minutes."

"I need coffee. Do you mind?" Sofie asks.

I shake my head and scratch my chin. I'm not going to drink it. Only in extreme situations is coffee consumed. I'd rather drink Red Bull than coffee. Hell, I'd rather go thirsty.

I pick Ella's tablet up and read through the rest of the story. She's on her phone, and Sofie is consumed by the coffee machine, so I take my time as we wait for Leila.

Every claim—aside from the obvious—in this is total bollocks. Pretty good for my ego, I admit, but I think the girl has a career in writing romance novels as opposed to modeling. She's very...thorough...in her descriptions. No-holds-barred, erotica kind of descriptions.

Great. The entire world will know of my fictional sexual prowess by lunchtime.

If I wanted that, I'd have been a porn star.

Bloody heck.

I look up when there's a knock at the door. Sofie gets to it before I can even move and opens the door to reveal a sleep-disheveled, tired-looking Leila. She obviously hasn't brushed her hair, much left removed the traces of yesterday's mascara from her eyelashes, and she's wearing the shortest shorts I've ever seen.

At least she's wearing a bra. Jesus.

"Seriously. I need new friends. I'm sellin' y'all on freakin' Craigslist and advertisin' for new ones." She grumbles each word out as she pushes past Sofie and comes into my suite. "What do y'all want?"

"Don't look at me," I tell her, leaning back when she turns her bright-blue eyes on me. "I didn't bring you here."

"Yeah, but I'm guessin' you did something."

"Actually, I didn't."

"But it's your fault."

"Wrong again."

"Well, fuck me," she drawls, folding her arms around her chest. "There's a first for a guy I know."

"Do me a favor," I say to Ella. "Don't ever wake her up again."

Leila's expression turns thunderous. "I swear to god, y'all, spit it out or I'm gonna go back to bed right and you can fuck yourselves."

Ella spits it out. Literally, the situation explodes out of her. She runs through the whole story a hell of a lot quicker than she did when she told me, and I don't blame her. Leila already looks like she wants to kill someone, and that's just from having been woken up.

"Where's the tablet?" Leila asks. "I want to read it."

I hand it to her despite Sofie's frantically shaking head. I guess that was a mistake. Oh well.

She knows better than anyone exactly where I was that night.

"'Model, Stella Porter, twenty-one,'" she reads. "Ha! Model! They're always models. Someone should tell them that putting their tits up on Instagram doesn't count. What a load of shit." She hands it to Ella without reading any more.

"You're stopping there?" I question.

"Yeah. She's a *model*. She's no model. She's a store clerk wannabe who'll get paid ten bucks to promote some small-time company on her social media using pictures her brother probably took for her." She shrugs. "Plus...she's blond."

My lips twitch to the side, and we share a look. Hers strong and certain, mine amused.

"What's wrong with blondes?" Sofie sniffs, patting her own golden hair.

"Nothing. He just doesn't like them." Leila nods toward me and stalks toward the coffee machine.

Fuck, her arse.

"Why not?" Sofie asks. "Oh, wait. Attracted to. Never mind. Good. Okay."

Leila rolls her eyes and shoves a mug under the machine.

Sure, everyone drink the coffee. They're lucky I don't live off it.

"Okay..." Ella says, looking at Leila. "I was expecting a little more..."

"Drama?" Leila glances over her shoulder, one eyebrow raised. "Sorry to disappoint. It's clear shit. And why do I need to know anyway? We're not in a relationship."

Both Sofie and Ella swing around to look at me.

I shrug. "We're not."

Sofie cuts her eyes between us before grabbing her purse and finishing her coffee. "Y'all are weird."

I hear Leila's snort before Ella gets up.

"Oookay," Ella says, looking at me. "We'll leave you both to it. Jen is awake, so I'll call her and we'll pull together a statement to refute the claims. She'll also call Lawrence and inform him so he can have his team keep an eye out in London. We might need more security." She nibbles on her lower lip. "Don't worry. I've got it figured out."

"Come on, Rambles," Sofie says, grabbing Ella's arm. "You're rambling."

"She guessed when you called her 'Rambles,' idiot!" Leila yells when they leave. She pushes the button on the coffee machine to end the stream and adds her sugar and one of the little of pots they leave that I hate. The spoon clinks against the sides of the mug as she stirs it.

She's too quiet. If there's anything I've learned this week, it's that, unless her nose is buried in a book, Leila is never quiet.

"You have an awful habit of staring at me."

"You're here in practically underwear. What do you expect?"

She glances down at her legs. "Ah. I dressed in the dark. No wonder the man in the elevator kept shifting uncomfortably."

I thin my lips and nod, adjusting my sweatpants so my own half-hard cock isn't obvious.

"I thought I had something on my face. Oh well." She shrugs and joins me on the sofa. "You don't mind that I'm drinkin' your coffee—stupid question, right?"

"Right." I grin and rest my arm on the back of the sofa. "You can go back to bed now. I didn't even want to wake you up, but they're persuasive."

"They're pests," she corrects me, putting down her mug and running both of her hands through her hair. All it does is make her boobs rise up, her shirt expose a strip of tantalizing skin above her waistband, and the curve of her neck look too tempting to ignore. "They should know better. Why did they even think I'd care? What did you tell them?"

"Me? I didn't bloody tell them anything. They woke me up with their bollocks, too, you know."

"Bollocks," she repeats. "That word is fabulous."

"I'll write you a glossary," I say dryly. "Us British have plenty of words I think you'll find 'fabulous.'"

"Tell me one now."

"I just did."

"No. Another."

"Uh... Tosser."

She grins and claps her hands in delight. "What's a tosser?"

"Basically an idiot. It's a pretty versatile word. Tosser, tosshead, tosspiece, tosspot."

"Shit. I can't decide which I like most." She giggles. "Tosspot. That's the best, I think. Toss. Pot. Toh-ss-poh-t," she attempts in a British accent.

"Don't do that again. Ever," I laugh. "I'm pretty sure I already told you your British accent is the worst thing I've ever heard."

"Yep, but practice makes perfect. How am I supposed to learn to talk right if you won't let me practice with you?"

"Because I can't help but think it's an awful waste of your mouth."

"Only if you're plannin' on kissin' me."

I lean over the sofa, cup the back of her neck, and pull her mouth against mine. She wraps her arms around my neck and falls back, taking me with her. I soften the fall by flattening one of my hands on the sofa cushion beneath her head, but it doesn't stop the way her leg bends upward, inviting my cock to press against her pussy.

Involuntarily, it does.

Leila grips me tighter, digging her nails into the top of my back, teasing my lips with the tip of her tongue. She presses herself against me, flexing her body and pulling me down farther until our bodies are flat together.

My muscles twitch. My cock is throbbing hard, and the desire to take her again, to feel her again, to get lost her again, right now, is overwhelming. Temptation is consuming me, and she is it embodied.

"Thought you weren't into booty calls," I murmur.

"Not a booty call. Friends with benefits," she murmurs right back while kissing along my jaw. Her tongue flicks a trail down my neck, and she wraps her legs around my waist. She flexes her hips against mine, rubbing her pussy along my cock.

I'm trying not to get in her pants, but she's intent on getting into mine, it seems. A groan rumbles deep in my throat. "Leila, you're making this very hard for me."

"I know." She grins cheekily and reaches down between us. She tugs at my shirt, her nails trailing up my sides.

I don't move, so she moves her hands to my front and runs her palms across my stomach, right down to the waistband of my sweatpants.

And dips her hand under.

"Leila..." I swallow hard when her fingertips brush the head of my cock.

She leans up, her breath tickling my ear. "Your cock gives you away, Jase." She slides her hand beneath my boxers and grasps me.

Her soft palm against the hardness of my dick makes my hips push into her hand. Slowly, she moves her hand up and down, twisting gently.

My balls tighten.

Jesus. This wasn't the plan when she walked in this morning. Hell—at all today. But I can't resist her any longer. She's a vixen hiding beneath a hardened exterior, and she's using it to her advantage. The article bothers her, and she's using sex to deflect her feelings.

If that's what she wants right now, it's what I'll give her.

Sooner or later, she'll have to talk to me about how she really feels.

I pull her hand off my cock and walk into the bedroom. I grab a condom from the nightstand, and when I get back into the front room, she's standing in the middle of it, her back to me.

"Where are you going?" I ask her.

She turns, the corner of her top lip in her mouth. "My room. You just—"

I cut her off by holding the condom up. Then, in a flash, I have my arm around her and I'm throwing her back onto the sofa. She laughs as I throw my clothes off and lean over her for hers. Her shorts and her underwear join the clothes on the floor, and she pulls her top over her head, reaching for me and kissing me between each piece that falls.

I sit back to roll the condom on and then run my fingers along her pussy, kissing her. I slide two fingers inside her, putting my thumb on her clit and rubbing. She moves against my hand, gasping, and I swallow her sharp inhale with a kiss as I replace my fingers with my cock.

She curls around me, her legs at my waist and her arms at my neck. She's so tight and wet, hugging me perfectly as I thrust in and out of her. Each harsh breath she releases between our kisses spurs me on, the quiet moans behind them telling of her advancing orgasm.

I can feel it too. My body is hot and covered in sweat, and my muscles are tense and twitching as I drive into her.

There's nothing else.

Just Leila. Just this.

These moments when I'm inside her and my name is falling uncontrollably from her lips are my favorites.

She cries out, her pussy tightening around me, and arches her back. I see the orgasm wash over her face and feel it in the way she clenches and digs her nails into my back. I move faster, desperately teetering on the edge of my own, some crazy part of me needing to join her in her pleasure.

I do—in a flood of heat and pleasure so blinding I have to close my eyes against its force. And then I collapse on top of her trembling body, barely able to stop myself from suffocating her with the weight of my body.

She relaxes, huffing happily, and I laugh.

"I need to go to back to sleep now," I mutter, burying my face in her hair.

She shakes with a silent giggle. "I needed to go back to sleep before. I just took advantage of the situation I found myself in."

"Are you staying or are you going?"

She opens her eyes and looks at me. A little frown mars her forehead. "I should go. My brothers will be down here as soon as they find out. If they find me here..."

"An hour," I reason. "Sleep for an hour and then go."

She hesitates for a moment, and then... "Okay. One hour."

chapter eleven

Leila

The sound of loud knocking tugs me out of my sleep. I move to grab the sheets and then freeze. There's a hard, hot body behind me, and... Shit.

Jase.

And there's knocking at the door.

Double shit.

"Jase!" I whisper as loudly as I can, sitting up and nudging him.

"Hm?" He grunts, rolling over.

"The door! Someone's at the freakin' door! Wake up!" I shove him one more time and clamber out of the bed.

At least I put my panties back on.

I peer into the main room. The knocking has paused, so I run in, grab my shirt, my shorts, and my room key, and run into the bathroom.

"What are you doing?" Jase asks, amused.

"Hiding!" I hiss, hugging my clothes tight to me. "I bet you a hundred bucks that's my brothers."

"Bloody hell!" He grabs some jeans and tugs them up his legs. He pulls a shirt out of one of the drawers and turns to me. "Lock the door. I'll try and get them to talk about this in the restaurant so you can leave. And—shit. I've missed that call from Madison..."

I purse my lips.

He notices, shaking his head. "There's a voicemail. It'll be here. I need breakfast first anyway."

I nod, letting go of the mention of Madison and focusing on the more important stuff. Right. Concert tonight. They're going to be working all day.

"Okay," I say.

I close the door, but Jase stops me and kisses me. It's quick but firm, and I get a little dizzy when he pulls back, a smirk playing on his lips, and closes the door.

The lock clicks when I turn it, and I put my clothes and my key on the counter, taking in a deep breath. Jesus... Idiot. Idiot, idiot, idiot!

One hour, he said. It's been two. No alarm. Fuck, I shouldn't have even stayed. I should have gone right back to my room, and I'd still be asleep, not hiding from my brothers in Jase's bathroom.

I dress quickly and put the toilet seat down to sit on it. I have no idea how long I'm going to have to wait here. I hope he's right and he can convince them it's better to talk somewhere else.

I hear Jase greet my brothers and let them into the room. My stomach is churning with nerves. Nothing good can come of this. Nothing at all.

"We heard about the article. Ella said it was all shit." Kye's voice travels through the suite.

"Yeah. She reckons I picked her up at the meet-and-greet I wasn't even at, and I was back here watching your sister try to drown herself in tequila," Jase answers.

I take offense to that. I wasn't drowning myself in tequila. I was floating on it, thank you very mind.

"Ah! I remember that," Tate says. "She had to take you for great food to apologize for being a prick, right?"

"Something like that."

I take offense to that too. Assholes.

"So the crisis meeting is less of a crisis and more of a 'hey, here's what's up and what we're doing about it,'" Aidan sums up. "Ella already has it under control."

"Ella has everything under control," Tate says.

"Even you," Con chuckles.

Jase laughs. "Yeah, she has it figured out. I just have to read over the statement, apparently, but Jen will have it out before the concert tonight."

"Good."

I can imagine Tate nodding as he says that.

"We're drafting in a few more members of security tonight," he continues. "They'll all be assigned to you... Just in case."

Just in case of what? He accidentally looks at some girl who isn't even there and gets her pregnant? That's how these shit stories start, right?

Bitches should write books instead of picking on real people.

"Cool. Thanks," Jase says. "Did you get breakfast yet? I went back to bed after Ella and Sofie left and just got up now."

"Nope," Kye answers. "We were woken up at to eight-thirty because, apparently, our sleeping in doesn't fit with our schedule."

Damn right it doesn't. Lazy shits.

"Well, I'm gonna head down to the restaurant right now, and I wouldn't mind the company."

"Sure." Kye again. "I don't think anyone's eaten."

"Has Leila?" Tate asks.

I freeze at the sound of my name. *Nowhere. Not here! Not here!*

"I haven't spoken to her since yesterday morning when she left with Jase," he goes on.

Sound a little more accusatory, Tate, why don't you? Geez...

"In bed," Con answers. "Sof said she and Ella called to tell her about the article and were met with several inventive uses of the word *fuck* and a threat to buy new friends on Craigslist before she hung up."

Ah. I love them. Now, anyway.

"Why would they need to tell Leila?" Aidan asks.

I freeze again. Shit, shit, shit!

"They said something about her needing to know everything," Jase answers. "They said, before they left, they were going to call her and tell her so nobody lost a body part when she found out she was the last to know."

"Ah. Of course," Aidan and Kye say together.

"Whoa," Jase says, shocked. "That was...strange."

I cover my mouth with my hand and bite my tongue so I don't laugh. Oh my god. He's never heard the twins do their voodoo talk. Admittedly, it's weird as fuck, but I'm kinda used to it.

Times like this, I wish I could see Jase's face.

"Yeah, shut up," Tate says. He always has been freaked out by it. "Let's get breakfast. I'm starvin'. Hey, can I use your bathroom before we go down?"

No! I think right as Jase exclaims the same.

"Sorry," Jase says. "Nah, there's a problem with the flush. It's why the door is shut. I called the desk this morning and they're sending someone up this afternoon."

"Fuckin' hotels. Pay them a shit-ton of money and they can't even flush your piss right."

Charming.

"Let's go," Kye says. "We've figured out that the issue is a nonissue and Ella's on the ball. Let's go stuff our faces with pastries and shit we won't get in London. Well, not this good. No offense, Jase."

"None taken," he laughs back, and the door opens. "There's no way pastries are this good in London."

The door shuts behind them, and I let out a long breath.

Jesus.

That was closer than close.

And one more reminder of why this is the worst idea I've ever had. The stupidest choice I've ever made. The wildest thing I've ever gone through with.

But, hell...it's fun, too.

Hiding in the bathroom from my brothers.

I giggle into my hands. How crazy. Now I get why people have relationships they shouldn't. The hiding is...fun. The sneaking and the...dirty little lies...are fun. Exciting. Thrilling, even.

I'm so dead.

So, so dead.

Like a freakin' dodo.

Deader than.

A few minutes of silence pass, and I finally feel safe enough to leave the confines of my bathroom. I have to praise Jase on his quick thinking about the toilet flushing. That excuse was on point.

Safety aside, creeping through his suite when he isn't here makes me feel...dirty. Mostly because I just kinda wanna go on back to his bedroom and rifle through his drawers.

He's so perfect—with his good looks, his sexy accent, his bedroom ability, and his singing talent—that there has to be something wrong with him. Has to be. It's a given fact. And the sole reason why I want to peek through his drawers.

I'm judging myself right now. Like I wouldn't turn around to a friend and say, "So do it," if they called me with this predicament.

Somehow, I force myself out of the room, the niggling desire to peek in his stuff bugging the crap out of me, and shut the door behind me. It puts an end to my peeping tom quality because I can't get back in. That's that, and well done, me. Self-control isn't usually my forte.

Lack of self-control is how I ended up in this freaking situation.

I make it back into my room without running into anybody. The first thing I notice is the notification light at the top of my phone blinking. Oh, boy. That usually means I'm in some kind of trouble, but I'm going to place a wager on the fact that it's my brothers trying to get ahold of me.

Ugh... Such pains.

I check my phone as I go into my bedroom to get changed. I'm kind of hoping there's an invitation for breakfast in here somewhere. I'm hungry, and if they're all working all day, I'm going to need to find something to do. Preferably find a bakery, buy my weight in carbs, and sit outside the Eiffel Tower while reading all day.

Wine breaks are obvious.

Yep. There it is, but it's from Jessie, a few minutes ago.

Jessie: *Breakfast? Now? Your brothers are about to implode.*

Me: *I'm naked. Give me five minutes.*

Jessie: *Classy chick.*

I laugh and get dressed.

Jase will be there.

Oh, boy.

Why am I bothered about it? I've screwed the guy twice in twelve hours, and since my feet hit French soil, I've spent more time with him than anyone else.

Maybe it's the fear of knowing I'm not fighting this connection we have. By agreeing to be friends with benefits, I'm agreeing to give in to this crazy attraction we have.

I'm more than a little afraid of what that attraction could morph into. What it potentially is morphing into. Because, when you wake up thinking about someone the way I'm afraid I will tomorrow and when you think of them more than anyone the way I'm doing right now, that's beyond attraction. It's...something else.

Attraction doesn't consume you.

Desire consumes you.

But desire is fickle... Desire is the thing you believe for the longest time until you think you can't believe it's just desire. It changes too quickly.

I'm hard. I'm the girl who will keep her heart long after she's given you your loyalty. My heart is the most precious part of me, and I don't care what anybody says. She can't be stolen or swooned. She can't be romanced with words or actions.

She'll give up when she's ready to.

I've never been so afraid of the possibility.

Jessie: *Are you coming? I think Tate is going to come find you soon. He looks strange.*

As opposed to his looking normal normally? Right.

I quickly brush my hair and do my makeup, choosing a natural look. My hair needs washing and looks like it's gone ten rounds with a bramble bush, but the rough bun on top of my head hides it for the most part. It'll have to do. I can't be bothered to be human today.

I grab my purse, tuck my phone inside, and head down to the restaurant. I get the feeling I'm about to have two different breakfasts for the second day in a row.

I need to check out the hotel gym the moment we get to London and hope to god the food there isn't nearly as good as it is here.

Yeah, right.

I remember that starchy, carb-filled pub-food heaven the Brits love so much.

I find their table in the restaurant immediately. Mostly because Mila is yelling about something I can't make out from this distance. Seriously, the kid could bring boats into harbor with the way she screeches when she's annoyed.

"Good morning," I chirp, slipping into the empty seat next to Jase.

Coincidence? Probably.

"Where have you been?" Tate asks, staring hard at me with his blue eyes.

"I was sleeping. Sorry, Dad. Should I ask your permission tonight?"

"Mom told me to look after you. S'all I'm doin', kid."

"Call me kid one more time and you'll have to look after yourself a whole lot more, bro."

He cuts his eyes away from me and shakes his head. "If Mom heard you..."

I pick my glass of water up. "She'd give me a high five and tell me to keep givin' you shit."

Sofie chokes on her own water.

I'm taking it as agreement.

Mila shoots her arm out. "Oo-ro, pwease."

"What now?" I question her. Why do I always have to sit next to her?

"Oo-ro." She blinks at me, her bright eyes innocently hiding beneath her crazy, dark curls. "Oo-ro." She shoves her hand at me again.

"Euro," Jase mutters. "She's gotten two from me already."

"Really?" I turn to him. "Two? Y'all can't have been here more than fifteen minutes. I'm impressed."

"At her or me?"

"Honestly? Both." I pick my purse up from my feet, secure two euros from my wallet, and put them in the hand of my little cuss-word-nazi niece. "There you go, Mila. Don't spend it all once."

"My won't." She hands it to Sofie, who dutifully tucks it into a cartoon coin purse.

Ah. It's like that.

"Did you order already?" I ask everybody.

Kye shakes his head. "Nope. Chels said not to. Somethin' about you being hangry."

"No, I said I was hangry," Chelsey corrects him. "But I know, if we ordered without her, she'd be hangry."

"Lies," I mutter, rolling my eyes. I pick the menu up and quickly scan it to choose what I want. Honestly, an almond croissant and fruit. I'm easy like that.

We order as a group, and then everyone descends into an easy chatter. The low hum from the table is occasionally broken as Mila giggles and sings to herself—or perhaps Bunna, it's up for debate—but I find my lips tugging into a gentle smile.

I love my family when it's like this. I must be one of the only people in the world blessed to have her best friends as a part of her family this way.

"You're grinning like a fool," Jase whispers, leaning over to me.

"Did your toilet get fixed?" I whisper right back.

"Not yet." His lips twitch up, and he grabs his mug. Filled with tea—of course.

"Shame." I sip my water.

He knocks his foot into mine under the table. I glare at him, but he just flashes me a grin before turning back to Tate, who just asked him a question.

"Obvious," Sofie mouths to me across Mila.

I poke my tongue out at her. If she doesn't want me to be obvious, maybe they shouldn't leave the only empty seat at the table next to him. They should put it between the twins or something. Then I'd be...safe.

Our food is brought to us, and the low chatter descends into silence as everyone eats. I barely pick at my fruit, although the croissant lasted all of a few minutes. I guess I'm in the mood for super-heavy, pastry carbs and not much else.

"Jennifer said she'll have the statement written before we leave," Ella says, looking up at Jase. She flits her eyes to me. "Are you coming with us?"

"Am I supposed to be?" I ask, a grape held halfway to my mouth.

Ads shrugs. "You can. Just sound check and rehearsing."

"Well...I was going to stuff my face with carbs and read all day," I say hesitantly.

"You can do that at the arena," Jessie reminds me. "Just send someone to get your carbs and sit at the back with your freakin' book."

"You'd probably like this book if you read it."

"Great. When you're done, I'll borrow it so I don't have to waste my money on your trash."

I poke my tongue out at her. Honestly, my friends are making me regress into a six-year-old.

"Do I have to come?" I ask. "Can't I just stick to my plans?"

"What's wrong with a sound check?" Jase looks at me out of the side of his eye.

"Nothing. They're just boring as hell and don't interest me whatsoever."

"So, plenty wrong, then?"

"Oh, Jesus, fine. I'll come with y'all. Don't complain about the grumpy girl in the back, yeah?" I finish my glass of water. "I'm going to get my book. Or two."

I can't believe I stayed there for six hours.

My butt is numb. My ears are ringing. My fucks are totaling zero. And I left an hour ago.

I love my brothers; I do. I'll support them until I'm blue in the face and struggling to breathe, but if I'm ever talked into attending one of these freakin' checks again, I'm going to lose my ever-loving mind.

Never mind I wasn't so much "talked into" as I was kinda convinced, and it was mostly Jase, but whatever.

And as for Jessie sending someone to get me pastries? Yeah, right. More like Sofie and I had to go find some.

My day has been completely wasted, and I'm not the happiest person in the world right now. I can't wait until we get to London tomorrow and I'll be refusing anything remotely related to sound checks or rehearsals or whatever.

The craziest thing about this was the way the media mobbed Jase before and after we left the arena. Jennifer, their publicist, put out the statement refuting Stella Porter's claims right after we arrived, so they wouldn't have gotten the memo by then, but leaving?

It was worse.

Tate was right to demand extra security for him. Carlos, as good as he is, can't handle it alone. The reporters are too crazy and the photographers are too pushy. They're all desperate to get his story—even if there isn't one.

And there isn't. How can there be a story when half his evening was spent drinking tequila and kissing me?

Is it wrong that I'm smug about that? I feel like it might be. This girl has sold her lies, made a quick buck, and hasn't thought about the repercussions of it. I mean, come on. That lie isn't even believable. It's so untrue that it stopped being a lie half an article ago.

Why am I so annoyed about it?

I know. I don't want to admit it, but it's because I saw how worried he was. Ella and Sofie called me because they were worried how *I'd* react, but I knew the moment they told me that it was a lie.

It was the apprehension I saw in Jase's green eyes that bothered me. Like...I don't know what he was thinking, honestly, but it was worry for me and him.

I'm wondering if, already, saying we're friends with benefits is wrong.

I don't want it to be.

I wasn't lying when I told him I don't want the life my brothers' girlfriends have. I don't want to deal with the shit Jessie took from the Dirty B. fans when she was fake-dating Aidan. I don't want the abuse Sofie got when Mila was revealed to the world. I don't want the quiet crap Ella took or the hated invasion of privacy Chelsey had to accept.

I want to have fun loudly but fall in love quietly. Simple as that. I don't want to hand my beloved heart to someone whose every movement will be stalked and documented, whose every decision will be scrutinized and ripped apart.

I don't want to live in such a way that every Tom, Dick, Harry, Marjorie, Betty, and Eleanor feel the need to comment and judge me.

I want happiness. And I don't know if you can truly find it in the public eye.

Keeping out of it, when your brothers are one of the world's most famous boy bands, is definitely harder than it seems.

I look down at my feet, which are stretched out on the bed. My fluffy, stripy, mismatched socks are glaringly bright against the pure-white sheets. I wriggle my toes as I reach for my phone and check the time.

The concert will be starting in less than an hour, but I have no desire to go with them. I'd rather stay here, curled up in bed, or go out and enjoy my final Parisian night. Maybe go up to the roof... Who knows?

One or the other will be fine.

Anything but the damn arena.

Maybe even a nap, but first, room service.

I skim through the menu before I call and order a burger with fries and a bottle of white wine. Since I managed to finish my book and start another earlier today, moving from billionaire hero to cowboy, I think the wine will work just perfectly.

My phone lights up with a text message, and I unlock it.

Jase: *Meet me on the green outside the tower at two minutes to ten.*

I raise an eyebrow. What? Two minutes to ten?

Me: *That's precise.*
Jase: *Don't be a smartarse.*
Me: *In my DNA. Sorry not sorry.*
Jase: *I know. Will you be there?*

I draw my lower lip into my mouth and peel a small bit of dry skin off with my teeth.

Me: *Yes.*

෴

I tug my jacket around me as I step out of the hotel. The light wind that whips around me casts a slight chill in the night air, and when I look up, the very faint twinkling of stars just about breaks through the haze from the city's lights.

A handful of media people are waiting outside the hotel, ready for my brothers to return, but I stalk right past them as they talk among themselves. None of them pay me the slightest bit of attention.

I put my hands in the pockets of my jacket and grip my phone and my key. Walking through the streets of Paris at night doesn't feel like you're in the center of a major city at all. The old buildings and tiny streets are worlds away from the traditional high-rises of a city center. It's one of the things I love about it here—you're surrounded by thousands upon thousands of people, yet it doesn't feel like it.

It's like being in a very, very big small town. If that even makes any sense at all.

I gaze around almost dreamily as I follow the streets to the tower. I've left myself more than enough time, mostly because I've had three glasses of wine and I wanted to make sure I wouldn't suddenly get all woozy when the fresh air hit me.

Don't judge me. The book made me drink.

I walk for a few more minutes through the streets before reaching the turn for the Eiffel Tower. It stretches up high into the air, reflecting down onto the River Seine. Momentarily, I lament the fact that I never got a chance to go on one of the *bateau mouche* boats for a tour of the city, but I think Jase and I pretty much covered the sights as it is.

Before we were stopped when he was recognized, that is.

My mind's flip to Jase has me focused on him now as I walk toward the tower. This is hands down the strangest request I've ever received—and Mila's given me some strange-ass requests since she came into my life a year and a half ago.

I glance at my phone as I walk into the park, beneath the bright lights of the tower. I'm a few minutes early, and now that I have time with nothing to do, I'm equal parts excited and apprehensive over why Jase wants me to come here.

Excited.

To see a guy.

I can't remember the last time I felt like this. The last time I had good butterflies—not the type that make you want to throw up all over the guy you're meeting.

Oddly enough, I've never felt that way with Jase. Except when I saw him in the restaurant after we'd landed, but that was just because I was shocked, so it doesn't count.

The park is pretty much empty except for one couple holding hands and one solo person walking their dog. I watch the dog as it sniffs around the grass before stopping to do its business against the leg of a bench.

Jase's voice sounds behind me. "Close your eyes."

"Wha—" I make to turn around, but his strong arms grasp my shoulders and keep me in place.

"No," he says. "I said close your eyes."

"You've lost your mind, Brit Boy."

"Do it. Now."

I huff but close them anyway. His hands fall from my shoulders, and his fingertips leave goose bumps in their wake as they trail down my arms despite the material of my jacket.

"Jase?" I ask, but it comes out barely louder than a whisper.

"Just...wait."

"I'm so confused."

"Leila, love, shut the bloody hell up."

"Fine."

I lick my lips as I wait for...I don't freaking know what. It seems like forever passes before I see a flash behind my eyelids, his warm hands cup my cheeks, and he kisses me.

The tower sparkles on the hour.

His kiss is tender, his lips soft against mine. It's not forceful or deep, yet I feel the easy touch right down to my bones. It feels like a thousand stolen moments all rolled into one simple kiss.

Such a simple thing shouldn't make me feel so much.

But it does.

I feel everything everywhere. Tingles, shivers, softening, relaxing, warmth, comfort, safety... I lean against him, hold his waist tight, let myself drown in the feeling of this moment. Let myself be swallowed by the rush that barrels into me from the simple touch.

Let myself be taken over by him, just for this moment.

"You came to the sound check because I teased you," Jase whispers.

I finally open my eyes and look up. The flashing twinkles of the tower illuminate his features and dance off of the brightness of his green eyes.

"Yeah, and?" I ask.

"I know you wanted to see it one last time. So here. You can see it." He drops his hands from my face and steps behind me. Then he wraps his arms around my shoulders.

I glance down at his loose hold on me and instinctively lean back. He tightens his grip as my back presses against his solid body, and I swallow as my hand creeps up to his arm and my fingers wrap around his wrist.

I breathe in and turn my face toward his. His cheek brushes the side of my head, and I'd swear he turns his face toward mine too and kisses my hair.

"Thank you," I whisper as the flashing of the tower ceases and my eyes travel back to it, still gorgeously lit.

"Any time," he whispers right back, pulling me back against him. His lips brush my temple, and I close my eyes.

I didn't think I'd like anything more than the Eiffel Tower.

I was wrong.

This... This is better.

Jase is better.

And I don't quite know what I'm supposed to do about this.

chapter twelve

London.

I put my key in the lock of my flat and walk in, wheeling my case behind me. I shove it through the doorway and against the wall of the hallway, breathing in the peace of my own space. Home.

It's only been a few days, but bloody hell, I'm glad to be home.

No more having to gesture my way through every conversation or eating out. I can cook in my own kitchen and eat on my own sofa.

Well, for nine days, that is. Before a quick two-day trip to Manchester and Newcastle for shows before coming right back here to close out the tour. I think they all forgot that, because only London was mentioned until Ella decided to remind everyone this morning.

That was fun.

Now, it's past lunch, they're all checking into their hotel, and I'm happy to be here. Some space from everyone is exactly what I need—not because I don't like them, but because I'm afraid I'm liking one of them a little...too much.

Leila.

I huff and drop onto the sofa. I only ever meant to tease her, mess with her because of how we met before, but her attitude took over and grabbed hold of me. My sassy, Southern girl is taking my life over —and it's the worst possible thing that could happen.

Neither of us has a place for the other in our lives. Sure, we could make them, but with an entire ocean between us, it's harder than it'd seem. Least of all because my working visa approval is taking its sweet-arse time coming through.

I make a mental note to check on that this week and get right back up. I bet there's nothing worth having in my fridge or any of the cupboards, which means I'm going to need to go out.

How fucking unappealing right now.

"Oi, knobhead. Nice to see you too."

I jump at the sound of my brother's voice. "Kian? What the fuck are you doing here?"

He grins and rubs a towel over his wet hair. "My water cut out again. I borrowed your shower."

"Yeah, no problem," I say sarcastically. "You're welcome, bro."

"Hey, thanks!" His grin widens, and he throws his towel on the kitchen side.

I stare at it, and he snatches it back up and throws it in the laundry basket. Three feet away. So fucking lazy.

"I bought you milk, bread, and orange juice. Oh, and teabags. I used those too."

At least he replaced them this time.

"One day," I say "I'm gonna take your damn key back. You're almost thirty. Get your shit together."

"I'm waiting for the bank to process my mortgage request for the house." He sits at the small island in the middle of the kitchen. "They're taking their bloody time about it, because apparently having more than several million pounds sitting in an account isn't good enough. Believe me, nobody wants to get out of that shit little flat more than I do."

"I know. Thanks for the milk and stuff. I still need to go out though. You didn't take my car too, did you?" I give him a side-eye.

He laughs. "No. Looked for the spare keys but couldn't find 'em."

"Took them with me." I smile smugly, opening the fridge. "How's the leg?"

Kian winces and stretches it out. "Mum didn't call you?"

"No..." I put the orange juice on the counter. "What happened?"

He scratches his eyebrow, pain twitching across his face. "I saw Dr. Hargreaves on Wednesday. He's ninety percent certain I'll never play again."

"Shit. I'm sorry, Ki."

My brother was—is—signed to one of the top teams in the English Premier League, but several months ago, he took a bad tackle during a match. He snapped his leg in two places and tore his ACL. He's only recently been able to walk without a stick or any help, but the big question has always been whether or not he'll get back on the pitch.

I guess the answer is no.

"Yep. He said it'll probably heal to the point it'll be almost like new, and there won't be too many lasting effects, but it was torn so badly that almost new is all I can hope for." He takes the glass of juice I slide toward him. "Unless there's a miracle, he won't clear me for play."

"Doesn't the team doctor have the final say?" I ask, putting the juice bottle back in the fridge. "What if he thinks you're okay and you can prove your fitness?"

"Hargreaves is one of the top doctors in the country, Jase. If he says no, I doubt bloody Barker will clear me. He's more anal than the category on PornHub."

I smirk. "What are you gonna do instead?"

He shrugs. "I don't know. The season is almost up, so I'll probably retire on the first of July when the transfer window opens. I don't think the club is expecting me back, and they need my wages to buy another player."

"True. Walker is shit."

"Yep. He's got more luck shooting at the moon than the goal." Kian shudders. "He's killing the team single-handedly." He sips. "Enough about that crap. I saw that article about you." He waggles his eyebrows like a teenager.

"Aw, man. It's not even true." I rub my hand across my forehead. "I've never met the girl in my life. It's all crap."

"I know. I'm just messin' with you." He grins. "How's life on the road with every teenage girl's dream?"

This is why I need to get his spare key back. "It's hardly on the road, and yeah, it's good." Somewhat of an understatement, admittedly.

"Good? Just good? I've heard you more excited about taking a shit, Jase."

"Just...good." I grab my glass of juice and walk through the open-plan space, into the living area, and sit on the sofa.

Kian follows me over, limping ever so slightly, and puts his glass on the coffee table. "I hoovered, too. You're welcome," he says, dramatically sweeping his arm across the carpet.

I look up at him. "You brought a date back, didn't you?"

"To the spare room!" He holds his hands up, smiling. "I swear. I couldn't take her back to my place without the bloody shower working, could I?"

"You're a millionaire. Get a fucking hotel room, you cheapskate."

He laughs. "Yeah, yeah, I hear you. Now, back to your little singing road trip. Just good?"

Fuck me, he's not gonna let this go. This is what happens when you grow up close with your older brother—everything is dissected before you can take it back.

"Remember that song I was stuck on before I signed with Lawrence?"

"Yeah, sure. 'Tonight,' wasn't it?"

I nod. "Do you remember me saying I met that girl in Waterstones? She helped me write it."

"Yeah. Then you took her for dinner and... Shut up. She's on the tour?"

I grimace. "She's the sister of the band."

Kian stares at me for a long moment before he bursts into a booming laugh that fills the walls of my quiet flat. "Shut the fuck up. You're kidding me."

"Dead serious."

He laughs again. "Please tell me you've behaved yourself."

"All right, then. I won't."

"You're screwing their sister?"

"Once. Pretty sure she screwed me the second time."

She sure as hell initiated it, anyway.

My phone rings, so I pull it out of my pocket and look at the screen. Leila.

"Talk of the devil," I mutter, hitting accept. "What's up?"

"Hey," she replies. "Is there, like, a supermarket or somethin' around here where we can get Mila some snacks? This hotel pretty much wants an ovary in exchange for a bag of chips."

"Bag of—oh, crisps." I press two fingers into my temple. Chips. Honestly. "Yeah, I think there's a Tesco or Sainsburys not far from you."

"What's a Tesco or Sainsburys?"

Oh man. Here we go. "Let me make it easy for you. Do you have a car seat for Mila?"

"Hang on. Hey, Sof? Do you have a car seat for Mila?"

"Yeah, why?" I hear her answer.

"She said, 'Yeah, why?'" Leila says to me.

"I heard. You're all quite loud."

"Shut up."

"Do you want me to take you to the shop or not? I'll come pick up you, Sofie, and Mila and take you. As long as you shove your attitude back up your arse where it belongs."

"I'll shove it up yours, smartass."

"Arse," I correct her. "You're in London now, babe. It's arse."

"Smart*arse*," she fires back. "Fine. How long will you be?"

"Probably twenty minutes. I need to put petrol in my car."

"Petrol? Ah, gas. Yeah. Forgot y'all have strange words for normal shit."

"Yeah, we're the weird ones." I roll my eyes even though she can't see it. "I'll text you when I'm outside. I'm not paying the parking fees."

"Yeah, yeah. See you soon." She clicks off the line.

I hear my brother snort.

"What?" I demand.

"You've fucked her three times and you're her bitch." Kian chuckles. "I gotta meet her."

"I'm not her bitch. I'm just not willing to let a three-year-old go without snacks." I get up and check my pockets for my wallet.

"So, you're a three-year-old's bitch?"

"If I've learnt anything since I met the Burke family a week ago, it's that *everybody* is Mila's bitch." After finding my bank card in my wallet, I pull my keys out, put my wallet back into my pocket, and head for my door. "Get your arse out of here before I get back."

"Why? Bringing that girl back?"

"No. I'm just fed up of seeing your ugly mug already." I turn, opening the door, and shoot him a grin.

He flips me the bird.

Yeah. It's good to be home.

"Ah. So this was a Tesco." Leila looks behind her and up. "I've never been here before."

"Really?" Sofie frowns, pulling Mila out of the seat in the trolley. "Mila, pull your legs through the holes to get out, please. Then what did you do when you were here before?"

"Spent all my money in those adorable little shops they have. They're like drugstores but without the drugs. Just magazines and foods and drinks and stuff."

"Corner shops," I offer, pushing my own little, but very full, trolley.

"Why are they called corner shops? Mila, please!" Sofie grabs her foot, pushes it up, then sets her on the ground, much to Mila's displeasure.

"Because they're usually on the corner." I push the trolley down the path toward my car as Mila swings on Leila's hand.

"That's real cute." Leila grins, a bounce in her step as she follows me. "Will you take me to one?"

I raise an eyebrow as I reach inside my pocket and press the button that will unlock my car. "Sure?" It came out as more of a question than an answer, but that's the oddest thing I've ever been asked.

"Like right after we get back to the hotel?" She looks way too excited at this prospect.

"I...guess so." I open the back door so Mila can climb into her child seat and go around to the boot. I open the door while Sofie and Leila switch places, and I start loading the bags into the car, keeping them separate using Mila's magazine.

I can already tell Sofie will forget it before they leave the hotel. She already whispered once about her being a tiny magazine hoarder.

"What do you call that?" Leila asks as we take the trolleys back. "The thing we just put the shopping bags in."

"The boot?"

"The boot." Her eyes light up the way they always do when I speak and something is strange to her. "Wow. That's way more fun than trunk. What about the front? The hood?"

"Bonnet. Are you going to do this for the next two weeks? Because it's going to get old really quickly." I take the trolley from her and push it under the shelter.

"Okay, okay. Can I ask random people in the street, then?" She sounds really hopeful about that.

"You wouldn't."

"Are you challenging me, Jase Masters?"

"Sssh!" I clap my hand over her mouth and cup the back of her neck with my other. "We've discussed speaking my full name aloud in public. Say it too many times and they flock like seagulls looking for chips at the beach."

She flicks her tongue out and licks right up my palm.

"That was gross." I let her go and wipe my hand on my jeans. I pause at the back of the car as she walks to the right side—the driver's side—and reaches for the handle. I clear my throat.

"What?" Her blue eyes find mine.

"You driving, love?"

"What?" she repeats, looking down through the window at the steering wheel. "Shut up." She releases the handle and stalks around the front of the car, mumbling to herself.

I can't understand a word of it, but I grin anyway, mostly because she's kinda cute when she gets grumpy like that.

I get in the car and start the engine. Leila has her arms folded across her chest, and Sofie is giggling quietly in the back while Mila just looks confused.

"Good to see you found your seat," I tell Leila, smirking.

"Shut your face," she mumbles, looking out of the window. "Easy mistake to make, all right?"

"I suppose. But it really is common knowledge that we drive on different sides of the road and have the wheels on different sides of the car."

"You're messin' with me, aren't you?"

"I hope so. This is way too fun not to be otherwise."

"I hate you."

"You want me to take you to a corner shop?"

She groans, lolling her head onto the window. "I don't hate you."

I grin.

"This is like watching a sick verbal sex tape," Sofie mutters from the back.

"Mama, what a sex tape?" Mila asks.

Leila snorts, laughs, and then coughs all in quick succession. Hell, even I'm trying not to choke on my own laugh. I glance into the rearview mirror.

Sofie's frozen, obviously trying to think about what to say.

"It's a grown-up thing," she answers. "Like when Pops says you can't say the bad words until you can touch the ceiling with your head without being picked up or climbing on the sofa."

"Ah. Otay." Mila nods and looks out the window. "Wed. Gween. Back. Back. White. Oooh, lellow! Look, Mama!"

"Spotting the cars," Sofie sighs. "I can't see, baby. Aunty Leila will play with you."

Leila rolls her eyes. "All right, Mi. Find the...blue car!"

"Wed. Wed. Wed. Lots of wed. Oh! Boo!" Mila knocks on the window. "I find it."

"Okay. Now...orange."

"Onnich. Otay."

Onnich. Oh, Lord. This kid is seriously cute.

They keep this game up the entire drive back to the hotel. I have to give Leila props. That's some serious patience she has there, which is ironic because she's one of the most impatient people I've ever had the chance to meet.

Still, it's quite funny, listening to her play with Mila. I remember playing it myself when I was a kid, and it drove Mum mad when Kian and I would fight over who saw what car first. Let's just say that road trips were kept to a minimum, and it was a groundable offense whenever we were forced onto the motorway.

Didn't stop us playing it when we got phones though. Not that she minded much then—it was the loud fighting she got pissed off about.

I pull up outside their hotel after having braved central London traffic, and immediately, a valet comes over to us. Leila rolls the window down and tells him what's happening, so he grabs a bell cart and wheels it over while I get out and open the boot.

"Is there anywhere I can pull up for a few minutes while she runs this upstairs?" I ask the valet, nodding toward Leila.

"Of course, sir. Just pull up at the end here and you can wait there for up to fifteen minutes." He motions to the end of the slip road.

They really need to get some better car parks in this city. Even a couple of temporary parking slots would be a win.

"Thank you," I tell him, shutting the boot just as Sofie hands Mila to Leila. "Do you want a hand, Sofie?"

Leila sets her on the floor as Sofie gets the seat out. "Nope! I'm good. Thanks though." She smiles as she straightens and the guy takes the seat off her hands.

Why use me for free when you'll have to tip his arse in a few minutes, eh?

"Hey, Lei, I'm good. You can go find your corner shop or whatever it is."

"You sure?" Leila looks her over. "I can come up."

"No, it's okay. I've just gotta wrangle Mila and I do that anyway." She grins. "Have fun. And behave." She said the final word with a sly look across to me.

I hold my hands up. "I'm a gentleman, thank you very much."

Leila snorts and gets back in the car.

I guess I don't need to wait after all.

"What was that snort for?" I shut my door behind me. "And hey! You got in the right side this time!"

"I swear to god, Jase, I will kill you." She glares at me and flings her arm out. Her fingers slap my arm quite sharply.

I bat her hand away.

"And the snort was because you're no gentleman."

"That's rude. I hold doors for you all the time." I pull away from the hotel.

"Oh, well, forgive me. I must have you confused with some rough-fucking, ass-slapping other guy."

I raise one eyebrow and look over at her when the traffic light goes red. "I thought the arse-slapping was a given if you're a gentleman. Not to mention that a gentleman knows how to give a woman what she wants, and unless I was mistaken, you wanted it exactly how I gave it to you."

"So...the entire point of this conversation is that you're right, I'm wrong, and you're actually a gentleman?"

"Not just any gentleman. I'm an arse-slapping gentleman who isn't afraid to give you a good, hard fuck."

She contemplatively narrows her eyes and tucks some hair behind her ear. "I don't usually like admitting I'm wrong, because I'm never really wrong, but you make a good case."

"Do you need me to convince you?"

"That you're a gentleman?"

I glance at the clock on the dashboard. "We've got time."

"Aren't you supposed to feed me first? Isn't that also a rule of the gentleman?"

"Now you're just making it up as we go."

"Because you haven't been doing that at all, have you?" She turns in her seat, hugging one knee to her chest, and watches me as I drive. "All that ass-slapping, good-hard-fuck nonsense is just that. Nonsense. A gentleman is...holding a purse or getting the car door. Or any door, really. It's holding her arm while she crosses a road and taking the longer route just because she wants to."

"All right, Queen Victoria. Did Doctor Who drop you off in his Tardis?"

"You're so cocky."

"Your traditional view is really cute, Leila, but I'm a modern-day gentleman. So I'll get the door for you and stare at your arse on the way out. I'll carry your purse full of pastries *you* insisted on buying. If I had to, I'd carry you across a damn road and cop a feel halfway. But I'll also let you get your own door, carry your own purse, and get yourself across the road because you're an independent person. Just like I'd let you flip me onto my back and ride me until I come if that's what you really want to do... But don't forget that I'll also put you on your knees and fuck you until you have to bite a pillow to muffle your screams."

I pull up outside my block of flats and unclip my belt before I look at her. Her cheeks are flushed bright red, and her blue eyes sparkle with her own embarrassment—or is it lust? I can't tell. Either way, she's shifting in the seat.

"Well played, Brit Boy." She clears her throat. "And I'm gonna hold you to that last one. Both of them."

"Like I said... We've got time."

Her gaze flicks to the building. "This ain't a corner shop."

"No. It's my flat. I need to put away my shopping." I pull the key from the ignition. "Are you coming up, or are you going to wait in the car?"

"I'll come up." She unclips her belt and gets out before I have a chance to.

I go around to the boot and pull out my four bags, close it, and lock the car. I lead Leila inside and to the lift. It's in the lobby, so the doors open straightaway and we fly up to the fourth floor, where my flat is.

"Do you live alone?"

"Yes. My grandfather lives with my parents on the weekends and he's slightly...forgetful." I put my bags down so I can unlock the door.

"Oh. Does he have Alzheimer's?"

"No. He just can't remember a bloody thing." I snort and grab my things before motioning for Leila to follow me inside.

"Then why is he only there on the weekends?"

"Because my mother is smart enough to placate my father with weekends but not stupid enough to give in and have him there full time. Granddad's forgetfulness makes him eccentric. He once forgot he was almost eighty and decided to play limbo against our protests. One hip replacement later, he still swears he won."

Leila laughs, shutting the door behind her. "He sounds like a hoot."

"I'll bring him to a concert one night. He'll probably mistake your brothers for Elvis Presley and assume he started a band." I dump the plastic bags on the small island. "I'll only be a minute. You can sit down if you want."

"Can I just stare at your kitchen?" she asks, pulling a stool out at the island and looking around a little dreamily. "You have a hot kitchen."

"A hot kitchen," I repeat, emptying the contents of my shopping onto the counter in front of me before I put them away. "Well, the cooker isn't on, so I'm assuming you mean nice."

"Ha ha ha. And you say I have the attitude."

"I've refined mine. It's easier to deal with your bollocks."

"Seriously the best word ever," she mutters. "Whatever. I like to think I'm teachin' you, and that works. How far away is the nearest corner shop?"

"Like a ten-minute walk. Why are you so obsessed with it?"

"I like saying corner shop."

"Really. You like saying corner shop."

"Yes. Try it. It's real fun."

"I've said it a million times."

"Corner shop. Corner shop. Cor. Ner. Shop." She smacks her lips together at the end of *shop*, creating a big *puh* sound, then laughs.

"Don't you have corner shops?" I frown. "Or something like them."

"Convenience stores are probably the closest. I've heard them called corner stores once or twice." She chews the inside of her cheek. "But it's 'shop.' Shop

sounds so much more fun than store. Y'all get all the fun words."
   "You had them too, until you changed the language up."
   "Shop. Shop. Corner shop."
   "Leila. Stop."
   "Shop."
   "Leila..."
   "Shop. Shop. Shop. Shop. Bollocks shop."
   I stalk around the kitchen island and kiss her.

chapter thirteen
Leila

Oh, okay.

Jase kisses me, silencing me. Tingles erupt across my skin, and I reach up and touch the side of his face, leaning back.

Bad idea.

Bad, bad idea.

I shriek as I almost fall backward off the stool. He wraps his arm around my waist, pulling me back up and loudly laughing. My heart thunders against my chest, having narrowly missed dropping so suddenly that it'd fall out my ass, and I slap my palm against his chest.

"That was your fault!"

"How the hell was it?" he asks, still laughing at me.

Shit, he's laughing so hard that he's doubling over.

"You kissed me!"

"You leant back. That's not my fault, love."

"If you hadn't kissed me, I wouldn't have leaned back." I fold my arms across my chest and glare at him. I think I'm going to stay standing now. "Are you done with your shopping now?"

"Why is shopping not funny to you, but shop is?" He stops laughing, barely, and puts some yogurt and a bag of apples in the fridge, finishing it off.

I shrug and look at him. He's got his head tilted to the side, his hand against the fridge door, and he's staring at me. His white T-shirt hugs his muscular body and the ink that wraps around his bicep seems extra dark against the fabric. My mouth dries, and my tongue runs over my lips several times as I desperately try to wet them.

I've never really looked at someone and thought *Shit. You're kind of perfect.*

Until right now.

"You know," I say, dragging the words out and, walking to the door, "we spend way too much time together for people who are friends with benefits."

"Is that right?"

"Yep. Way too much time talking and not enough fucking."

Jase's sneakers squeak against the tiled floor, and he grabs me before I can touch the door handle. He tugs me against his body, one of his strong arms wrapping around my waist, and he kisses me again, but this time, it's harder. It's hungrier. He wastes no time as he slips his tongue between my lips and strokes it against mine.

I grab the collar of his T-shirt and push against him. My breasts rub against his chest, and god, this... This is addictive. The unexpected touches, kisses... Yet they're baited by me and always fallen for by him.

The desperate way he touches me.

That. That's the addictive part. Every time he touches me, I believe it. I believe he wants me.

And there's nothing sweeter than feeling wanted, whether that touch is a desperate clasp of your waist or a gentle brush of fingertips.

"You didn't want a booty call," he says in a low voice, wrapping his hand around the back of my neck. "You wanted friends with benefits. Well, beautiful, guess what? Friends spend time together. Then come the benefits. Unless you want to change up the friends part and just do the benefits."

I don't answer.

How do I answer that?

I don't. I...like the friends part. More than like it. I like spending time with him. He makes me smile all the time, makes me laugh almost as much, and doesn't take my shit. I do give him shit—I know I do. And it's refreshing that he flings it right back at me.

Even if it feels like we're pushing the line of friendship.

"Exactly." He looks into my eyes, captivating me with that compulsive, green gaze of his. "And shoot me for saying it, but I like being your friend."

I draw in a long, deep breath. My thumb stretches up and brushes along the underside of his jaw, touching upon his chin, and I whisper, "I like being your friend too."

He doesn't move, just looks at me, right down at me. Chills run over me, and before I know what I'm doing, I'm reaching up on my tiptoes and pressing my lips to his. His are warm, and I breathe the touch in before I lower myself back down to my heels.

Jase runs his hand around the side of my neck and then rests it against my collarbone. He trails his thumb along my jaw in a mirror movement of what I just did, but he swipes right the way around to my mouth. The tip of his thumb brushes the lower curve of my bottom lip, making me shiver at the softness of the touch, and his mouth quirks into a tiny smile as he fully presses the pad of his thumb to me.

Then, oh so slowly, he drags it along the soft curve. I close my eyes and inhale sharply as he does. My heart beats quickly as he cups my chin and tilts it up, only to kiss me one more time. It's slow and easy.

The most perfect kind of kiss.

The one that ignites fire in your veins and chills them with ice at the same time.

The one that breathes life into your soul, makes it sing, dance, fly.

It's a kiss for no other reason than being a kiss.

"That didn't feel like a friend kind of kiss," I whisper to Jase, my lips still brushing his.

"It wasn't," he hoarsely whispers back.

"Then what was it?"

"It was anything you want it to be." His exhale is shuddery, his shoulders heaving as it leaves him.

I want to stay here, in this "anything you want it to be" moment. I want to hold onto it, keep it held tightly to my chest, lose myself in it. Lose myself in the knowledge we're not defined by anything, because behind every 'friend' line we throw, there's the whiper of more.

Except, maybe, it's not whispering anymore.

Maybe it's screaming.

"Come on," he says quietly, breaking the moment by dropping his hand from my face. "Let's find your corner shop and I'll buy you some real chocolate."

"Cadburys?"

"Of course Cadburys. I'm not a sadist, Leila, love." He flashes a grin, and just like that, it's back to the way it was ten minutes ago.

"Okay." I swallow the small lump that formed in my throat. "Let's go."

I think I just ate my weight in chocolate. Sampled it, really. One or two squares of each bar. Cadburys and Oreo, Cadburys with Crunchie—which is *amazing*—and Cadburys with minty, puddly things in the middle.

Long story short, and this could easily become a long story of my love for British chocolate, Cadburys is the greatest thing I've ever eaten. And, if I eat a little more, I'm going to explode. Like, boom. Pow-wow-boom.

I'm also lying in the middle of Hyde Park, next to Jase, the chocolate wrappers on the grass between us, while people bustle past us. Some people are whistling to their dogs as they run off. Others are riding along the paths on their bikes, and some are groups of teenagers, laughing and giggling to themselves.

Jase has been lying with his arm over his face for the last ten minutes after he was sure he was almost recognized. It's odd, being with someone who doesn't want to be noticed. He wants everything that comes with the life of being a famous singer—except the recognition.

I don't blame him. I wouldn't want to be bothered while buying stuff in a store either.

"I'm never going to eat American chocolate again. I'm ruined," I moan, resting my hands on my stomach.

Jase chuckles quietly. "I tried to warn you before you ate fifty million squares."

"It wasn't that much." I swing my foot to the side and kick his calf. "Only maybe ten million. At least, that's what it feels like."

"Like I said, I tried to warn you, but you didn't listen to me. I said it was sweeter than American stuff."

"Oh, but it's so good." I roll my head to the side and look at him.

Even with his arm over his eyes, I can see how handsome he is. Maybe because of that, because I can't see those eyes that captivate me so easily.

His sharp jaw dotted with rough stubble. His soft, plump lips unfairly bestowed on a man. His dark hair cut short at the sides, longer and swept back on top. Strong shoulders, toned, inked arms, and the kind of neck that curves so perfectly that it was made for snuggling into.

Jase Masters is perfect.

I swallow hard and roll onto my side. I reach one fingertip out and trail it along the line of his hourglass tattoo. The inked sand is halfway dropped, and I can't imagine how excruciatingly long that must have taken to do. He doesn't even flinch as I trace the lines, scrutinizing every last inking.

"You going to be a tattoo artist in your next life, love?" he mutters, turning his head to the side and peeking out at me from under his forearm.

"No. Just thinking that it's interestin'."

"How so?"

"Tattoos have meanings, right?"

"Mostly. For most people."

"Right. Jessie has a half-sleeve of just about every flower under the sun, and every flower's meaning has something that directly matters to her. Sofie has Mila's name on her wrist, and Ella has her mantra on her... I want to say shoulder..." I scrunch my face up as I try to remember. "Never mind where. But my brothers do too. At least half of their tattoos mean something to them...like a permanent reminder of something that once was."

"So your question is...do mine mean anything to me?"

"I guess so." I keep tracing the lines of the hourglass, and now, I notice the tiny bumps that are coating his upper arm although it isn't even cold. Goose bumps.

I give him goose bumps.

My heart flutters. *Down, girl.*

"Some do, I guess. Not all when I had them done, but after? Sure. Like the one you're practically redrawing with your nail." His lips tug up to one side in a kind of half smirk. "The hourglass. I had it done with the sand halfway dropped because I liked the design. But, now, it means something—that time can stop when you least expect it to."

I pause my finger in the middle of the sand and look up to meet his eyes. They're covered again by his forearm, so I reach up and lift his arm just enough that I can look into the green sea of his gaze.

"Like when?" I ask quietly.

He searches my eyes for a long moment, one that causes my heart to skip a beat, before he says quietly, "Like when you walked into the restaurant at the hotel in Paris."

I don't know what I expected him to say, but it wasn't that. "Really?" *I can't believe that's my response.*

"Yeah. I was so shocked to see you that I didn't know what to think. You just kind of...stared at me. I stared back before I realized everyone was looking at me. Then I took your hand to shake it and everything froze again. That was the moment the tattoo made sense to me."

"It kind of stopped for me too," I say so quietly that it's almost a whisper. I let my hands fall from him and roll back onto my back, looking up at the sky.

The sun is setting, casting a golden glow across the trees. Rays peek through the leaves and branches, spilling onto the grass around us, somehow missing us entirely.

Time. Stopped.

Was that really what happened when I saw him in that restaurant? I remember feeling total shock and freezing, sure, but was that me, or was it my entire world stopping right along with me?

"That was strange, wasn't it? The freakiest coincidence." I talk without knowing if he's listening to me at all. "I had no idea who you were when Con told me, yet I knew your name. Knew you. I would have laughed at anyone who told me you'd be the person I find."

"Divine intervention." Jase laughs. "Gotta be, right? It's more than coincidence. It's bloody freaky. We met more than a year ago in the world's tiniest fucking coffee shop in the corner of your favorite place in the world, and then, suddenly, we're thrust back into each other's lives in such a way we can't escape it."

"We could."

"But that would involve self-control, and I just watched you devour an entire bar of Cadburys single-handedly, if you add all the squares together. Self-control, you do not possess."

"What are you, Yoda?"

"Self-controlled, I am not."

"You're an idiot."

"I know. It's one of my more charming qualities, don't you think?"

I roll my eyes and wriggle to stop grass blades from tickling my neck. "It is kind of crazy, isn't it? Kinda like that Timbaland song with Katy Perry. 'If We Ever Meet Again.'"

"I think I remember that." He half mutters, half sings a few of the lines, and I grin.

I've never really heard him sing before, so even when he's muttering like an old man telling himself his to-do list, it's grin-worthy. "That's it. Now, sing it properly."

"Uh... No." He shakes his head, which is still beneath his arm.

"Yes!" I roll back toward him and push at his arm. "And, for the love of god, move your dang arm."

He shakes his head again. "They might find me."

"They're photographers. Not extra fuckin' terrestrials."

"May as well be." He laughs, but he rolls onto his side, laying his arm over the side of his face instead of over his eyes.

Anyone who walks past us would be hard-pressed to work out who he is without getting super close. I'm actually amazed we've gone this long without him being spotted. Maybe his name is more recognizable than his face. I don't know. Then again, don't they say there are some celebrities who can walk down the busiest street and never be noticed?

I guess it depends on whether or not you're looking for the person walking past you.

"There's nobody else around, really. You don't have to hide anymore." I tuck my hand underneath my cheek as our eyes meet. "Besides, I'll junk-punch anyone who gets close enough to take your photo without zoomin' in super high."

He raises an amused eyebrow. "What if they aren't male?"

"Then I'll vagina-punch."

"You'd touch another woman's vagina for me?"

"Punch it. Through their clothes. Hard." I kick him. "Don't get ideas."

"I wouldn't dream of it." He grins lopsidedly, his eyes glinting with playfulness. "Although..."

"No!"

"Kidding! I'm kidding!" He jerks back when I go to kick his shin again. "Stop that. You've got a kick like a donkey."

My jaw drops. He did not just say that.

I prop myself on my elbow and stare down at him. "I can't believe you just called me a donkey!"

He laughs. "I didn't call you a donkey. I said you kick like one. That's a compliment!"

"On what world is that a freakin' compliment? Do I have hooves? Large thighs? A giant butt?"

"You just have to twist my words, you don't?"

"Answer the question, Jase!"

"You have a very nice bum, lovely thighs, and I haven't seen your bare feet to comment on the hooves."

I purse my lips and fight my smile as he attempts to keep his laughter in check. I'm doing a better job at fighting my amusement than he is. His entire body is trembling as he holds it in. Honestly, he's bad at concealing shit like this. I don't know why he bothers.

"I don't have hooves. And my butt is only 'very nice'? That's, like, a three out of ten. I don't squat like a boss to be a three out of ten on the butt scale. I squat to be a twenty at least."

"Okay, then you have the best bum I've ever seen."

"Well, now, you're just sayin' it!"

"Bloody hell, woman. There's no pleasing you, is there?"

"Actually, there is. It's just inappropriate to do in public."

His smile stretches so wide that I think his face might break. "True. Then I'll have to do this." He finally removes his arm from where it's been lying over the side of his face, shoves the chocolate out of the way, and grabs my butt.

I squeak as his fingers dig into it, involuntarily moving away from his touch and closer to his body. My breasts are now brushing his chest, and our hips are dangerously close together.

"What are you doin'?" I ask.

"Evaluating your bum." He raises both his eyebrows, his smile becoming a sexy smirk.

"Isn't this a family park?"

"Your niece demands money every time you swear and is the richest three-year-old I know. I've seen you alone hand her the equivalent of probably twenty dollars in the last week. I'm not sure you're in a position to be throwing out the 'family park' line." He wriggles closer. "Besides. My hand is outside your underwear. Unfortunately."

"You're kind of a pig. You know that?" I look down at him.

"From the girl who told me six hours ago we spend too much time being friends and not enough fucking," he says dryly. "But sure. I'm the pig."

"I never said I wasn't a pig. I'm just a cute pig."

"So, you're okay with being called a pig but not a donkey?"

"Pigs are incredibly clean animals, I'll have you know."

"They roll around in mud all day, Leila. How is that clean?"

"Good for the skin." I pat his cheek. "You'll never see a pig with acne."

"I don't know if pigs get acne."

"Exactly. It's all the mud."

Jase draws his eyebrows into a frown as he stares at me. "You are full of completely random shit. Has anyone ever told you that?"

"The last person who did got a knee to their balls," I tell him honestly.

All right, so he'd just dumped me, but he did say I was random. And not in a nice way. If there's such a thing.

"You're really violent," he mutters.

I teasingly jerk my knee against his thigh, but he's stronger and quicker than I am.

Before I know it, I'm on my back and he's on top of me, his knees on the outsides of my hips and his hands pinning mine above my head.

He looks down at me, his green eyes sparkling dangerously. "I don't know if I can quite figure you out, Leila Burke."

"Good." I defiantly raise my chin, our gazes still locked. "If you can do that, I won't be nearly as interesting as I think I am."

"Honestly, I can't imagine a world in which you're anything close to boring."

I bite the inside of my cheek, but the smile I'm fighting wins and my lips creep up on one side. "Boring isn't a word I understand. Random? Crazy? Impulsive? Yep. But boring? Who has time for that?"

"One would imagine being random and crazy is far more time consuming." He squeezes my hands, which are still pinned against the tickly grass. "And hey. You read a lot. Isn't that boring?"

I still. Not that I'm moving anyway, but I still. "Take that back right now."

"What did I say?"

"You asked me if reading was boring. Take. It. Back."

"Or you could just answer the question..." he says. Then he pauses and grimaces. "You know what? I'm a little afraid of the look in your eye right now. Really glad I have you pinned under me."

I glare at him and sigh. "Don't you understand what a book is?"

"Obviously."

"Then how can it be boring? It's not just twenty-six little letters all mushed together to make words that link together to tell a story. It's the creation of another world where anything can happen and anyone can be whoever they want to be. It's a crazy, special kind of magic that can transport you out of the real world, to anywhere you want to go. It doesn't matter if it's a made-up universe or it's written in a city you can drive to within an hour. It's what happens within the pages that makes reading so...not boring." I hesitate for a moment, realizing that I sound like a crazy girl, but Jase isn't laughing at me.

He's...watching me still, his eyes narrowed the tiniest bit, but not in a mean way. Like he's...processing what I'm saying. Trying to figure it out and understand it.

"Sometimes, when I read, it's not just fiction while I'm between the pages. It's real. My heart races when they kiss, and I get shocked when they do dumb stuff. I yell at their bad choices and the bad guys, and sometimes, I even cry. If a book can elicit such real emotion from somebody, if a story can be so powerful you feel everything the characters are feeling, then reading can't ever be boring." I swallow as I finish.

My heart flips with the stunning thought that I just bared a piece of my soul to him. That my *heart* just opened up and allowed him to see a piece of me nobody else has ever seen.

Not my brothers. Not my family. Not my friends.

Just him.

Terror filters through my veins. I didn't…I didn't mean to do that. Say all that stuff. God, now he's going to know I'm totally crazy. Only a crazy person says that out loud.

Hey, I prefer fiction over reality, but don't worry. I'm as sane as they come.

This is the moment it all stops, isn't it? Where he realizes he's wasting his time hanging out with a hard-hearted romantic sap.

"Is that why you carry a book with you wherever you go? And don't lie. If you have your bag, you have a book inside it. I bet there's one in it right now," he says quietly.

I take a deep breath. "Yep."

"And why you can pull it out at any given moment and ignore everybody for five minutes?"

I nod. "It's not because I want to escape real life. It's because, sometimes, I just want to go somewhere else. It's like a vacation without paying extortionate plane ticket prices. And there's no risk of being frisked by security."

Jase's chuckle is quiet, and he lowers his face until our noses are almost touching. "You just keep on surprising me. Every single day."

"Then buckle up," I say quietly, my lips frozen into a mischievous little smile as the panic slowly recedes. "Because you ain't seen nothin' yet."

"Oh," he replies, his mouth tugging up on one side into a determined smirk that reflects in his eyes. "I'm counting on it."

"I am not datin' Jase."

"You spend a lot of time together."

"So? You spend a lot of time with Jennifer. Does that mean you're suddenly not with Jessie and are with Jennifer?"

"Entirely different situation." Aidan shakes his head. "She's our publicist. You don't work for or with Jase."

"No, but when y'all aren't workin', y'all are loved up and he and I have nothing to do." I shove a strawberry in my mouth and say, "So there."

"Gross," Kye mutters.

Like he's never been more disgusting than that. I wasn't even chewing.

"We're just worried you're spendin' too much time with him," he continues. "That's all. We know what you're like."

They what? "Know what I'm like?" I swallow the fruit. "What does that even mean?"

"You tend to get...full on."

"In my threats, yeah, but that's about it."

Aidan rolls his eyes. "Leila, you flit in and out of relationships like a moth gets burned on a flame. This isn't one you can steamroll in and out of like normal. Hell, it's not one you can even steamroll into. Tate'll lose a ball if you date Jase."

"I'm. Not. Dating. Jase." I punctuated each word by banging my fist against the table. "And I do not steamroll in and out of relationships! I date, and none of them have been the right guy for me. Do you expect me to stick around after date two if I can't even get a zing in the old vag after a goodnight kiss?"

"Whoa!" they say together, wincing.

"I don't need to hear that," Kye continues. "I feel like I need to bleach my ears."

"Word," Aidan mutters. "Way too much info."

I shrug. "Y'all will keep on at me. Expect to need ear bleach every single time, 'cause I'm getting real sick of it."

No joke. This is too regular. I'm not dating Jase. We have a mutual agreement that benefits us both, but we're not dating. I'm going to stick to that until I'm blue in the face because *we've never been on a date.*

And dat*ing* implies more than one date. And, if we haven't been on one date, we sure as hell haven't been on more.

Ergo... Not dating.

"It's just a lot of time to spend with a friend," Aidan says. "That's all. I don't want you doing something stupid like get feelings for the guy and then mope around like a wet fish when we go home."

"You're ridiculous." I stab my fork into a piece of bacon. "Completely ridiculous."

"We're lookin' out for you, Lei," Kye says. "The way you did for us. That's all."

"Okay, first, I wasn't looking out for you. I had front-row seats to the panto that was your love lives, and y'all know you'd still be clueless and single if it weren't for me."

They both share a look that I know means they agree.

"Second, you don't need to look out for me. How many times do I have to say that? I'm twenty-three. I'm an adult. I don't need you to baby me, as much as I appreciate your concern."

"We're still gonna look out for you."

"I know," I grumble. "Can you just do it a little quieter? And away from me?"

"Why are you so bothered anyway? If you don't like Jase, it shouldn't be a problem that we care."

"How did you get from my independence to that? Honestly. You're insufferable pains in my ass."

Aidan snorts. "Yeah, we're the pains."

"Can you hear yourselves? Really? Y'all're like records stuck on freakin' repeat. I got it the first time. Why don't you trust me?" *Because you're kinda, sorta lying to them, idiot.*

"You think we don't trust you?" Ads frowns.

"I know you don't trust me. And I know you're just doing Tate's dirty work so I don't dick-punch him with a vase!" I point at the twins with my fork, half a bacon rasher stuck to the end of it. "Now, you're up here while I'm eating my breakfast, bugging the crap outta me. Don't you have anything better to do?"

"Yes. But we were forced," Kye admits.

"You're adult men. How can your brother force you into bugging your sister?"

They share a look.

I put my fork down with a clatter. "Tell me. Now."

They share another look.

"The vase dick-punches can be shared," I threaten.

Ads pulls his phone out of his pocket, taps the screen a few times, then walks across my room and hands it to me. "Ella got this Google alert this morning."

Her Google alerts are out of control. Seriously. Someone needs to give that girl something else to do.

I drop my eyes from my brother's down to the phone screen. I can tell it's a screenshot from the double notification bar at the top—Ella also needs to sort her notifications out. But the other thing I can see? It's a shot of a story with a picture, albeit grainy, of Jase kissing a girl with dark hair, lying on the grass.

"I don't follow." The lie is blatant—to me, at least—but I meet Aidan's eyes, unblinking.

"You were with Jase yesterday after he took y'all to the grocery place."

"Tesco. The giant supermarket that's like a baby Target," I correct him.

"Whatever," Kye says, walking up to the table to join us. He leans against the side of it and looks down at me. "You were with him and this story is running everywhere."

"I wasn't with him all night."

What? I was back here at nine p.m. That's not all night.

"So, you're saying this isn't you?"

"I wasn't with him all night," I repeat.

Oh, man. Lying by evasion is way less guilt-inducing than outright lying.

"All right." Aidan exits the screen and locks his phone before putting it back in his pocket. "I believe you."

"You do?" Kye frowns.

"She says she wasn't with him all night, then she wasn't with him all night." Ads shrugs and looks back to me. "You're right. You are an adult. We just don't want you to get hurt, Lei, yeah? We love you."

Aw, man. What's that bug gnawing its way through my conscience? Oh, yeah. The guiltbug. Ugh...

"I know," I say. "I love you guys, too. But does this mean you'll let me pee without questioning it?"

"We'll tell Tate to back off. Promise. What are you doing today?"

"I'm going to Convent Garden to read."

"You know how to get there?"

"I'll get a cab."

"You can get back?"

"The Oyster card is paid and ready."

"You'll tell us if you get lost?"

"I thought I could pee without question?"

"Yeah, but you ain't peein'." Kye grins widely, taking over for Aidan. "Now you promise to tell us if you get lost?"

I flatly stare at them both. "I'd rather eat my own eyeballs for breakfast."

Aidan laughs and pats my shoulder twice, causing me to shift away from his touch. "All right. We'll leave you alone. Want me to see if Chelsey and Jessie want to go with you? I think their ears will bleed if they have to do another sound check."

"What about Sofie? Mila?"

"She said she's gonna take her to the zoo," Kye answers. "I think Mila's a bit overwhelmed by everything and Sofie wants some quality time with her. Con's gonna meet them as soon as we're done."

I nod. It was easy to see that Mila was getting tired of everything, and Sofie can only bring herself to leave her with the temporary nanny for so long. Getting her to agree to a temporary nanny was the hardest thing I'll ever do in my life, I'm sure.

"Sure, then. Company won't be bad." I smile as they head for the door.

They wave as they leave, and the second the door shuts, I shake my head, but my eyes flit back to the screenshot.

I'm lucky it was grainy. So grainy that they must have been able to see Jase clearer with their own eye than with the camera to know it was him. I'm also lucky they didn't recognize me—I've been pictured with my brothers more than enough times. Although I've pretty much avoided them since we landed in Europe, so there are no recent pictures. Or maybe he was just hiding me... I don't know.

Either way, I'm not sure Aidan believed me. He gave in way too easily. I know him, and when he wants to know something, he'll go on and on and on and on until he gets the answers he's after. Even when it's a person—Jessie didn't exactly date him by choice. He did kind of lie about being her boyfriend in the start and screwed it there, and in the end, he wanted her, so he got her.

I have a horrible feeling he's going to be biding his time where I'm concerned. And there are more of my brothers than there are of me.

I'm gonna have to talk to—

"Let us in!" Chelsey demands, banging on my door.

—Chelsey and Jessie.

I get up, chewing on a bit of bacon, and open my door. "Morning."

"It's early is what it is," Jessie grumbles, shuffling past me. "And Aidan drank the last of our coffee."

I hook my thumb over my shoulder, toward my coffee machine. I'm not engaging in a long conversation with her until she has a mug in her hand. If you cut her open, she'd bleed coffee, I'm sure.

"That was quick," I say to Chelsey.

"Yep. Apparently, they think, if we come here right after they did and ask questions about Hot Brit, we'll get answers." She grins and jumps onto the spare bed.

It's why I never make my bed.

"They're idiots," I say. "And you need to get them under control."

"Why? Are they close to finding out you're bonking his balls off?"

"I am not bonking his balls off!" I say a little too loudly.

"We already know you are," Jessie says behind me. "We're not gonna tell them. We're not that dumb."

"You're dating my brothers."

"Which means all of our stupid is taken up for that portion of our lives, leaving our smarts to cover your tracks." She flicks my hair and starts the coffee machine.

Lucky me, eh?

"Thanks," I say dryly as soon as the coffee machine stops. "That's what I always wanted. Your smarts to help me."

"So, the pictures weren't obvious, then?" Chelsey asks, grinning.

"No." No point lying about it. "You couldn't really see me. They just assumed it was me because I was with him last night."

"What did you tell them?"

"That I wasn't with him all night."

"So, you didn't deny it?" Jessie asks, one dark eyebrow disappearing beneath her bangs as she raises it.

"No. I was attempting not to lie."

"How is that not lying?"

"I was back here by nine."
"Ah. Sneaky." Chels nods. "Now what?"
I sigh heavily. "I try not to get caught again... Or stop."

chapter fourteen

Me: *Sorry.*
Leila: *What for?*
Me: *The photos. I know how you feel about the media.*
Leila: *It's okay. They must have been well hidden. Plus nobody knows it was me.*
Me: *Your brothers keep mentioning it to me.*
Leila: *Yeah... They're kind of annoying like that.*
Me: *They asked me who it was.*
Leila: *Uh-oh. What did you say?*
Me: *Some girl I know. I didn't know what else to say. They put me on the spot.*
Leila: *They're annoying like that too. Sorry they're bugging you. Maybe this isn't a good idea after all. You and me. We've almost been caught twice in 3 days. Idk if I'm okay lying about it. Makes me feel like crap.*

I scratch my ear and read that last message over and over again. I know she's right. Her feelings about the media's invasion of someone's private life and the sneaking around behind her brothers' backs... It isn't a good idea.

I never pretended it was. But she's right. We've almost been caught twice. First, at the hotel room in Paris. Then, twenty-four hours later, in Hyde Park by a photographer.

I don't know what I would have said to her if the photographer had recognized her. I'm holding out hope that they didn't see her face at all, if only for her protection. It was stupid, kissing her out in public like that. What would have happened if one of her brothers had happened to be walking through the park and seen us? Extreme situations and all that, but it could have happened. I know they were all out seeing some sights last night.

One second. That's all it would have taken. One second of seeing me on top of

her, kissing her slowly, and it would have been over.
I pick up my phone and hit the reply button.

Me: *Is that what you want?*

I watch the screen for a reply, but it doesn't come.

Me: *If it is, all you have to do is say. I'll respect your choice.*

I put my phone back in my pocket and lean back on the sofa. Waiting for Dirty B. to finish the concert feels like it's taking forever, but I'm not going to risk any more crazy stories coming out from wannabe models, especially since Stella Porter was just forced to retract her story and admit she was lying.

From now on, I'll be photographed leaving every concert with them and an added bonus in the backstage meet-and-greets. Good for me and my profile, bad for my privacy.

The band gets back with just enough time before the meet-and-greet. Within seconds of their arrival and downing a bottle of water each, security is controlling the girls who are stopping by for a photo and signatures.

It passes in a blur for me. I smile, take photos, sign things, take more photos, take selfies. It's a whirlwind of excited girls and twenty-something women who have paid out their arses for this experience. I'm here physically, but my mind is elsewhere—with Leila. With the unanswered text message.

I'm glad when it's over and we're being hounded out of the O2. I keep my head down for every photo, not in the mood to see my miserable mug plastered across every page tomorrow. I'm tired and the sister of the guys in front of me is taking over my mind.

My life, even.

I'm hustled into another car to take me home, while the others go to the hotel. Carlos is sitting in the front seat next to the driver, and I drop my head back against the seats as flashes from the cameras of photographers hoping for one last photo glare through the tinted window. They won't be the best, but all they'll see is one tired guy with his eyes closed.

Nobody told me how tiring large concerts like this are. I'm learning a lot and I'm learning it quickly, and I'm slowly remembering why I told myself that getting involved with Leila was a bad idea. I knew she'd be a big distraction from what was happening to me—a big and pointless distraction given that we live thousands of miles apart—but I couldn't resist her.

Still can't.

If she says to carry on this game we're playing, will I? Or will I step back and focus on my career, on my dream?

Or will I continue to give in to the mystery that is her? The one that's unraveling itself piece by piece, bit by bit.

Leila Burke is a mystery of epic proportions. She's sarcastic and sassy, playful and teasing, hard as nails. Yet she's soft, too, beneath all that. She's a tornado of complexity and intrigue, and I'm caught in the eye of her storm.

It's uncontrollable.

I'll never say no.

And I'm not sure I can let her say no, either.

I check my phone. It shows one message from her from a few minutes ago.

Leila: *We can't have this conversation over text. Can I come over?*
Me: *Tonight?*
Leila: *Yes. I told Sofie I was going to bed. I can get a cab to your apartment if you give me your address.*

I think about it for a moment. She's right. We need to talk about this. She's obviously way more bothered than I thought she was, but now I'm wondering what's gotten her so worked up, because she sure as hell wasn't this bothered when we talked yesterday.

I send my address in the next text and lock my phone after she responds with a thank-you. I'm fucking glad I bought some Red Bull when I had to take her and Sofie shopping. I have the feeling I'm going to need it to wake myself up enough to have this conversation with her.

The car pulls up outside my block of flats, and I look out the window. Nobody's here.

"Either we beat them to it or your address is still secret." Carlos looks back between the seats, a sneaky yet smug smile on his face.

"Thanks, mate." I reach forward and shake his hand. "Appreciate it."

I get out of the car, dragging my bag out behind me, and shut the door. I throw a wave into the air as I look around. It could be paranoia, but now, I'm wondering if having Leila come here is even going to be a good idea. I can't see anybody, but then again, I couldn't at the park yesterday either...

I was somewhat distracted then though.

I go up to my flat, taking the stairs instead of the lift. By the time I get up there, my phone is buzzing in my pocket, and when I pull it up, the message is from Leila. She's downstairs. I unlock my door and press the button to release the door. Then I text her back telling her to come up.

I dump my bag just inside the door and wait for her to come up. It takes only a minute before I hear the lift whizzing up and stopping at my floor. I watch the doors as they ease open and she steps out, her head down, a hood covering it, and her hair tucked in. She looks up instantly, her bright-blue gaze colliding with mine, and in the girliest fucking thing I've ever felt, my heart stutters at the sight of her.

She looks so hesitant. Almost like she doesn't want to come in and have this conversation. She's the quiet, vulnerable Leila I keep getting glimpses of, like last night when she talked about her books and what they are to her and why she reads so much.

It's a peek into the cards she plays so close to her chest.

"Coming in?" I ask her when she doesn't move from standing in front of the lift.

"No. I came to talk to you in the freakin' hall," she snaps halfheartedly.

My lips tug to the side. There's that fire that's so hot.

"Then get your arse in here so I can shut the bloody door."

"You're so demandin'." She does as I said anyway, walking past me and into the flat.

I shake my head, smiling, and push the door shut. It clicks as it swings into place, and I unzip my jacket and hang it up on one of the hooks. Leila pulls her hood down and untucks her hair before taking the jumper off.

"Jesus. There are people outside, by the way," she says, neatly resting the jumper on the arm of my sofa. "Not many, but I think you're getting discovered."

"Brilliant. Do you want a drink or anything?"

She shakes her head. "Honestly, I just want to get this done."

"Get this done? Sounds like you've already made your choice, love." I fold my arms across my chest. "I don't understand why we need to have this conversation in person. Do you want to continue what we've started? Yes or no. It's not exactly multiple choice where you can select bloody 'other' and write yourself an essay."

Her eyes flash with hardness. "I don't like lying to my family, Jase. It's not easy. I feel like a bitch."

"So, what are you doing here?" Harsh—but I'm not in the mood to mess around. If she doesn't want us to continue the relationship we have, all she's gotta do is fucking say it.

"Because," she says quietly.

I raise my hand to run it through my hair.

"I don't think I can give you up."

I still, my fingers buried in my hair, and then drag my eyes to hers. "Sounds like you've got to decide which you hate the idea of most. No, don't look at me like that, Leila, love," I hurry out when she widens her eyes and her lips part. "This isn't on me. I understand what you're thinking, but this is your choice. I'll respect it whatever it is, just respect me and don't fuck around making it."

She stares at me for a long moment, and the air buzzes between us. Her rapidly growing annoyance is palpable. I can almost taste it, almost reach out and touch it, grab hold of it and meld my own with it.

It's not hard.

She wants this or she doesn't.

I know what I want.

Her.

That word—that one tiny word, those three little letters—hits me hard. My head swims with the impact of my realization, because this isn't like before. This isn't just wanting.

I don't just want her.

I *want* her.

Fuck.

I can't let her walk out of here like it's nothing.

Shit no. I won't let her walk out of here like it's nothing. I won't let her fucking walk out this goddamn building without her knowing just how badly I want her. Even if she hits me or screams at me, even if I only get to kiss her to show her, I'm gonna fucking well do it because she needs to know it.

She has no idea. About anything. About how I feel. About her. About us.

She's not leaving here until she realizes that our stupid agreement has become so much more.

"Jase," she whispers, looking away from me, at the floor.

Instinct makes me move. Desire propels me toward her.

Raw need makes me grab her and kiss her like she's fucking everything I'm ever gonna need.

She gasps as I tilt her head back to take her mouth better, to taste her more, to take whatever is left of the reality that could easily become a memory. It feels so hopeless, but I put everything into it, put everything I have into the touch of my lips to hers, and slowly...

No.

Nothing about what she does is slow.

Not the way she grabs my shirt. Not the way she wraps one arm around my neck and holds me against her. Not the way she kisses me back like *I'm* everything *she's* ever gonna need.

The way we grasp at each other is desperate and driven by emotion, fueled by carnal desires. She's so fucking soft and small in my arms, and I drink her in, greedily taking every kiss she'll give me.

Blood rushes to my cock, but I fight it. Somewhere inside my brain still works even though my heart is pounding harshly and my cock is throbbing. Still, somehow, she ends up against the wall that hardly separates my living room and my kitchen, her teeth tugging my bottom lip, her hands creeping up my body beneath my T-shirt, pulling it up.

I tear it over my head and reach down for hers. I kiss her as I pull it up, only breaking to pull it over her head, and it hasn't even touched the ground when her arms are back around my neck and our mouths are melded back together.

I grab her thighs and lift her, wrapping her legs around my waist. A tiny moan escapes her lips as my cock presses between her legs. Her skin is soft but not enough, so I slide my hand up her back to her bra strap and unclasp it without even a fumble. She throws it to the floor, and when she brings her chest back to me, her hardened nipples press against my skin, making my cock throb harder.

Temptation runs rife through my body, uncontrollably red hot. I pull her from the wall and carry her through to the next room, my bedroom, once I've kicked the door open. My fingers dig into her arse cheeks as I get a grip on her to throw her onto my bed.

No sooner has her back hit the bed than I'm back over her, slipping between her legs, pushing her into the middle of the mattress. She winds her fingers in my hair as my mouth leaves her and journeys down the silky-smooth curve of her neck to her exposed breasts.

My tongue rolls over her nipple and she arches her back, pushing it farther into my mouth despite my touch being anything but desperate. She does the same when I turn to the other, grazing my teeth across it.

Grasping her tiny waist, I move farther down her body.

I kiss her flat stomach, feeling the goose bumps beneath my lips as I near her hips. Her jeans are no match for me as I deftly unbutton them and slide them all the way down her legs, leaving her in her panties. I slide my hands up the insides of her thighs, and my thumbs brush against her wet pussy through her underwear. She bucks her hips up to me, inhaling sharply, and I roughly tug the material down her legs.

Before she can do anything, my hands are parting her thighs and my tongue is circling her clit.

"Oh, god," she moans, rolling her hips against my mouth.

I explore her wetness with my tongue, dipping inside her, sucking her clit, teasing her. Her moans go from breathless to loud. Her hands go from tugging on my hair to grasping the sheets. Her breathing goes from shallow to rapid.

Her body goes from soft to hard as she winds her fingers in my hair, crying out one last time, as she comes on my tongue. I continue to tease her with my mouth as she rides it out with tiny, breathless whimpers until she's lying on the bed, spent, in front of me.

I can't help the smirk my lips form as I stand and look down at her in the middle of my bed. Cheeks flushed, lips dry and parted, tits heaving as she catches her breath.

And all from my mouth.

I step out of my jeans, pulling a condom from my wallet. I'm rolling it on before I've even kicked my boxers away. I lean over Leila, sliding my hands up her body, probing her soft skin with my fingertips. She turns her face up to mine, runs her hand up my back to the back of my head, and pulls my mouth down to hers.

She's slowly coming back to life beneath me, and as hard as it is not to push myself inside her, I'll wait until she's ready, until she pulls me into her. I shake with the restraint as my cock touches her wet pussy and hovers at her opening.

She wraps her legs around me and takes me in one.

"Fuck," I hiss against her mouth.

She smiles, but it drops when I pull out of her and push back in. "Jase," she whispers.

It undoes me.

The restraint she knocked through when she took my cock inside her has been shattered by the whisper of my name on her lips.

I flatten one hand next to her head, grab her arse with the other, and thrust into her. I'm unapologetic with every movement, but the hottest fucking thing is watching her. Watching her eyes flutter shut every time I bury myself inside her. Watching her lips part as she draws a breath when I move out. Watching her cheeks flush redder and redder as I move again and again. Watching sweat bead on her forehead as moans escape between her lips.

My body tightens as the hotness of watching her coming to her orgasm mixes with the pleasure of fucking her tight pussy. My heart is pounding so fiercely I can hear my blood echoing in my ears as it floods my body.

Fuck—she's incredible.

She cries my name, squeezing me tight.

I groan hers as my own orgasm hits.

"Fuck," I whisper, wrapping my arms around her lithe body, taking care not to squash her as I relax as quickly as I came.

Leila nods beneath me. Then she leans up and buries her face in the curve of my shoulder, her arms sliding easily around me. Her fingers splay across my back, soft in their touch. She sighs softly when I pull out of her and roll to the side, quickly reaching down to pull the condom off. I tie the top behind her back. Then I drop it off the side of the bed to the floor and pull her against me.

"Are you cold?" I ask her hoarsely, remembering last time she was.

She half laughs but shakes her head. "Not right now."

"Hold on." I let her go and half get up to pull the quilt back.

"What are you doin'?" she asks, amusement teasing her tone.

"Getting you warm before I get really comfy and don't want to move." I hook my arms beneath her neck and her knees and kinda lift her against me, making her let out a tiny scream. I attempt to push the quilt down the bed with one foot, but I end up falling backward in my attempt not to knee Leila in the back. I fall against the headboard with an oomph.

She laughs. Throws her head back and laughs before bringing her face back to my chest. "You're such an idiot."

"Almost...got...it..." I mutter, giving the sheets one final kick.

She rolls her eyes through her laughter and gives the duvet a damn good shove.

"Nice one." I drop her next to me, making her laugh even more, and fuck, I love her laugh.

It's literal music to my soul, that breathy laugh.

I lie down next to her and pull her against me again. Together, we pull the covers over us, and she snuggles into my side, our legs intertwining and locking together.

"That was unexpected," she murmurs into my shoulder.

"Leila." I open my eyes and look down at her.

She tilts her head back, and her blue eyes are crystal clear as they meet mine.

"Did you mean what you said about not wanting to give me up?"

Her tongue creeps out and wets her lips. Then she nods. "Yes. And it's just not because of the sex."

"Although that's pretty fucking convincing, right?"

"Very." She half grins. "It's because of that. Because...you're an idiot."

"You don't want to stop seeing me because I'm an idiot," I say flatly. "I guess that could be a reason for you to stop. Could be worse, although I've heard better reasons, not going to lie, babe."

She buries her face in my shoulder, her body shaking with silent laughter. "That!" she manages to spit out. "That's exactly why." She props herself up on her elbow, resting her other hand on my chest. "You make me laugh," she says quietly, her lips pulled into a small, shy smile. "All the time. I don't know. There isn't a real reason half the time. You just...do. And I don't want to let that feeling go."

I bring my hand up and brush my thumb over her cheek. "I don't want to give you up, either, Leila. Not yet. Not until I have to."

Her breath audibly catches, and she turns her face against my hand. "Then don't."

"It's not my choice."

She wraps her fingers around my wrist, leaving a chill to dance over my bare chest, and pulls my hand away from her face. "So, if I got dressed right now and walked out of here with nothing more than a goodbye, you'd let me go, would you?"

Possessiveness bolts through my entire body, sending shivers down my spine and clenching my muscles with determination. My gentle grasp on her becomes tight, and my fingers dig into her skin at her hip. Fuck no.

"Not a fucking chance."

"Then it's not just my choice." She lets my arm go and rests her palm back against my chest.

I tuck a lock of hair behind her ear before letting my hand fall back to her waist. "Geez, love..." I huff out a long breath. "How can I keep you if you're unhappy lying to your family? What are you going to say when you get back if they realize you left? They're more important than I am."

"Doesn't my happiness matter more? I know they're worried about me being hurt, but we both know what this is. It's not like I can stay here once the tour is over, and you can hardly come with me. I can't be hurt by something I'm prepared for."

"So, why not tell them?" I draw tiny swirls on her skin with my finger.

She shivers.

"Just be honest with them. If they give me shit, then I'll take it. I deserve it for creeping around with you."

"Because they won't see it the way I do," she mutters, or she tries to. "They won't see you the way I do."

"And how's that?"

"An idiot."

My lips quirk. "Pretty sure that's exactly how they'll see me. They'll just add some strong words in front."

"Several," she agrees. She blows out a long breath, her lips pouting. "I'll figure somethin' out. I guess I just had a real crazy moment earlier where I realized what we were doin', and it seemed wrong, and then I came here and I saw you and you kissed me and—"

I do it again. Kiss her. Because, if I don't stop her right here, she'll get herself worked up.

"You're getting yourself in a tizzflap."

She abruptly pulls back from me. "What the ever-loving fuck is a tizzflap?"

Oh, good. Another British word for her to obsess over.

"A tizz. A tizzflap. Worked up."

She blinks. Several times. "Are you sure y'all speak English here? Is that a real word?"

I shrug. "I don't know."

"Tizzflap." She giggles.

"Here we go again."

"Tizzflap."

"Leila?"

"What?" She flutters her eyelashes at me.

"Don't make me shut you up again," I warn her.

She leans in, a sexy yet mischievous glint in her gorgeous, blue eyes, and whispers, "Tizzflap."

It's the last thing she whispers too.

chapter fifteen

I'm in trouble.

I'm in big, biiiiig trouble.

Why? Oh—because I'm not at the hotel and it's eight in the morning. That's right. I fell asleep here last night after Jase decided fucking me to shut me up was the only way to get me to stop saying tizzflap—he was right—and I'm still here.

In Jase's bed.

I'm gonna need a dang good explanation for this one.

Jase yawns next to me, absently slides his hand up my side, and cups my boob. My eyes widen at the unexpected move, and I peer over my shoulder. He's fast asleep. And, now, his erection is prodding me in the butt.

Freaking awesome.

I feel gross, and I'm dying for a shower. The only problem is that I don't want to move. Now, I guess I can't actually move, so it's a bit of a moot point. I'm trapped here until he decides to release my breast from its hostage situation. Who knows how long that will take?

Oh, Jesus. I need to pee.

I clench my legs together as the thought grabs my mind and becomes a literal compulsion. My bladder hurts. I look over my shoulder again, but he's still sleeping peacefully, so I bite down on my lower lip and resign myself to the fact that I'm going to have to perform the equivalent of a Navy SEAL operation if I want to free my breast from his grasp so I can pee.

Slowly, I peel his fingers back one by one and actually lift his arm so it's out of the way. Then I shuffle forward. He half snores, and I freeze, but another cursory look back shows he's still fast asleep.

Come on, Leila. Let's do this.

Quick is best. I scoot right out of the bed then pause because I'm completely naked. Shit.

I grab my underwear and put it back on, wincing as I straighten the waistband of my panties. *Note to self: Carry spare panties in my purse.* This is the most disgusting thing I've ever done and I have four brothers. I've been an accomplice to some vile crap in my life.

I throw my shirt and my jeans on—lotta effort to pee—and tentatively open the bedroom door. Jase doesn't stir as I pull it to behind me and find the bathroom. Thankfully, it's right next to his room, so I lock the door behind me and go about my business.

When I'm done, I look in the mirror and squeak. Jesus fucking hell, I look like I've been thrown under a bus and dragged backwards through a bush. I desperately run my hands through my hair in an attempt to smooth it down so it's kind of presentable to the outside world. Does he have a brush here?

Why would he have a brush?

He's kind of put together. Like a rough-edged pretty boy.

Wait. No. He's not a pretty boy. He doesn't undo the buttons of a shirt to his freakin' belly button like those idiots do. Still though...

"Leila?" Jase's voice travels through the door. "You in there?"

"Yeah." I abandon my thoughts to ransack his cupboards and unlock the door. I open it and look at him. "I need a hairbrush."

Jase blinks harshly, rubs one eye, and then focuses on me. "Don't take this the wrong way, but bloody hell, you do."

I give him my best screw-you look. "It's your fault. Do you have one?"

"Uh, yeah... If you don't mind using mine." He comes into the bathroom, wearing nothing but his underwear, and opens the drawer in the unit next to the bath. He pulls a brush out and sets about cleaning it. He runs it under the tap before he hands it to me. "There. It's clean-ish, at least."

"Thank you." I pull it through my hair in the first arduous task of my day. "If I go back to the hotel looking like this, my excuses will be useless."

"Shit. Yeah. What are you going to say?" He grabs his toothbrush and squeezes some paste onto it.

"Well..." I run the brush through my hair one last time, finishing with a final few tugs on a particularly knotty section at the front. Then, after running my hands through it to liven it up, I still. "Hey, let's go back to Tesco!"

Jase pauses, his toothbrush in his mouth, and meets my eyes in the mirror. "'Nndom," he says.

Random, I assume. "Yes! But I can say I ran out of shampoo so I called you this morning and you took me to get some."

He spits paste into the sink. "You could call the concierge. You're staying in a five-star hotel. They'll have shampoo."

I wrinkle my face. "I don't like hotel shampoo."

"So you called me at... What is it? Like, eight? In the morning to take you to get shampoo because you're a diva who can't cope with hotel toiletries."

"Yes!" I clap my hands together. "That's exactly it!"

"All right."

"All right? Really? You're agreein'?"

"I don't have much of a choice," he says in a resigned tone. "Plus, if I take you to buy shampoo and you actually buy it, you're not entirely lying."

"I did only bring a small bottle," I muse. "Okay. Get thinkin', Brit Boy. We've gotta come up with a whole bunch of these in case this happens again." I slap his arm and turn away.

He laughs, slapping my ass. "You're bossy on a morning."

"It's how I get through the day." I flash him a grin. "Plus, when you're the only girl out of five, you have to develop survival techniques."

"No shit. I thought being one out of two boys was bad."

"Two? Oh, right. Your brother." I nod and slip onto a stool at the small island. "How old is he? Wait. How old are you? Why don't I know this?"

Jase fills a kettle with water and looks over his shoulder, smirking. "Because you never asked. I don't know how old you are, either."

"You never asked. Besides, that's rude. You never ask a lady her age."

"I wouldn't call you a lady..." he says hesitantly, clicking the kettle to boil.

My jaw drops, and I gape at him.

"More like a force."

"Force of what?"

"Just...a force. You're something to be reckoned with."

Is that a compliment? I don't know. I think it's good.

"How old are you?" I ask.

He raises an eyebrow. "Twenty-six."

"Hey. You're the same age as Tate."

Now, it makes sense. Tate knows what single guys in their midtwenties can be like because he was the biggest man-slut I've ever met in my life.

"Are you a man-slut?" I clap my hand over my mouth because I wasn't actually supposed to say that out loud.

He almost drops the mug he's pulling from the cupboard. "Uh... Define man-slut."

"That's never a good response." I sigh and rest my chin on my hands, my elbows resting on the counter in front of me.

"Are you asking if I've been with anyone since I saw you last week?"

"I'm askin' if you're a man-slut." Hell, I'm in deep. May as well enjoy the hole I've dug myself.

"And again—define man-slut."

The kettle finishes boiling with a click, and he opens a cannister that has teabags in.

"A slut that's a man. I don't know how to define it further. I always thought the term was self-explanatory."

But, while we're here, his question is exactly right. Has he? I don't know. Unlikely. You know though. While the point has been thrown out there.

"No, Leila, love. I haven't been with anyone since you walked into the hotel restaurant. I was too busy being fucked up with the knowledge I'd be stuck with you for a while."

"Stuck with me? You're staying at home here, Brit Boy. You don't have to see my ass at all."

"I know. Although the main problem here is that I'm particularly fond of your arse. The rest of you too, actually." He pulls milk from the fridge.

I tilt my head to the side as he spoons in two sugars over the teabag then pours the hot water over it. Man, he's concentrating pretty hard on making that cup of tea. Like it's a damn art or something... Then again, if I really focus on the view...

He's standing there in his tight boxers, every other part of his body on show. Thick, strong thighs. Trim waist. Broad, muscular shoulders. Tattooed, toned arms. Messy, unkept hair. Rough, stubbly jaw.

Hot British guy makes tea.

That should be a porn movie.

It's actually a very strange turn on. Maybe it's just seeing a guy in the kitchen.

Jase spoons the teabag out of the water, squeezes it against the side of the mug, and puts it on a tiny ceramic dish next to the kettle.

Oh, boy.

I have no idea why a shiver runs down my spine, but lord oh lord.

Hot British Guy Makes Tea should definitely be a porn movie.

"You doing all right over there, love? You seem distracted."

I snap my eyes upward from his ass—who knew it was that tight? "You're not wearing anything. It's a nice view."

"I love it when you compliment me."

"It won't happen often. Don't get used to it."

Jase laughs loudly, putting his mug of tea on the counter. "I wasn't even thinking about it. Let me drink this and get ready. Then I'll take you to buy your shampoo." His lips move up on one side. *That smirk.* "Then you get to field more questions from your family while I see my mum before she starts calling me and wondering why I haven't called her yet."

Mum.

He said mum.

"You're dying because I said mum, aren't you?" He looks way too smug.

"No."

This has to be the world's most blatant lie. I have no idea why I'm even pretending. He knows. Of course he does. That's evident by the dirty smirk creeping onto his face and the laughing glittering at me from his eyes.

"Can you drink your tea so we can go, please?"

He says nothing as he hides that smirk behind his mug and walks out of his kitchen.

Against my will, my head turns as my eyes follow him. Jesus Christ, the guy is hot. Hotter than hot.

I still say there has to be something wrong with him.

I bet he picks his nose. Yeah, that's gotta be it. Maybe flicks them at passersby out of his bedroom window. Or bites his toenails. It has to be something super gross, because perfect always comes with a side of yuck.

I silently laugh at my own thoughts and bite my thumbnail, staring aimlessly at the light oak cupboards that make up his kitchen. This apartment is real airy and light. The kind of place that'd see raindrops at their finest and the sun at its brightest. Where you could sit happily with a book, of course.

I almost want to pull mine out of my purse and read a few pages while he gets ready.

So I do. I hop off the stool and go to the sofa, where my purse is sitting next to my sweater. I reach inside and pull my book out. Then I drop onto the sofa and tuck my feet under my butt while I get lost in the world of the story.

I don't know how long I read for.

I don't know how long I've been reading when I feel his eyes on me.

"How long have you been standin' there?" I ask, turning to face him, sliding the bookmark between the pages.

Jase shrugs, shoving his hands in his pockets. He's leaning against the wall he had me pinned against last night. "Few minutes. Not long."

My cheeks flush as a slow wash of embarrassed heat washes over me. I snap the book shut and tuck it back into my purse. "You should have said you were ready to go."

"I did." He smiles the kind of smile that lights up his entire face, making his jaw appear sharper and his eyes greener and brighter. "You were so engrossed you didn't hear me, so I didn't want to interrupt you."

I stand up, grabbing my things, and stop in front of him with one eyebrow raised. "So, you watched me read?"

"Yes."

"Why?"

"Because I think you're beautiful."

He said it so easily, so simply, like those five words were nothing. They rolled right off his tongue freely, as though they were lyrics to one of his songs and he's sung them a thousand times. More than anything, though, he said them so honestly.

I believe his words, believe him.

"I love it when you compliment me," I say softly, only half teasing him.

He cups my chin with his finger and his thumb and tilts my face up to his only to catch my gaze in the intricate web of his. "It'll happen often. Get used to it."

Honestly, I answer, "I don't think I ever will."

"Good," he replies softly. "Because then it'll stop meaning something to you." He leans forward and kisses my forehead.

The kiss burns my skin with its tenderness, and briefly, my eyes flutter shut as I bask in the intimate touch.

No. I don't think it will.

I've come to the conclusion that my brothers are either playing along with me or just downright fucking stupid.

They bought the shampoo thing without blinking yesterday morning, and now, I feel oddly better about this whole sneaky-sneaky scenario. I almost wish, if they're playing along, that they'd just turn around and come out with it so plainly that I wouldn't be able to deny it. Although, if they're not, I appreciate their turning a blind eye to me as I do the very thing they forbade me from.

They must have known forbidding me to do what I wanted would never work out well for them.

If they're just stupid and really did believe the shampoo line, then, well. The dumb shits deserve to be lied to.

I like to think they're playing along. It assuages my guilt a little more. Okay, a lot more. I don't feel like my pants are gonna light on fire at any second. It was starting to feel like it'd be a real possibility. That we'd be talking about something totally unrelated then, pow, my ass would set alight.

This is the third day in London and all I've seen is Hyde Park. I feel like a total loser because I was so excited to come back but all I've done is read. My brothers are all back to their usual loved-up, vomit-worthy coupled selves, which pretty much leaves me alone.

It's hard to drag your ass out when you're alone. When I was here before, it was an exciting adventure, like a whole new world to be discovered. But now... I've seen it. I've done it, and it's maybe not so exciting this time around.

Not to mention Jase lives here, so I can't exactly ask him, can I? Not when he's already shown me everything before. It wouldn't be the same as it was then, when I didn't know where to go or what to do. When I had no idea how to get anywhere or the difference between the one- and two-pound coins. (The two pound coins are the pretty ones with the silver middle, for the record. I like those.)

Plus, you know what? Jase is right. I hate tourists. I don't wanna be a damn tourist. They're all in the way with their cameras and those fucking selfie sticks that get in the way of everybody else's pictures. *Sure, that's okay. I always wanted your phone on a stick in my shot of Big Ben.*

Maybe that's also another reason why I should just stay in my room. I'm not the most patient person and may or may not have threatened to break a guy's selfie stick last time I was in this city.

Everybody has thought it at least once.

I huff out a breath and drop back onto my bed, reaching for my phone. The sun is shining—contrary to the stereotypical weather of it always raining—and I'm lying on my bed in my room. This just goes to prove that I'm the worst American ever. I know that my brothers will be out doing their thing with my friends before they have to go film some live TV appearance on a talk show tonight. I almost wish I'd tagged along with them just for something to do.

I could text Jase.

No, I can't text Jase. We've spent too much time together lately and I'm starting to definitely cross the line of friends with benefits. It doesn't freaking help when he keeps being so sweet and...honest. I'm not used to guys being honest. They usually want me for my brothers.

He had my brothers before he had me.

Kind of.

Crossing the line between friends with benefits and real feelings isn't in the plan. In a week and a half, we're gonna get on a plane back to South Carolina and this whirlwind trip will be done. Jase and I will be done.

I don't want to think about why that makes my heart clench.

I don't want my heart to clench. I can't start falling for this gorgeous guy—any more than I have, that is. 'Cause I have. A little. You don't laugh at someone as much as he makes me laugh at him without falling for them just a little, teeny, tiny, itty, bitty bit.

That's where it's going to stay. The falling. The feelings. A little, teeny, tiny, itty, bitty bit. Like a blood-cell-sized bit.

If I keep telling myself it, maybe I'll believe it soon. Preferably within ten minutes.

I groan and roll onto my front, burying my face in the pillow. I inhale deeply, turn my face to the side, and stare at the plain, white wall. It's a futile fight, I know. They're hopeless feelings, destined to live buried in me, because I've said so.

Some things just can't be shown.

These are some of them.

I need to compartmentalize. Stop seeing him as...god, him. How can I stop that? How can I stop seeing Jase as everything he is? How do I stop him from being everything I want? Everything I crave?

His laugh. His smile. His touch. His taste.
I crave it.
All of it.
It's not supposed to be this way.
It's supposed to be a chain of late-night dirty little rendezvous after dirty little rendezvous. Secret, forbidden, hidden. Life-changing, earth-shattering, heart-thumping, but in the dirtiest, most delicious, most provocative way.
Not secret, forbidden, or hidden because there's more to it.
Not life-changing, earth-shattering, or heart-thumping because he's someone so much more than just a person to warm my bed for an evening.
Butterflies aren't supposed to be because I know he's coming, but because I'm wondering what he's going to do to me next. Breathlessness isn't supposed to be the way his laugh rumbles across my skin and sets my hair on end. It's supposed to be because he's so deep inside me that I can't open my eyes for the pleasure. Need isn't supposed to be because I miss him. It's supposed to be because I want his body over mine.
But it is.
The butterflies are because I know he's coming.
The breathlessness is because his laugh is the deepest, most melodic, most spine-tingling sound I've ever heard.
The need is because it's so quiet without him... Because it feels so cold without him around me, warming my soul with his compelling, green eyes and tender touches, whether they're with his hands or his soft mouth.
I squeeze my eyes shut as I unlock my phone and tap the icon of where I know my texts will be. Simultaneously, I love and loathe international plans. If I didn't have it, I wouldn't be able to text him or anything, but here I am, opening my eyes and tapping his name at the top of my message inbox.

Me: *What are you doing?*
Jase: *Writing. You?*

So busy writing that he can text me back right away, right? Still, I smile as I hit the box to reply.

Me: *Lying on my bed, lamenting the boredom that is my life.*
Jase: *How Shakespearean of you.*
Me: *Why? Because it's tragic? Romantic? Hardly comedic.*
Me: *It's tragic, isn't it?*
Jase: *Terribly, love. You could help a poor guy write some lyrics.*
Me: *Did that once. Look where it got me.*
Jase: *?*

Jase: *Regular orgasms with a hot guy who can make a shit hot cuppa?*
Me: *But can you sext?*
Jase: *I prefer to turn you on when I can do something about it.*
Me: *That was a half sext. 5 points for Slytherin.*
Jase: *Was that a pun? As in... 5 points for when I slytherin you?*
Me: *I saw that joke on Buzzfeed.*
Jase: *Fuck. That Tom Felton always steals my thunder.*
Me: *Could be worse. Neville Longbottom could.*
Jase: *I long to touch your bottom.*
Me: *That's the worst thing I've ever heard. Literally ever.*
Me: *Don't ever say it again.*
Jase: *Ever? Are you sure? Is three times the charm?*

I read back over my last two messages and realize he's a cocky little shit. That's it. Payback.

Me: *And here I was about to send you a really dirty sext about your cock and my mouth.*
Jase: *On my way.*
Me: *That wasn't an invitation...*
Jase: *Taking you up on it anyway. Be in the lobby in 20 minutes. I have plans for you.*

I stare at the screen. Oh, boy. That sounds...dangerous.

chapter sixteen
Jase

"This wasn't what I was expecting when you said you had plans for me," Leila says with a sigh, climbing down the stairs of the open-top bus.

I roll my eyes as I take her hand so she can step off the bus. "Why not? You said you were bored. What other way not to be bored than to get a ride around London on a bus? And nobody even recognized me. That's a win, babe." I wink.

"I suppose..." She glances back at the bus. "Why is that?"

"Nobody recognized me?"

"Yeah. I thought you were hot property in the UK."

I shrug. "None of them care. It's not as crazy here as it is in the US."

"Really? So, you won't get photographed going to into Tesco with spilled soup on your sweats or something? Because that happened to Conner once, except it was Mila-puke, and he thought getting her medicine was more important than changing his puke pants." She runs her hand through her hair and covers her beautiful eyes with her dark sunglasses.

"Rich people don't really go to Tesco. More like...Waitrose."

"What's Waitrose?"

"A high-end supermarket."

She slows down and peers at me over the top rim of her glasses. "You have fancy supermarkets?"

"You don't?"

"Shelton Bay has five hundred people on a busy day. We barely have a cheap supermarket." She laughs, lightly swinging her purse at her side. "It's the oddest thing. The next town over has the swimming pool, the schools, and the bitches... And Shelton Bay has the shops and the famous boyband." She laughs again, to herself this time, then glances over at me. "Meanwhile, London has everything."

I nod in agreement. "I actually grew up just outside London. I didn't move farther in until it made sense for work." That and it's stupid fucking expensive to live here. "London traffic is insane. Not to mention the bloody parking charges."

"So, why do you drive instead of take the Tube?" She raises one eyebrow above her glasses, and I can only see it because she's got her fringe clipped back from her face.

I also don't have an answer to that. I want to... Damn it. Nope. Nothing.

"Shut up, love."

Another laugh. Her smug laugh.

Yeah.

That's right.

I've named her fucking laughs.

There's the smug one that sings that she's right and she knows it. Then there's the sad one that says she's thinking over whatever she just forced herself to find amusing. The sarcastic one that's a cross between a giggle and a chuckle that screams *ha, fuck you*. The angry one that literally yells *ha!* The sleepy one that's slower than the others and almost always punctuated by a yawn. The happy one that's like the spring sunlight coaxing flowers out of their buds.

Then there's my favorite.

The uncontrollable one. It's a whole other ball game. A fucking strike at bowling. A hat trick of goals. Match point at Wimbledon.

Chilling. Beautiful. Soul-pulling. Unforgettable. Haunting. Indescribable, because nothing I've just said even comes close to how I feel when she throws her head back and lets that laugh go.

I glance over at her as she walks beside me, the sun dancing off her dark hair, her lips curved up with the ghost of her smug giggle, and can't help but smile right at her.

Bloody hell.

She's the girl you write songs about. Not just any songs though. The songs that make albums that go to number one worldwide and go on to be platinum. The songs that sell out world tours.

She's the girl who makes the songs you write come from your heart.

She's the girl who makes you sing them from your god damn soul.

This. Right now.

I know... *I'm a goner.*

For her. For my sassy, Southern girl. For her smart mouth and her dirty thoughts. For her pure heart and her honest soul.

I'm a total bloody goner for Leila Burke.

And it only took ten-ish days to lose myself to her.

I quickly close my eyes as the sun hides beneath a cloud. Shit. This is wrong. I can't feel this way. Not this strongly. I can't be this lost to her so quickly. It's not normal... Not this natural.

Or is it?

I don't know. I've loved before. I've been closer to love than this before. I'm not a guy destined to spend my life as an eternal bachelor. Nor have I done it in my life. I've had a relationship that's have lasted two years and others that've barely broken three months.

But they've never felt like this.

But then we don't have a relationship.

We have an embellished friendship. Hidden intimacy, a dirty little secret, forbidden nights. A "How was your day? Great, let's fuck" kind of relationship.

I rub my hand down my face and open my eyes before I slam into somebody who isn't the girl I really want to slam myself into. Fucking hell, thinking of her in all kinds of ways is messing with me big time.

I just want her to be Leila, the girl I can't resist. Not Leila, the girl I can't stop thinking about.

Hell, her being Leila, the girl I can't have, would be better.

If it were possible, I'd regret ever having met her, ever having touched her, ever having kissed her, ever having been with her.

A part of me wishes it were.

The rest of me knows that it never will be, and if I ever regretted it, I'd be lying to myself.

"Y'all have opticians here, right?" Leila lifts her glasses. "I'm gonna book you an appointment. You almost walked into a post back there—you can't stop staring at me."

"I wish you'd get ugly," I mutter, shoving my hands in my pockets.

"I wish you'd watch where you're goin'!"

"I do when you're not here distracting me."

"I'm not a distraction. I like to think of myself as an enhancement of the surroundings."

I slide my eyes toward her for a brief moment. "You all right there, love? Want a hand carrying your ego?"

"You know," she says, setting her sunglasses on top of her head when the sun disappears fully behind the clouds. "If I didn't grow up with four brothers, I'd have your balls for that. As it is, you're on strike one. You got two more chances, Brit Boy. Then your balls are mine."

"Pretty sure they already are."

She coughs, flattening her hand against her chest. I raise an eyebrow, glancing at her. Obviously she wasn't expecting that. Good. I like surprising her. Her reactions get better and better.

"Are you callin' me out?" she demands.

"Nope. Just a general statement. A notification."

"That I own your balls?"

"I own your arse. It's only fair."

She stops in the middle of the path and rests one of her hands on her hips, her eyes focused on my face. Her sudden cease in movement causes a runner with a dog to divert their path around her.

"Did you just—never mind." I shake my head.

Nothing surprises me with her. Honestly, I didn't know the runner was behind us. She probably did though.

"Since when did my *arse* belong to you?" she asks me, defiance flaring in her eyes.

I take a step closer to her, running my gaze across every inch of her face until it finally comes to settle on her blazing, blue eyes. "Since you stood half inside your hotel room in Paris, perfectly sober by your own insistence, and all but begged me to follow you into your room and fuck you."

Her cheeks brighten with a light hue of pink. "I did not beg you."

"I distinctly remember you asking me several times and getting incredibly offended when I refused." My lips twitch to one side.

She replaces the twinge of embarrassment in her gaze with defiance. "I didn't get offended!"

"Yeah, no, you did, babe."

"Only a little," she says after a second or two of hesitation. "But anyone would be offended by that. It was offensive!"

"My turning you down because I thought you were drunk is more offensive than my potentially taking advantage of you in a disorientated and highly intoxicated state of mind?" I raise an eyebrow and keep my eyes focused hard on her.

She can't still be bothered by the choice I made that night.

"You're such a gentleman," she mutters, childishly kicking the ground and turning around.

"No. Don't walk away." I grasp her hand, forcing her to turn back to me.

There's the hint of defeat in her eyes, and she keeps looking away from me before her gaze flits back only to move away again.

"Does that still piss you off?"

She opens her mouth. Then she closes it, sighs, and looks at me, resignedly flinging her other arm out. "I never thought about it that way, okay?" Her fingers twitch around mine, their grip barely tightening. "I don't know why. So...thank you for turning me down. Even if I was totally capable of making that decision. I wouldn't have forgotten it the next day."

"Now you're pulling at the straws of excuses. We both know you wouldn't have forgotten it."

"Because you made me scream so loud an entire floor heard me. Yeah, yeah, I know."

"You want a public demonstration?"

"Exhibitionist? Ooh, there's somethin' I didn't know about you."

I burst into laughter at the challenge that sparks to life in her eyes. She can look at me like that all she wants. That's definitely crossing the flipping line. I'm pretty sure she's joking anyway, but still... No. Daft girl.

I shake my head, fighting with the smile on my face, and walk again. She doesn't pull her head away from mine, although I do hear her take in a deep breath.

"Are you hungry?" I ask her, peering over at her.

"A little. Is it time for dinner? I promised everyone I'd be back at the hotel for it..." She trails off. "Then again, they'll be loved up and I'll want to vomit and end up getting room service instead."

"And it's cheaper because you won't have to pay Mila when you inevitably get frustrated and end up swearing every two minutes."

She nudges her elbow against mine, our fingers still loosely linked. "I'm not that bad. Tate's the worst."

That I can agree with. He swears like a bloody sailor when something doesn't go right. Hell, he swears like one when it does go right. There's really no casual in-between for him. It's all or nothing with the word *fuck*. I kinda respect his inventive usage—I'd teach him all about knob, wank, and tosser if I didn't think he'd send me the bill for Mila's swear jar.

"Okay," Leila says after a moment of thinking. "Let's get food, but then I have to go back or they'll ask too many questions."

"All right. You got it."

There are many things about this job that bother me.

Madison is one of them.

It's not even that she spends half her time flirting with me or anyone with a pulse. It's that she can somehow magically turn the shortest and simplest of conversations into a novel. She'll never use five words if five hundred will do, and to be honest, "conversation" is bloody pushing it for what it is.

It's more her talking while I nod and make the occasional agreeable sound, all the while wondering when this fucking fresh hell will end.

Like I've been doing for the last thirty minutes while she enjoys herself, regaling me with a tale about the last time she went to this place I'm supposed to meet some fans.

I want to ram my face into a brick wall. Dramatic, and perhaps a bit of a reaction I've stolen from Leila, but also accurate.

If I hear about Madison's friend Debbie one more time, I'm going to remove my ear drums with a fork.

She doesn't even realize that I'm bored. That's the worst bloody part. She thinks I'm yawning because I'm tired and tapping my fingers against the table because I'm waiting for Tate to come down to get a ride to the O2 to prepare for tonight's concert.

I'm tapping my fingers because it's helping to drone her out. And her seduction attempts.

Even if I weren't wrapped up in Leila, I wouldn't be interested. I can't say it's because I don't want to mix work with play, because that's kind of what I'm doing with Leila, but Madison is...

Annoying.

There. I fucking said it. She's damn annoying.

And now... Shit. She's looking at me with wide, suggestive eyes that are also expectant. What was the question? I spaced. Shit. Shit.

"You didn't hear a word I just said, did you?" Madison says, annoyed, pursing her dark-red lips.

I grimace. "I stopped listening somewhere around Debbie and her third date with... I want to say Brian?"

"Dennis," she grinds out. "Brian dumped her."

"Yeah, I really couldn't give a shit."

Madison rolls her eyes. "Anyway, like I was saying, Dennis is taking her out tomorrow night and she's nervous, so she's asked me to double date."

"Great. I'm sure you'll have fun."

"We will!"

"We?" I missed something. Again. Shit.

She blinks at me. "I asked you if you'd join us and you nodded."

Didn't I just say I'd stopped listening? She's nuts.

"I didn't agree to that," I say.

"Ready?" Tate says behind me, slapping his hand onto my shoulder.

Never been so glad to see another guy in my entire life. "No idea how ready, mate," I answer, relieved, pushing my chair back. "Sorry, Madison. I'm busy tomorrow."

"I can have her reschedule."

"I'll be busy then too," I assure her. "Look, if Lawrence has put out that I'll be at the VIP meets after the concerts, I'll be there. It's not a big deal. It makes sense, and I'm happy to do it, especially if fans want me there. I can't talk anymore because I have to go."

With that, I follow Tate out of the hotel's restaurant and outside, where there's a swarm of photographers waiting—for him. I'm just the bonus, but by the time we get to the car, I'm seeing rainbow spots every time I blink because of the flashes.

You'd think they'd turn those damn things off. The rate they go, there's probably nothing in the pictures but everybody else's flashes.

"Why do I get the feelin' I just saved you from your own personal fuckin' hell?" Tate looks across the car at me, smiling.

"Because you did." I blow out a long breath. "She's incessant. She was only supposed to tell me that I'm now required to do the post-concert meet and greets."

"And she couldn't have done that on the phone?"

"Not without telling me about whoever Debbie is and trying to corner me into a date. Can't hang up on her in person."

Tate laughs. "I think you just did, man."

"I hope so." I slump back in the seat and rub my hand down my face. Jesus, I'm exhausted from that conversation. I'm ready to go home and sleep until tomorrow, never mind going and singing in front of tens of thousands of people.

Madison has that effect on people. Well, maybe just me, but still. The effect is strong.

"Surprised you were at the hotel. Thought you'd meet us there," Tate says.

"I was going to until she called me. She originally wanted to come to my place to talk to me, refused the office, and was forced into taking the hotel." A conversation which set off the chain of events which has me exhausted. "She might do what my manager tells her do, but she does it in a roundabout fucking way."

"Course she does. She's a woman. Never do anythin' simply, them." He chuckles quietly to himself. "Hey, did Leila speak to you this morning?"

"Only to ask me where the nearest bookstore to the hotel was," I reply dryly.

He grins. "Did you tell her?"

"I sent her the link for Google Maps with the walking route. She didn't reply after that."

"Yep. She tried to talk me into going. She eventually convinced Ella, who spent almost the entire trip on her phone organizing us."

"Does she ever get a day off?"

"Have you tried suggestin' that to her?" Tate's eyes go wide. "Last time I did, I almost had to sleep on the sofa she was so offended."

Noted. "I won't even think of it."

"Did Leila tell you what she plans on doing tomorrow?"

"No. Why would she?"

"Y'all're spendin' a lotta time together."

"She doesn't like Google Maps. I know where I'm going. Plus, she's really insistent."

"Yeah..." Tate scratches the side of his nose, and I wonder if he's bought it.

Not that it was a lie. She does hate Maps, because she told me to fuck a shark's mouth this morning when I sent it to her, and insistent is kind of a weak word. She's downright obsessive when she wants something because she knows I'll give in.

Except taking her to a bookstore. Half of her suitcase must be filled with books.

She can't need more. Even if she does look damn peaceful when she's reading.

"I know it's hard for her. We're datin' her best friends. She'll never admit it, but she gets lonely a lot. I think that's why she's spendin' time with you." He slides his eyes over to me. "I just don't want her getting hurt or anyone takin' advantage of her."

I meet his gaze. "Your sister is the craziest person I've ever met, but believe me when I say I'd never do either of those things to her. Her wildness is refreshing."

Tate stares at me for a long moment, holding my gaze, and the air between us tightens for a brief moment before the tension dissipates. "I believe you. I know it pisses her off real bad when I get protective of her, but she's my baby sister. I helped Mom change her shitty diapers before she could say my name."

"I get that."

"Just know that she's a total bitch, but she wears her heart on her sleeve." He pauses. Then he slowly turns his face back to the front of the car and stares at the back of Ajax's seat. "And, if she thinks you're good enough, she'll give it to you, no matter what I think."

The question sits on the tip of my tongue, lingering there on the edge of my consciousness. Unspoken. I want to ask it, but shit, I'm a little afraid of the answer. His questions have proved that he suspects more than friendship with me and Leila—but he suspects the kind of relationship I'm trying so desperately not to have with her.

Emotional.

The car turns toward the O2, and already, I can see the flashes as photographers attempt to get snaps of us before we enter the building.

"What do you think?" I ask, finally forcing the words to roll off their perch on my tongue. "Do you think I'm good enough?"

"Well," he drawls, barely looking at me, readying himself to leave the car. "I haven't beaten the fuck out of you yet, have I?"

chapter seventeen
Leila

I roll onto my stomach and stretch out, clasping my hands as they reach out over my pillow. I wince as my knuckles bang into Jase's headboard. "Bollocks."

Jase snorts and flips onto his side from his back. "How do you know when you spend too much time with someone of a different nationality?"

"When you start saying crazy-awesome words like bollocks?" I offer, turning my head to look at him, a smile on my face.

"Ding ding, we have a winner." He grins and, propping himself up on his elbow, rests his hand on my back. "I forgot to tell you Tate spoke to me last night."

My stomach drops. Right through my belly button to the pits of everlasting hell.

"Are we busted?" I ask.

"Yes and no?"

"You don't sound so sure there, slick."

He laughs quietly then pauses to yawn. "I think he's worked out there's something going on."

"Good. I was starting to wonder if he was as dumb as I always figured he was." I tug my pillow down so it's beneath my cheek and hug it, still looking at the hot guy lying next to me. "What did he say to you?"

"Nothing much, really. Just pretty much warned me that, if he doesn't think I'm good enough for you, he's going to beat the shit out of me."

Yep. Sounds like Tate.

"He's got a pretty mean right hook. Broke Ella's ex's nose."

Jase stares at me for a long moment. "Why?"

I look up at the ceiling as I recall the story Sofie told me that had me hightailing my ass on a plane to find out what the hell was wrong with him. "Ella's ex was an abusive fuckhead, so she ran away right before their wedding to work for Dirty B., and when he found her, he snuck into the hotel room she'd been sharing with Tate for her *protection*. He tried to beat her up. Tate saw him, beat the life out of him." I think that's it. "That's the important stuff, anyway."

"That's...romantic?" Jase says.

I push up onto my forearms a little. "So, if you walked in and some guy had me pinned to a wall, you wouldn't go a little mad?"

Something flashes in his green eyes—a dark, possessive glimmer of a side of him I've only seen once, when I almost left and ended this. A tingle shivers down my spine as that glimmer lingers in the back of his emerald gaze like a dangerous shadow.

"You probably don't want me to answer that question, love," he responds roughly, his finger drawing circles across my bare back.

"Why not?"

"Because it wouldn't showcase my stunning personality very well."

"Um, we're both naked in your bed, my ass is sore, and I'm pretty sure there's a bite mark on my boob. You're not really in the market for a stunning personality right now."

"Did I or did I not give you three orgasms last night?"

Well... "Yes."

"Then, babe, I *am* the market for a stunning personality." His grin is lopsided, and there's the light hint of a dimple hiding under his stubble.

I reach out and touch his cheek with my fingertip, dragging it down until it reaches the shallow indent in line with the corner of his mouth. "I rarely see this." I prod it a little. "Why?"

"Dimples are like erections. They only pop up when I'm really happy."

I run my tongue over my lips to wet them before I smack them together. "Yep," I say, lightly patting his cheek. "We've spent too much time together."

I won't tell him about the warm fuzzies I have from his inadvertent comment about being really happy. But they're there, and they're the equivalent of lying on the floor and letting twenty tiny, fluffy puppies crawl on top of you and climb all over you.

I want this feeling to stay.

"I'm not sure it's possible, actually," Jase says, rolling on top of me and covering my back with his body. His hard cock pushes against my butt cheeks, and I crane my neck back to look at him. "Do I feel like I've spent too much time with you?"

"I'm not sure your cock is qualified to make that decision. I mean, you could hate me, but if I'm fuckable, it'd want to fuck me."

"You're definitely fuckable," he murmurs, moving hair away from my face. He brushes his lips down my cheek to my ear.

I shiver when his exhale makes my lips part. The smile I feel against my skin is smug, but my head drops back down to the pillow when it falls just as quickly as it formed and he kisses the tender spot just beneath my earlobe.

"That's a compliment, right?" I breathe out.

But Jase doesn't respond, instead kissing down my neck so slowly but tenderly that my head spins a little. My blood thunders around my body as he continues his journey over the curve of my shoulder, dipping his tongue into the hollow of my collarbone, right along to the top of my arm. I open my mouth, but the words die on my tongue as he drags his mouth right across the top of my back, pushing my hair out of the way once again.

He pushes himself up onto his knees, and with them on either side of my hips and the head of his cock barely brushing my pussy, he runs his hands up my back firmly, keeping his mouth on me. His thumbs slide together on my spine, and the pressure feels so good that a moan escapes my lips.

His laugh annoys me.

"Fuck you," I mutter, closing my eyes as he massages my shoulders and the back of my neck. Jesus. *Feels so good.*

"That's the plan," he mutters right back, kissing the underside of my jaw before he sits back up and massages my entire back. From top to bottom, neck to butt, he gently works his fingers into my muscles.

I'm never moving. That's it. I'm going to stay here, in this bed, with this guy massaging me and his cock teasing my now-wet pussy. I'm torn between lying flat and letting him continue his unexpected foreplay or pushing myself back onto his cock and putting an end to it.

Both seem equally good.

"Stop wriggling against me. You're making me want to fuck you."

"Was that supposed to deter me?" I deliberately open my eyes and glance over my shoulder at him.

His muscles are tensed as he clearly tries not to carry out what he just threatened. All looking at him, all tight and toned and tensed, does is turn me on a little more.

Jase places two fingers at the base of my neck and pushes them against my spine before running them right down the center of my back. It's not quick and it's not slow—somewhere in the middle, quick enough that my heart thumps but slow enough that it feels as though he has a grasp on my desire and is pulling it downward.

He keeps going, right to the very bottom of my back, where my spine meets my ass. Then he drags his fingers over the curve of my behind, just ghosting between my ass cheeks to where they rest against my aching pussy.

I take a deep breath as he slowly eases them inside me, his cock falling and rubbing against my clit. He pumps his fingers inside me as his other hand creeps up my back and winds itself in my hair. His cock keeps teasing against my clit, and the pressure of both his fingers and the head of his erection moving against me swiftly brings me to my climax.

I feel Jase lean over me and reach for the nightstand.

And I say something that I know will change the dynamic of our relationship.

"Jase?" I whisper, turning my head so I face the other side. To face him. "I'm clean."

He stills. Literally freezes over me. "So am I."

"And..." I lick my lips. "Protected."

He doesn't make a sound before he brings his mouth to my ear. "Beauty... The first time I fuck you without a condom won't be a spur-of-the-moment decision you make in an orgasmic haze. It'll be because I've just worshipped the life out of your body and I'm going to make love to you. Not because I'm desperate to fuck you because I've spent half the night having dirty dreams about you. So, good to know, but right now, Leila, love, I need to fuck you, not love you."

The slamming of the drawer as he opens it and fiddles inside masks my surprise.

I'm going to pretend he never said that last sentence.

He does what he promised seconds after he rolled the condom on. With one hand grasping my hair, me on my knees and him behind me, he fucks me hard and deep, grabbing my ass, alternating between the odd spank and a palm, until I come undone and scream into my pillow.

When he's joined me, he collapses on top of me, pressing his face into my back, still inside me. Our breathing is shallow and quick as we both deal with the come-down of our pleasure.

"Know what I want?" he asks me, still breathless, flattening his cheek against my back.

I wriggle as his stubble tickles me. "A nap?"

Jase laughs quietly. "No. A full English."

"I just had one."

This time, his laugh is anything but quiet. "Truth. And, in case you didn't realize, you're still full of English." He flexes his hips.

A tiny, "Mm," escapes my lips as he pushes against my tender skin. "That's either the best thing I've ever heard or the corniest." I sigh when he pulls out of me and sits back on his heels. I curl onto my side, bringing my knees up, and look down at him. "What's a full English?"

He pauses, the condom pinched at the top and hanging between his fingers, and stares at me.

"Freakin' hell, Jase. Put that in the trash!" I lamely flail my arm in his direction, causing him to laugh and get up.

He drops it in what looks like an oversized leather tub with a plastic bag in the middle and turns to me. "It's the best thing ever."

"The full English or the dirty condom?"

"I swear you and your attitude are going to be the death of me, woman."

I grin.

"The full English. Bacon, sausages, hash brown, fried eggs, grilled tomato, mushroom, beans—"

"What?" I sit up quicker than I intended. My eyesight is fuzzy, and I blink harshly to clear the dizziness buzzing around my brain. "Beans? For breakfast? Like, baked beans? In a can?"

"What other beans would you eat for breakfast?"

"Are you a savage?"

He stops by the door and turns, still completely naked, his muscular body sweaty, red, and patchy, his dick still half hard. He looks at me. "You...you don't eat beans for breakfast?"

I pull the covers over myself and shake my head. "I'm getting more and more convinced that this"—I wave my hand between us—"is forged solely on our own personal horror regarding the shortcomings of the other's culture."

"Shortcomings? Speak for yourself. The English invaded America, don't forget. Your people fucked it, not mine."

"The English invade America a lot."

He stops halfway through the door and peers over his shoulder.

Lord that man's ass is something else. How unfair.

"Is that another sex pun?" he questions, one eyebrow raised.

I purse my lips. "Does it sound like one?"

"I think I'm impressed. Think. Eat beans for breakfast and I probably will be."

Baked beans.

For breakfast.

That doesn't even make sense. You don't eat baked beans for breakfast. That's one of the most disgusting things I've ever heard. Baked beans with breakfast!

The British are savages. That has to be the only explanation. I don't give a shit if Americans are descended from them. There are so many things wrong with them. They drive on the wrong side of the road. Their steering wheels are on the wrong side. They don't tip. They talk about the weather too much. They call their cookies biscuits. Their gravy is the wrong color.

And they eat baked beans for breakfast.

Literally the only good thing about the British is their fabulous use of swear words. Seriously. I can go home and fake-swear all over the fucking place and nobody will have a clue what I'm saying to them or that it's even supposed to be offensive.

"Here's what's gonna happen," Jase says, coming into the bedroom five minutes later.

Damn. I've been staring at the wall, contemplating the differences between us for that long?

And...double damn.

The guy is wet. Apparently showered. Naked apart from a towel.

Is this the view Madison had in Paris?

No. Not thinking about that. Not when there are water droplets dancing down his abs and soaking themselves into the fluffy, black towel or beading in little groups on his inked arms. Or just trailing down across his body, drawing paths of wetness behind them.

"Leila? Did you hear me?"

I say the first thing that comes to mind as I snap my eyes up to his. "Strawberry. That's my favorite milkshake."

Jase's tongue slides out and across his lower lip, and he struggles not to smile as his lips thin and he obviously bites the inside of them. "I prefer banana. But that wasn't the question."

"Okay, seriously? You come out here in your damn towel, all wet and hot, and you expect me to listen to you? I'm human, damn it. I get distracted. Especially by that." I flap my hand at his abs. Jesus... Abs... Lick-me lines... It's like a freakin' maze from his chest to his cock. "Fuck, can you put them away?"

"First time for everything." He walks to the dresser and opens the top drawer. Then, unashamedly, he drops the towel, revealing his tight ass as he bends over and puts underwear on.

I need a hobby.

Staring at him does not count.

I want to bite his butt. I've never wanted to bite someone's butt before.

"Stop staring at my bum."

"Now you know how it feels!" I snap. "I can't focus when you stand there like that!"

He smirks as he pulls a T-shirt over his head and grabs some jeans and a belt. "Think you can give me two minutes of your filthy little brain?"

"Starting...now."

"I'm going to Tesco and I'm going to buy everything to do a full English. Including the beans, and you're gonna eat them."

"You sound like Sofie when Mila doesn't want to eat something. Will you put me in the naughty corner if I refuse?" I grab the top of the sheet, tugging it back over my breasts, and look at him innocently.

"No," he replies, leaning over the bed and coming face-to-face with me. "But I will smack your arse."

I'm not eating the beans.

After the other day, I learned my lesson about the spare panties. And, I have to say, it's way nicer to put clean panties on after sex and a shower. That's all.

And that's exactly how I've ended up in the kitchen, wearing nothing but my underwear beneath one of Jase's T-shirts.

His T-shirts are bigger than they look—or I'm smaller than I thought.

"Right," I say to myself, picking my phone up as I stand in front of the kettle, braced with a mug and a teaspoon. *How to make the perfect cup of tea,* I type into Google.

What? The guy's gone out just to buy things for breakfast he's ultimately gonna have to make. The least I can do is attempt a cup of tea.

I've never made one in my freaking life, but it is what it is, right? How hard can it be? Thereare only like four ingredients, right? Water, milk, sugar, and a teabag.

How to make a decent cup of tea is the most ridiculous conversation I've ever had with myself, and I once lay in bed until two a.m. wondering whether or not penguins are jealous of other birds because they can't fly.

I huff out a long breath. What if I mess it up? He's British. He takes his tea freakin' *seriously*. Like, if tea were up there with taking someone's virginity, the virginity would be less of a concern kind of seriously.

That's it. I can't do it. I can't make him a cup of tea. Blow job? Sure. Tea? Nope. Not in this life.

The door to the apartment opens, breaking through my thoughts, and I turn.

"Hey, I..." I clap my hands over my mouth to cover my scream. Then I grab the teaspoon from the counter and hold it to my chest like it'll be a good weapon.

That isn't Jase.

He looks like Jase. But he isn't Jase.

"Hello." Mystery Guy grins widely. "You must be Leila."

I feel my eyes go as wide as saucers. "Who are you, and how do you know my name?"

"Kian. Jase's brother." He raises his hand, still grinning. "He didn't say you'd be here. Mind, I didn't tell him I'd be here, either." His eyes briefly drop to my legs before snapping back up. "I'd go put some trousers on before he gets back and thinks I've corrupted you."

Fuck! I'm not wearing pants.

My cheeks flame, and I put the spoon down before running into Jase's bedroom and slamming the door shut behind me. Oh my god. This is the most embarrassing thing ever. I don't know how I'm supposed to go back out there and face him.

This T-shirt barely covers my butt. Oh, god. Oh, god. Oh, god.

What if he saw my butt?

I cover my mouth with both of my hands. He saw my butt. I know he did. It could be worse—could have been my vagina. But still. My butt. I grab my phone from the nightstand and text Jase.

Me: *I think your brother just saw my butt.*

By the time he replies, I'm changed into ripped jeans and a tank top. Butt well covered.

Jase: *I'll be fifteen minutes.*

Yes! Thank you.

I stare at the door behind me. I'm gonna have to go back out there, aren't I? Can't stay in here for fifteen minutes. Well...

I force myself to open the door and go back into the kitchen. Kian is sitting at the island, sipping on a mug of hot tea, looking at his phone.

He glances up when I come in. "Hey," he says, putting his phone down. "Sorry if I frightened you. I should have called him first."

"Oh, it's okay. He probably should have told me his brother stops by randomly and I would have made sure I had pants on." I attempt a smile, but I think it comes out closer to a grimace than anything. I open the fridge and pull the carton of orange juice out.

"Yeah, I agree. Let's blame him. Looks better on me that way." He winks. "I take it he stopped behaving himself."

"Sorry?" I ask, putting the carton down and lifting my glass to my mouth.

"Jase. He said he was behaving around you."

I choke on my mouthful of juice as I swallow it.

"Shit. I should have been a bloody clown the way I keep scaring you today."

"It's okay," I squeak out, waving my hand dismissively. "I'm good. Since when was he behavin'?"

"Ah." Kian's smile gets wide. "I figured as much. He's a pain in the arse, isn't he?"

"From the one who rocks up without invitation or notice," Jase says dryly, coming in through the door.

"That was quick," I comment, screwing the cap on the juice.

"I might have run a red light." He nods toward his brother. "The idea of you being alone with him was repulsive."

Kian laughs loudly. "Because being alone with you is delightful."

"Depends whether or not you're an arsehole." Jase puts two bags on the island in front of him. "What do you want?"

"I was going to see if you had plans today," he answers, sliding his eyes to me for a brief moment. "But I see I'm interrupting them."

"Again, what do you want? Your last date get too interested?"

"I take offense to that. You're making me sound like an arse in front of your girlfriend."

My eyes widen. Again.

Jase's do the same.

In slow motion, we turn to look at each other.

This is awkward.

"We, um," I mutter, my eyes darting around the kitchen. Crap. Should have stayed in the bedroom.

"Yeah. We... Uh..." Jase trails off and scratches the back of his neck. "I'm gonna put this stuff away."

I look down at the floor, feeling Kian's eyes on us both, but now, the question has been posed. We're more than friends. Neither of us is stupid enough to believe that anymore. More than friends, less than official... We're like dirty little lovers or something.

Girlfriend though?

Wow.

That's... That's something. Ha. Um. Yeah.

"Well, this went downhill relatively fast," Kian observes, amusement playing freely in his tone. "The last time I saw two people this embarrassed was when I was seven and Marcia Greenway flashed me her knickers so I wouldn't marry Lily Daws."

"Ki, do me a favor?" Jase stops, staring into the fridge. "Get the hell out."

"Can't. I'm actually here for a reason that isn't to piss you off or create unnecessary friction with your..."

My gaze flies to him, my eyes narrowing dangerously in a warning.

"Friend," he finishes slowly.

Jase sighs and slams the fridge door shut. "What? Did Granddad forget where he lives again?"

"No. Not that crazy old man. I'm guessing neither of you have been online today."

"Nope," he answers for us both. "Why?"

"I don't want to hear this." I said it quietly, but they both heard me if the way they're both staring at me is anything to go by. "What? In my experience, that sentence is rarely followed by anything good and almost always followed by, 'There's this article,' 'You're in this paper,' 'You're trending on Twitter,' 'You probably shouldn't read this, but...' and I've had a lot of experience."

"You're good," Kian says. "Since he doesn't seem bothered, what do you think I was going to say?"

"All four of them," I reply dryly.

Kian smirks, swinging his gaze back to Jase. "Cozy meeting you had yesterday."

My spine straightens, making me sit bolt upright. If either of them notices, they don't show it this time.

"What?" Jase's eyes narrows, and an annoyed look flickers across his strong, handsome features. "Give me that."

Kian unlocks his phone and hands it to him.

His eyes flicker across the screen as he reads. His expression gets progressively angrier. The green gaze I've become so fond of hardens, and his lips thin.

"Son of a bitch."

"Daughter of a bitch," Kian corrects him, taking his phone back.

I don't want to ask, but... "What?"

Jase rubs his hand down his face and looks at me. "I met with Madison in the hotel yesterday before I went to the O2 with Tate. She hit on me several times. There are...pictures that would suggest something more intimate between us. I didn't think the media were allowed inside the hotel. How did these pictures get published?"

I inhale deeply. "She tipped them off and they snuck in," I say quietly, looking down at my hands. I slowly spin my glass between my fingers. Round and round and round. "You already said once she's desperate to get back into the spotlight. Why wouldn't she use an innocent meetin' and turn it into somethin' more?"

"That's pretty damning..." Kian says quietly.

"So was her turnin' up at his hotel room in Paris without notice and seein' him in a freakin' towel."

Kian snaps his head around.

Jase pauses, wincing as he does so. "Well. That might not have happened."

He's kidding me.

"You're kiddin'."

"You assumed. I just didn't...you know. Deny it." He steps back, holding his hands up. "It's not my fault you're irresistibly cute when you're jealous!"

I stare at him. Just stare. The swirling annoyance and frustration I'm feeling from a third article in two weeks melds seamlessly with the anger about his omission regarding something he knew bothered me.

"I wasn't jealous!"

"You were."

"I wasn't!" I feel my nostrils flare, so I take a deep breath. *Calm down, Leila.*

Calm has never really been my forte.

"You look stressed, darling," Kian offers, hiding his mouth behind his mug.

"Do I? I can't imagine why."

"Leila... I was just playing, babe." Jase rubs the back of his neck. "But you were jealous, and so cute..."

"I swear to god, if you say that one more time, I'm gonna show you freakin' cute when I choke you on your own fuckin' ballsac!" I snap, standing up. "I wasn't jealous. I ain't jealous. And it doesn't freakin' matter 'cause I'm not your dang girlfriend!"

I push the stool away from me and storm out of the kitchen and into his bedroom. As I slam the door behind me and fall back against it, squeezing my eyes shut, I realize the futility of my choice.

I can't escape here. I'm trapped in this room.

Shit. What's happening to me? I was jealous. I am jealous. I'm bothered by this whole goddamn freaking situation.

Can the real Leila Burke please stand up? Maybe get her tits out so I don't miss her? Shake 'em a little? Maybe twerk?

Maybe I need to print fliers. Missing: Leila Burke's identity. Search close to wine bars and bookstores. Probably stolen by a hot, tattooed British singer.

I dive my hands into my hair. They almost make claws as I rake my fingers through the damp locks and my back slides down the door until I'm crouching. I drop my head forward and close my eyes, taking the deep breath I so desperately need.

Hopeless.

I was afraid of this. Of this hopelessness that I knew would ultimately consume me.

Shoulda. Woulda. Coulda. All of those possibilities run through my mind too quickly to grab them and make any sense of them.

Shoulda. Woulda. Coulda.

Shoulda, woulda, coulda.

Shouldawouldacoulda.

Shoulda, woulda, coulda run away from this guy.

Not even from him. From the shitstorm that accompanies fame. From the bullshit and all the crap that swarms around the status like flies around shit.

I knew better. Do know better.

Which is why I'm leaning against his bedroom door, unable to move, instead of grabbing my stuff and getting the hell out of here.

Because knowing better isn't always best, and this will be over soon anyway.

Even if it hurts.

"Leila?" Jase softly knocks on the door. "You all right?"

"Fine." My voice half cracking in the middle of the word denies it. "Hold on." I push myself up and open the door, but I can't look at him. "Sorry. I should probably think about—"

"No." Jase's arms shoot out, and he grabs the doorframe. He's blocking my only escape path, almost entirely filling the small space. "We need to talk, don't you think?"

I shake my head.

"Then I should talk and you can listen."

"I don't want to," I whisper. The admission is lame, a total copout, but not wrong. I don't want to listen. I'm afraid of what he'll say next.

I'm afraid of what I might say that I won't be able to take back.

chapter eighteen

Her face is tilted away from me, her eyes fixed on some random spot on the floor. She hasn't moved since she opened the door except to speak.

I don't care if she doesn't want to talk. I'm so done with screwing around and not being honest with her about the way I feel. Fuck everyone else—fuck the lies we've had to tell to get to this point.

I'm done. I'm bloody done.

I'm not lying to her anymore.

I'm not going to lie about how badly I want her anymore. How badly I need her—how much her smile brightens my day and her laugh warms my soul. How it feels when she touches me or how my heart, goddamn that bitch, clenches whenever she meets my eyes.

I'm not going to lie about how fucking sick I feel at the thought of letting her go.

"I'm sick of fucking pussyfooting around this." My fingers tighten on the doorframe, and I focus even more intently on her.

On the way her hair falls just over her forehead, the way her long, dark lashes look like they're resting on her cheeks, the way her lips part every now and then as she breathes in and out.

I focus wholly on the way she's just so bloody perfect I feel nothing but utter terror at how strongly she makes me feel.

"We both know that what we feel for each other is more than just sex. You were right the other day. We spend way too much time together being friends and not enough time fucking—maybe we should have stepped back long ago. Maybe we never should have done this, but we did, and now, I don't know about you, but I'm in too damn deep to get out without a fight."

"Then fight."

"I will, but not to get out."

Her eyes lift, tracing over my face before they meet mine.

"I don't want to get out, Leila. If I have to fight every fucking day for this, for *you*, then that's what I'm gonna do. I'll fight until I physically can't anymore, until I'm broken and bleeding on the ground and my soul is in shreds. Because that denial you're forcing right now is the same reality I've embraced. I'm falling for you and there isn't a flipping thing I can do about it. Isn't a thing I want to do about it."

My heart thumps against my chest as I take a deep breath at the end of my words. The emotion seems realer now, stronger. The power the words hold has solidified the way I feel about her, and even though she's looking at me with fear in her eyes, I wouldn't take them back even if I could.

I'd say them sooner.

Say them louder.

Say them just because.

"And it's crazy, isn't it?" I drop my arms from the doorway, running one hand through my hair. "Because I know, I *know*, that you are the one thing I can't want. The one thing I can't have. The one person I can't kiss in the middle of the street just because I want to. Literally the only person I can't wrap my arms around and show off to the world because look how fucking *beautiful* you are, and that kills a little part of me."

She opens her mouth, but nothing escapes her soft, pink lips. Instead, she presses her right thumb against her left wrist, still watching me, her blue eyes wide and full of questions but also clouded with an emotion I can't make head or tails of.

I want to. God, I want to.

I want to tear into her soul and breathe her in until I understand her.

"But fuck it." I step back from the doorway, leaving her enough room to pass. "I'm not stupid. I know I'm gonna lose you long before I can fight for you, so you may as well know exactly how I feel about you, because god knows it's driving me crazy trying to pretend I don't want to be with you every single second. So...there." I wave my arm toward the door, letting out a long, tortured breath. "You wanna go now you know everything, now we've finally crossed the line and this secret finally has some truth breathed into it, then I'm not going to stop you. I'll just come bang your hotel door down before you wake up tomorrow."

Leila's lips twitch the tiniest, barest amount before falling back into their slight downturn. Her gaze slides toward the direction of the door, and her chest heaves as she breathes in deeply, her nostrils flaring.

Every second she stares at it, my heart clenches a little harder and hurts a little more.

chapter nineteen
Leila

*G*o, my brain whispers.

No, my heart argues. *You'll never find another him.*

My brain laughs. *Of course you will. Probably not the accent, but the rest of it. And he won't come with his own bunch of personal stalkers or teenaged lovebirds desperate for his attention.*

Maybe so, my heart says softly, squeezing. *But he'll never look at you in awe the way Jase does. He'll never touch you as reverently as Jase does. He'll never stand in front of you and tell you that he's falling in love with you as honestly as Jase just did.*

It would be so easy. Walk through that door. Give him, us, this, up. Give up a thing I didn't know even really existed until three minutes ago.

Give up looking into those intoxicating, green eyes, even if I only get to do it for another few days.

Or do I?

He wants to fight. Every day.

Maybe I don't want to give it up. Give him up.

No. I don't want to give him up. I don't want to forget what it's like for him to hold me in his arms and kiss my hair. I don't want to forget the crazy kisses when I won't stop saying his stupid British words and he wants me to shut up. I don't want to forget the shit he gives me when I get cocky, or the feel of his palm against mine, or his breath on the back of my neck when I wake up.

I don't want to forget any of that. I don't want to give any of that up.

He's right. We've lied. A lot. We've lied enough. To my family, my friends, each other, ourselves.

What if we could?

What if we could make this work, against all the odds, all the differences, all the tests?

But can we? Really? Can we really get past all the drama that comes with his career, the spotlights, the stories, the incessant hounding of everyone and everything?

Yes. I've seen it happen. Seen firsthand how it can be done if you want it badly enough. The people I love are living proof of it.

But what if a fifth time is one time too many?

No.

I'm not going to think like that.

He just bared his heart to me, and I've never seen him this open. This vulnerable. Every word was said with certainty, but I can taste his fear in the air. I can feel it in his eyes, set on me like stone.

I can feel it because it's identical to my own. It's one and the same with the grip on my heart, making each beat it takes feel like the uncontrollable shake of an earthquake.

Earthquake. What a perfect word to describe this situation—it's like the ground beneath me is cracking with the weight of the decision I'm afraid to make. I can fall through the cracks and give up, or I can avoid them and fight until we get the ending I've read about so many times.

I close my eyes and touch my fingertips to my nose, my palm hiding my mouth from him.

Jase Masters is my own personal tornado.

And, if I let him touch down, he could destroy me.

chapter twenty

It's written all over her face. The way her eyes are closed, the way her hand is covering her mouth...

I guess she's gonna leave.

I sigh heavily and turn away from her. I don't want to watch her go.

"Jase?" she whispers, her fingertips brushing my back and making me stop.

I turn back to her and look down into her fearful yet rawly honest, blue eyes. She rests both of her hands against my stomach, slowly winding them into the fabric of my T-shirt with a grip so tight she's anchoring herself to me.

And then, without blinking, she steps closer to me and takes a deep breath. "Will you catch me? If I fall?"

"Even if I'm falling right along with you?" I ask, my voice rough.

She nods. *Barely.*

"Baby...I'd hit the ground first just to catch you."

She sucks her lower lip into her mouth and buries her face in my chest, but not before I see the glimmer of wetness in her eyes. I wrap my arms around her and, closing my eyes, rest my cheek on top of her head. Her arms come to circle my waist, and she squeezes me tight.

"Promise me you won't give up," she says, turning her face so her breath ghosts across my arm. "Even when I want to because it's too hard or it's bollocks or people are *arse*holes."

I can't help but smile. "Only if you promise me the same thing. Because it's gonna be hard, Leila. It's gonna be bollocks and people are gonna be giant fucking arseholes."

"Starting with the people I share a last name with." She sighs. "Do you think we can do this? Really? With all the issues and—"

"Hey." I lean back and tilt her face up with my finger. "You can't doubt it already. That's not fair."

She purses her lips. "Just a question."

"You're an awkward bugger." I tap her nose. "Now, be quiet. I need to call Lawrence now to deal with this Madison thing. Then we're gonna get the hell out of this flat because I have a surprise for you in the car."

Her eyes light up to the brightest blue I've ever seen them. "What is it?"

"If I tell you, it's not a surprise anymore."

"What about my breakfast?" Now, she's pouting.

It's irresistible. I lean down and kiss her. "I'll buy you some. And, if any media bug us, we tell them to sod off."

"Sod off." She grins.

Here we go... "You do your thing with your new phrase while I make this call."

She nods, grinning, and I reluctantly release her from my hold.

"Leila, love?" I say as she moves toward the kitchen.

She stops and looks over her shoulder at me.

"We have time to figure it—us—out. I don't think there are as many problems as you think."

She tilts her head to the side but nods.

And, as she turns away, I smile and, the moment she's out of earshot, pull the envelope from my back pocket.

The logo on it makes me feel sick, but I flip it over and run my thumb beneath the flap, tearing it so I can pull the letter out. My hands shake as I unfold it, and I know the words written here are either going to make or break everything I just promised my sassy, Southern girl.

I take a deep breath and open the letter.

One word stands out from all the rest...making the rest all but irrelevant.

Accepted.

"I'm not very good at this instant photo thing."

"Well, you didn't read the instructions," I remind her, stealing a particularly crunchy-looking chip out of her tray.

She smacks my hand away. "They almost blew away when I tried!"

I shake my head and break the end of my battered cod off. "Read them now while you're eating. Hold them tightly." I nudge her bag toward her with my elbow.

"No! I'll get grease all over them." She pushes her bag back away from her knee and licks her fingers. "These are the best fries ever."

I stare at her for a moment. It's really not worth the argument, is it? "Chips. They're chips."

She drags her eyes toward mine. "Fine. Chips."

"Wow. That was agreeable."

"Only because fries are long and thin. These," she says, holding one up, "are chunky little bastards, and I like them."

Strange. She really is so strange.

"Okay," I say, "I'm done. Let me see the instructions for the camera."

Leila rolls her eyes but nudges her bag toward me, making me pause. "What? Are you such a modern gentleman you can't go into my purse?"

"You put strange things in them. Like...tampons."

"You're twenty-six and grossed out by tampons?"

"Well...no. They just make me uncomfortable."

"Don't worry. No tampons in my purse." She grins, biting half of her chip off.

"Great," I mutter, unzipping her bag. This still feels awkward—probably because the last time I went in a woman's bag, it was my cousin's, and she was "looking after a *friend's* vibrator." That was six years ago. I've avoided this situation ever since.

Plus, there's something awfully awkward about rifling through someone's most personal belongings. Sticking my dick inside her? Not a problem. Looking into her bag? Fuck no.

Leila's bottle of Coke fizzes as she unscrews it and watches me with total amusement. So what if I'm being hesitant? I don't know that she doesn't have vibrator like my cousin did. Or what other ungodly item I'm going to find. Don't women pack their kitchen sinks and the contents of the cupboard beneath it in these things?

Finally, I locate the small, folded piece of paper that contains the instructions for the damn instant Polaroid-esque camera that I thought it would be a good idea to buy her. She's never mentioned it, but pretty much every single time we've come out sight-seeing, her phone has died before she's taken all the photos she wants, and she got fidgety at least...oh, every single bloody time.

I figured an instant camera was the way to go, plus lots and lots of extra shots to go in her Mary Poppins bag. I just didn't consider that she'd find the use of such a simple creation as hard as proving the origins of the universe.

"It's amazin'—you're more bothered about the fact that I can't use a dang camera Mila could operate than the fact that you're manager-less."

I pause and glance up at her. "Babe, I don't want to talk about this. You know that."

"Oh, come on. How are you not bothered? Lawrence believed the bullshit she spun him, and now, you're where you were the first time we met."

"Not entirely," I answer, turning my attention to the instructions. "I have songs out, my album being released in two months won't change, and my lawyer can just do this stuff until I get new management."

She stares at me with those blue eyes. "How are you so blasé? When my brothers fired their manager, they pulled all sorts of dumb stunts and bullshit to get a company based in one of the Carolinas so they could record closer to home."

"I just... Can we drop it?" I ask, my voice harder than I intended.

She rolls her eyes but gives in with a huff and tears a small piece of fish off.

"I didn't mean to snap at you. I don't have to think about it right now, and I'd rather think about you than all that stuff, okay?"

She flicks her gaze back to me for the briefest moment before her lips purse in the way they do when she fights a smile. "Fine. You win. For now. One more thing though?"

I nod.

"Did you tell anybody yet? Like Ella or someone?"

I shake my head. "I was going to tomorrow. Like I said... Thinking about you and this bloody camera."

One hand flies up in surrender, and she goes back to eating while I fiddle with the lighting settings on the camera.

Now she's got me thinking about it though, hasn't she? Breaking up with Lawrence wasn't an easy choice, but Leila was completely right in her estimation of Madison. The only way the media could have gotten inside the hotel was if she'd somehow snuck them in, but if you ask Lawrence, I am responsible for those pictures being "leaked" and attempting to get Madison fired after I hit on her and she turned me down.

Yeah.

Bullshit.

Leila's now obsessed with the fact I'm without management, and I appreciate her concern, but I spoke to my lawyer right after to negotiate termination of the contract, and I know it isn't immediately necessary. Everything is already in place for the album release, and hell, if I have to, I'll just hire Jennifer to do some publicity for me.

I'll even steal Ella while Dirty B. is on downtime.

I'll make it work, one way or another.

Here or America.

I'm going to get all soppy and call this shit fate. The day I receive my visa acceptance is the day my management company needs to be dropped on their asses. I'm gonna take it. My world just opened up more than I ever imagined it would.

Everything I've worked for is coming true in a roundabout way. Everything I've wanted is laying itself out in front of me. Including the girl actually now lying on the grass in front of me.

"You look tired."

"I look like I just put on twenty pounds," she groans. "The breakfast, the fish and *chips,* and the Cadburys for lunch? I'm in trouble, Jase. It's amazing my pants still fit."

"I can help you out of them if necessary." I flash her a wolfish grin. "I think I figured this thing out." I hold the white camera up.

"Yeah, well, so did I right before I took a snap of Mr. Hawaiian Shirt's ass crack." Ahh... That wasn't her best attempt.

I hold the camera up and lean forward, peering through the tiny square. "Smile." She doesn't. She looks at me stony-faced.

"Come on, Leila," I attempt to coax her. "Let me try."

"Big Ben is right over there. Take a picture of his beautiful self."

"I want to take a picture of your beautiful self."

Her lips twitch, but she's strong enough to stop them from curving right up. "Nice try, slick."

"Obviously not that slick because you're still a grumpy bitch."

She gasps. "You meanie!"

"Meanie?" I peer over the top of the camera, taking care not to move it. "What are you, five?"

"You'll wish you were if you say that again."

"You're breaking my heart here, babe. I just want to take a picture of you. I promise I'll throw it out when it's done."

She looks up at the sky. "It looks like it's going to rain."

I have no idea what that has to do with this conversation. Oh, yeah. That's right. Bloody nothing.

"You've lost your mind, woman."

"Yes!" She points at me. "I have. But only because you stole it and turned me into this, this..." She waves her arm over herself.

"Happy?" I offer quietly, my lips tugging to the side.

"Yeah." She puts her hand down and peers up at me, her mouth slowly moving into a heart-thumping smile. "Happy."

I press the button on the camera.

"You bastard!" She launches herself toward me.

I roll away, laughing, and pull the picture out of the top of the camera.

"I'm gonna kill you, you sneaky little shit!"

"You wouldn't dare!" I point the camera back at her as I slide the instant picture down my shirt and press my hand over it to keep it dark. There aren't many other options outside in the center of London. "Leila Burke, stop right there or I'm taking another."

She pouts.

"That's not gonna work."

She pouts more.

"Nope." I shake my head. "You're not having the picture until I've seen it."

In her most mature move yet, she sticks her tongue out at me and dumps herself back on the ground next to our rubbish. She folds the paper around the polystyrene trays our dinner was served to us in, taking care not to leave anything on the floor.

I want to peek at that picture although I know it won't be developed yet. Then again, judging by her luck with the lighting so far today, she might end up as a feminine Voldemort without a visible nose.

I watch as she gathers our rubbish and takes it to the bin on the other side of the grass. She pauses before she turns back and looks out past the Houses of Parliament, toward the Eye, and over the Thames.

It's not late but it's not early, either, and the sun is halfway down. The sky is decorated in every golden hue imaginable, and seeing Leila stop and soak up the view I know she's experiencing right now churns something inside me.

I want to go to her, wrap my arms around her, and kiss her.

I also want to stand here and just watch her be at peace.

And I want to keep it for myself.

I look through the view hole in the camera and, after focusing her in the center of the frame, snap the picture. The camera whirrs as it prints the picture and churns it out, and I put it back in her bag after taking the second picture.

I replace the one in my shirt with the one I just took and look at the one I took a few minutes ago.

That smile.

Her happy smile, the one that's so warm and bright it could melt the Arctic and illuminate even the darkest, most overcast night, is shining through in this tiny, credit-card sized picture.

I pull my wallet from my pocket and slip the picture inside.

I don't care what she says.

I'm keeping that one.

Somehow, it's captured everything I see when I look at her.

"I saw that flash," she says, coming back over. "You're not as sneaky as you think you are."

I shrug. "I don't really care. I just wanted to get the moment."

"What moment?" She frowns, her dark eyebrows delicately drawing together. "Me thinking that going on the London Eye would be good if it didn't look like it was gonna pee down with rain?"

"You wanna go on the Eye?"

"Jase. I know that look."

"What look?" I smile, pulling the photo out from beneath my shirt. Jesus... Even from behind, she's gorgeous. "This moment. Look at it." I hand it to her. "You look so...peaceful."

"You can't see my face. You're silly."

"Maybe. But at least I'm serious when I'm silly." I grin and take it back, sliding it into my wallet behind the first. "You wanna go on the Eye?" I repeat.

"No." She pauses, pushing her fringe out of her eyes. "Jase, no. It's going to be busy."

I raise one eyebrow, smirking. "Don't you know who I am?"

"No! Don't you dare pull a freaky-ass voodoo 'I'm Jase Masters' trick just to get on it!"

I launch forward in an attempt to cover her mouth with my hand, but I miscalculate and end up knocking her onto her back. She screams halfway through a laugh as her back hits the grass, and I flatten my hands on either side of her head and look down at her.

"My name, Leila! You conjure them every time! Sssh!"

"Oh, please!" She laughs, rolling her head to the side. "You're not Voldemort."

"You'd be surprised. We'll probably find compromising pictures all over Twitter tomorrow and have to explain them to your brothers before they kill me then dump my body."

"That's dramatic."

"No, their leaving the country before I'm found is dramatic."

Leila rolls her eyes. "Then get off me and it won't be a problem."

"Can I take you on the Eye with my freaky-arse voodoo trick?"

"No."

"Then there's explaining to do."

She groans and half rolls onto her side. "Fine. Let's go. You can pull your shit."

She hasn't said a word for fifteen minutes.

It might have something to do with the fact photographers followed us from the London Eye to the bar we're currently in and are garnering us more than a little attention from the other people in here.

In my defense, I said my name was Jase and asked if they could they squeeze us in, and the girl at the ticket counter had a bit of a meltdown. Her manager had to take over and, after getting my autograph for the girl, who needed five minutes, arranged for us to get on the Eye.

And apparently also called every newspaper and media outlet in the city.

Although it is raining, much to the delight of Leila—but only because she can say, "I told you so."

I think the wine is helping to calm her down though. A little.

I hope, anyway.

I sip from my beer and look at her out of the corner of my eye. Her phone is lying on the bar—its battery only alive because of her new camera, not that she'll bloody admit it—and she's scrolling aimlessly through Facebook. With a heavy sigh, she presses the button at the bottom of her phone then locks it.

"What's on your bucket list?"

"What?" She snaps her head around to me, grasping the stem of her wine glass. Her thumb curves over the top, and she lifts it to her lips to sip the light liquid.

"Your bucket list," I repeat. "You have to have a bucket list. You've traveled too much not to."

"Maybe I got it all already." She spins the wine glass between her finger and thumb. "Most of it."

"All right, so what's left?"

"Boy, you're real insistent tonight, aren'tcha?"

"We can't sit here in silence."

"I sit in silence a lot of the time."

"Only when you read."

"Maybe I have a book with me."

I freeze. "You have a book with you, don't you?"

Leila grins and meets my eyes. "No. I have two."

I bury my face in my hands. Obviously she has two—because one just isn't enough.

"I want to swim the Great Barrier Reef," I tell her, dropping my hands. She's not pulling a bloody book out in a bloody pub.

"That would be cool." She turns her body on the seat and, resting her elbow on the bar, props her chin up with her hand. "What else?"

I see how we're going to play this. "I dunno... Hitting number one on the charts would be pretty cool. I almost did it with my second single. I got to two."

"Here, right? Where did you get in the US?"

"Twenty. So add number one in the US too." I pause as I pick my beer up. "Performing in Madison Square garden."

"My brothers did that." She thins her lips, her eyes betraying a giggle. "Kye and Aidan threw up at the same time and Tate hit them both with full bottles of water so they'd get their shit together."

I laugh. I can imagine. Kye and Aidan do a lot of things at the same time, I've noticed. Even when they don't realize it. If it weren't for their tattoos, they'd probably be able to trick Jessie and Chelsey on a daily basis.

"Wembley Arena too. That's probably the ultimate one because it's at home, you know?"

"Doesn't the tour close out there next week?" Leila raises an eyebrow.

I nod. "Ticking it off next Saturday."

"Wow. I might actually come to that one."

Of course. She hasn't been to a single one.

"Why don't you go?" I ask.

She shrugs and looks down, still playing with her glass. Her lips twist to one side, and I can almost see the thoughts forming behind her eyes as she obviously struggles to put things into words.

"I...don't know," she admits honestly. "I love them and I support them unconditionally, but it just doesn't..." She pauses. "It doesn't feel right a lot of the time. That's the best way to describe it. Maybe because I'm used to seeing them playing in the garage, on a dirty floor, surrounded by crushed cans of Pepsi and Red Bull and empty food packages and bags. Not to mention I get assaulted by their voices every time I put the freakin' radio in my car on."

I laugh at the disgust on her face. "I get it. My dad and I have season tickets for the football team my brother played for before he got injured, but I didn't always go. I usually gave it to my uncle. I spent way too much time on the sidelines, watching him, as a kid. We've both worked for our careers, but his success was pretty much immediate the moment he left the academy. I feel like I'm only just starting to get there. I lived in his shadow for a long damn time."

Leila stops playing with her wine glass and lifts her striking, blue eyes to mine. The smile that forms on her lips is sad, almost resigned, but the glimmer in her gaze tells me one thing: We're so different in so many ways, but in this...we're the same.

"That's it," she says softly, lifting one shoulder in a shrug. "I live in their shadow because they're successful. Meanwhile, I still live with my parents and will continue to live there because I got let go from my job right before we left. I have no idea what I want to do with my life, while they're made for the rest of theirs. God." She drops her head forward and runs her hand through her hair, peering at me from behind it. "Does that make me a bitch?"

"No. It makes you human."

"I'm twenty-three and I live with my parents."

"I was a millionaire at twenty-two from a record deal that flopped, and I lived with my parents until just over a year ago."

"That makes me a feel a little better." She smiles properly now. "Not the failed thing. The living thing."

"Here to help." I half smile, half smirk, and finish my beer. "You wanna go?"

She looks over her shoulder at the door. They seem to have left—or backed off, at least.

"Sure." She downs the last mouthful of wine and then hops up, grabbing her bag and zipping it shut.

I take her hand in mine, and we step out of the pub and into the darkness without being attacked by flashes. I guess someone better and more famous than me came along.

"What would you do if you were me?" Leila asks, falling into step beside me and swinging our hands between us.

I answer without thinking about it. "I'd find something I love and put all my energy into it until it worked."

"Like you already did?"

I look down at her, and her blue eyes are bright, even in the night. "I knew what I loved before it mattered. I know what you love."

"I'm not sure being a professional reader is a career. Although, if it was, I'd make a freakin' killin'."

I shake my head, smiling. "I bet you could write a book."

"That's ridiculous."

"Is it? You love books and romance so much so that you'd forget your phone before you forgot a book. It's not so crazy at all." I squeeze her hand. "You were moaning that the bird in your book was a wimp earlier and you wanted to staple her clit to a rhino."

"She's annoying!" Leila groans, dropping her head back for a moment. "When the guy isn't around, she's super cool. Then, the moment he turns up, she turns into a gasping, breathless, needy, naked idiot who doesn't even know his real name!"

"Sounds...kind of like a horror movie, actually."

"And she's not a bird."

"Not an actual bird." I snort. "We say bird the way you say chick. For a woman."

"You call women birds?"

"You wanted to staple a fictional person's clitoris to a rhino and you're worried about what the British slang for woman is?"

"Fair point." She nods in agreement. "So. what am I, then? Am I your *bird*?"

She said it so...confused...that I can't help but laugh at her.

"Do you want to be my bird?" I ask.

"Kinda feel like I need to take flight and go south for the winter, if I'm honest."

I let her hand go, still laughing, and wrap my arm around her shoulders. "How about this," I say into her hair, my lips brushing the side of her head. "You're just mine."

"I guess that's okay." She's dismissive, but her face turns toward me and betrays her real emotion about it.

"I don't care if it is or not." I stop us, barely taking notice of Big Ben right behind us, and face her. I look down into her eyes and cup her jaw, stroking my thumb over her cheek. "You're mine, Leila. I don't think anything could make me let you go now."

She looks into my eyes for a long moment before her lips move into a smug yet sassy smile, and she steps closer to me. "Good." She leans up and kisses the corner of my mouth, her hand flat at the side of my neck. "Jase?" she whispers, going back down off her toes as a couple of light raindrops fall onto the top of my head. "You really wanna know my bucket list?"

"I didn't ask you for no reason, love."

Leila smiles, her teeth grazing over her bottom lip, and steps back. My hand falls away, and she closes her eyes and looks up into the rain. It's only a light mist, but I can already feel it starting to trickle down my back.

"I have two things on my real bucket list, and I've never told anyone this. Ever," she says, righting her head and looking straight into my eyes. She holds two fingers up in the peace sign but wiggles one. "One: I want someone to love me the way they do in the greats. Elizabeth and Darcy, Laurie and Jo—because *everybody* knows it was meant to be them—Noah and Allie, Emma and Mr. Knightley, Jane and Mr. Rochester, Lennie and Lucky... You know? I want the kind of spine-tingling, gripping love that hits in the midst of insanity, maybe wavers, but never leaves. The kind that weathers any storm and the destructive aftermath that comes with it."

Her cheeks flush, and her eyes are bright as the passion for the books she loves screams through. It screams so loudly I almost feel it myself.

"Two." She wiggles her other finger, apparently not even having noticed the rain falling on her. "I want to be kissed the way they kiss in my books. With soul and desire and freeness. With everything except restraint or concern for the rest of the world. For even two minutes, I want to feel like I *am* the world." She pauses, dropping her hand. "So maybe I have read too many books with perfect endings, but that's just the way it is. The realist in me wants to see the world. The romantic wants to be someone's world. It's possible to be both, I think."

I don't know how to respond to that.

I might have half torn myself apart this morning telling her how I feel about her, but she just pulled her soul right out of her body and spoke it aloud. She just shared with me a part of her that is so intimate and beautiful that I'm the only other person who knows it exists.

She's the unexpected force in my life, and there are so many different little things about her it'd take me a lifetime to uncover them all.

And I don't... I don't know what it is, but something flicks inside me. Something I didn't know existed until now, and the idea of anybody other than me ticking those two items off her bucket list physically hurts.

I close the distance between us and, with my hands on either side of her face and my fingers slipping into her hair, kiss her.

Kiss her with everything.

Every last bit of me, all of my strength, all of my emotion... I pour it into the kiss, hoping to god she's feeling like my world, because fuck knows I think she just became it.

I bet even the darkest part of her is more beautiful than any ancient or natural wonder.

I already know her smile is.

"What was that?" she whispers, her eyes still closed.

"A kiss in the rain. That was me attempting my best Mr. Darcy impression." I stare at her face, still holding it as the rain trails down over her delicate features. "And hoping I ticked off item number two on your bucket list."

Leila takes a deep breath, and emotion—deep emotion, hard, swirling, consuming—swims in her eyes. Slowly, she nods, the barest lift of her chin.

And leans in, pressing her lips against mine, wrapping her arms around my waist.

She grasps my shirt, so I kiss her back harder.

And fall the rest of the way in love with her.

chapter twenty-one
Leila

"Leila!" Tate's voice breaks through my restless sleep, followed by endless banging on the door. "Leila Burke, open the goddamn door right now!"

My eyes fly open.

I'm in trouble, aren't I?

"Fuck off!" I yell, shoving the sheets away.

Ten a.m. and they're coming to wake me up—honestly. Don't they know how tired I am? I barely slept at all last night.

Not my fault. Jase's kiss kept popping up in my dream, even when I was dreaming about raccoons and otters fighting for their nests in a tree. Or maybe I created that myself while I was trying to stop thinking about that...

That kiss.

Oh my god.

I grab yoga pants, my bra, and a tank top from the chair where I flung them last night and get dressed. I almost trip over my own feet as I run for the door, and I right myself just before I open it.

"Good mornin'!" I swing my door open and plaster a wide smile on my face.

Tate... Well, he looks like he wants to murder someone. "My room. Now." He pushes in, swipes my room key from the side table where I dumped it last night, and grabs my wrist. He yanks me from the room before I can say anything and slams my door behind me.

"Hey! What the hell?" I tug my arm from his grip and punch him. "What cactus did you shit out this morning?"

"Never mind me and shit coated cactuses. I'm about to tear *you* a new asshole. What are you thinkin'?" he snaps, his voice deathly low.

"I have no idea what you're talkin' about."

Tate glares at me and swipes his card through the lock outside his door. Then he pushes me through it the moment he's opened it.

My other three brothers and my four best friends all stare at me.

"Awesome. A family meeting. Is Mom here making a chicken pot pie?" I put my hands on my hips and look around at everyone.

Sofie's eyes widen and she shakes her head, but she stops when she glances at Tate.

Aidan grabs a few sheets of paper and slams them down on the table. "Explain."

"Explain what?"

"Why this," Kye says, picking up the pictures his twin just put down, "is a series of pictures of you kissing Jase last night."

"Oh, like she can see them from here!" Chelsey snatches them from him and brings them to me. "Good luck," she murmurs. "We tried."

I take the sheets from her and drop my eyes to them. Yep. Sure as shit—someone caught the Bucket List Book Kiss. And there's absolutely no denying I'm the girl in these pictures. One has my face perfectly clear, so I can't brush it off like last time.

And here I was thinking I could approach this subject in a calm and sophisticated manner after Jase's and my big talk yesterday. And the Bucket List Book Kiss.

I have three ways to approach this. Shock. Grovel. Sass.

"And y'all needed a family intervention for a kiss? What is this? The eighteen hundreds?"

Sass it is.

"Leila..." Conner groans. "Come on."

"Come on, what? This buffoon"—I cock my thumb over my shoulder toward Tate—"just dragged me outta my goddamn bed, manhandled me through the hall, and shoved me in here before I even had a chance to piss."

"You've been lyin' to us!" Tate says loudly, walking around the front.

"I... Well. Just a little," I admit. "More omittin' information, if you wanna get it right."

He glares at me in the exact same way Dad does when he wants the truth. Hooey, that's some freaky shit.

"We knew somethin' was going on," Conner says before Tate can. "But we're a little pissed you kept it to yourself and we found out for sure like this."

"A little pissed?" Jessie snorts. "Tate looks like he's about to turn into a human steam train."

"Jessie, babe, shut up." Aidan covers her mouth with his hand.

She bites him.

"Okay, I get it." I hold my hands up, the papers flapping. "But can y'all just listen to me for a sec? Then I'll let y'all yell till you can't anymore if that's what you wanna do. Tate? Please?" I look at my oldest brother.

He opens his mouth before slamming his jaw shut and waving at me.

Jesus. Who died and made him king?

"Are you gonna tell 'em everythin'?" Sof asks, picking her coffee up.

"You knew?" Conner turns to her.

"Oh, don't look at me like that, Conner Burke. She's been my best friend my entire life. Of course I freakin' knew. You never asked me, so I never told you." She sips and looks back to me.

"Kinda don't have a choice." I grimace, wincing.

"Everything? What is everything? I swear to god, if you're pregnant—" Kye starts.

"What did I just say about y'all being quiet, huh? For once, can you listen to me?" I crumple the sheets of paper into balls, throw them onto the table, then fold my arms. "But, no, I am not pregnant, thank you," I snap. "I already knew Jase. Before y'all met him in Paris. We met when I was in London."

"As in…your trip before Chels and I got together?" Kye frowns.

I nod and briefly recount the Waterstones story. "We spent the night together and that was it. I didn't expect him to be the guy supporting you on tour." I look out the window, but not before seeing realization flicker across Conner's features. Now, he knows why I froze when I saw him. "We talked the day after we landed in Paris and agreed we wouldn't mention that we knew each other and we'd stay away from each other."

"Worked out real well," Tate mutters.

"Tate! Enough!" Ella smacks her hand into his stomach. "Let her talk."

"Did you know too?"

"We all knew," she admits Then she throws a, "Sorry," toward Chels and Jessie.

Jessie shrugs. "This isn't and never was our thing to share. It's Leila's. We bugged her until she gave in, and we promised not to tell you because it's *none of your business*." She sweeps her calculating gaze over everyone.

Whatever words were on the tips of my brothers' tongues die, and she looks at me, nodding for me to continue.

I take it back. I'm not selling them on Craigslist anymore. "Obviously, it didn't work. The night before the fake story broke? He turned me down because I'd been drinking. We agreed after that that we had a mutual itch that needed to be addressed and agreed to no strings. Somewhere between the Eiffel Tower, croissants, Big Ben, and a ridiculous amount of Cadburys, we became…more."

"More?" Con asks, his lips twitching up. "As in…"

"As in the idea of y'all givin' him a hard time about this though he was nothing but sweet and respectful toward me makes me want to gouge out my eyeballs with a rusted butter knife?"

"We can't have a conversation without your stupid, can we?" Aidan asks.

"I can gouge out other things with a rusted butter knife," I say flatly, refusing to look at him. I run my fingers through my hair then twist a lock of it around my finger. "I didn't want to hide this from you, but you were all so on my damn ass about being around guys when we got here that you literally made it impossible for me to tell you."

"Did we?" Aidan and Kye say together before they look at Tate and Conner.

In turn, all four of them meet the eyes of Sofie, Ella, Jessie, and Chelsey.

They all share their own look before they nod.

"Yeah," Sofie tells them, albeit reluctantly. "You were really kinda...over the top. Not even your dad would have been that hard on her."

"Shit," Tate mutters. He sits at the table and pushes the heels of his hands into his eyes. "What you're sayin' is that the reason this was secret is our fault."

"Actually, that's what we're tryin' not to say," Jessie adds helpfully. And a little too cheerfully. "But, now that you did, fuck yeah it was your fault."

"Helpful, Jessie. Thanks," I hiss.

She grins at me. "Anytime."

"That true, Lei?" Aidan asks quietly. "You keep it from us 'cause you were afraid of how we'd react?"

I halfheartedly pull my lips up on one side and shrug. "I guess, yeah. I didn't plan it, okay? Don't think I looked at him and knew it would happen. I didn't mean..." I take a deep breath and sigh it out heavily. "I didn't mean to fall in love with him," I say quietly, looking down at the floor.

It goes so silent that we could hear a needle drop on the carpet. There's more than one set of eyes on me, but the ones I feel the most are Tate's. My biggest, most protective, most pigheaded brother. The one who has always protected every single one of us because the thing he was most afraid of was all of us getting hurt. Conner when Sofie returned with Mila, Aidan when he was forced into a fake relationship with Jessie, Kye when he thought Chelsey would run out on him once and for all...

And me. Because it was finally more acceptable for him to consider punching the person who'd hurt me in the face.

"You love him?" Tate's voice is quiet and a little hoarse. "Really?"

"Yeah." I glance up at him and swallow. "He just...gets me."

And he does. It's like the rough edges of his soul fit right against mine.

"Fuck, Lei. I'm sorry." Tate rubs his hand down his face.

I walk to the table and wrap my arms around him, resting my head on top of him. "I'm not mad at you, Tate. I ain't mad at any of you. I know you were tryna look out for me, but I can do that too. Will you trust me when I say I know what's best for me?"

Slowly, all four of my brothers nod. It's the most reluctant bunch of nods I've ever seen, but nods all the same.

"Yeah," Tate mutters. "But I'm still gonna tell him I'm gonna break his neck if he's a prick to you."

Ella snorts. "If that's the criteria..."

"Hey!" Tate says, shaking me off and turning to his girlfriend. "I was a protective prick. I'm the oldest. You know how much work it is keepin' an eye on all of these?"

Ella flatly looks back at him. "You all need to be in the gym by ten, out by eleven. You have lunch being delivered to your respective rooms at eleven forty-five. At twelve thirty, you have a conference call with your manager regarding the Manchester-and-Newcastle leg of the trip. The moment that is done by one, you're all in cars and heading to the O2 for your final rehearsal before the next leg. At five fifteen on the dot, you'll have dinner delivered. Then it's time to prepare and one final sound check before you take the stage at seven. At ten, you'll all leave and come back here, where you'll find all your crap packed and ready to get on the plane to fly to Manchester tomorrow for tomorrow night's concert, where it'll happen all over again."

"You're such a bragger."

"Just proving my point." She grins.

"Damn," Con whispers. "And he can't even remember her birthday."

Ella casts her gaze toward him. "I know. He has an alert on the calendar on his phone every day for the week leading up to it."

"I do know when your birthday is!" Tate insists. "I wanna say...July."

"Month off. Go check your calendar and come back, you pain in the ass."

"And you're worried about me? Really?" I look at everyone.

Three knocks sound at the door, and I snap my head to it then back at my brothers.

They all refuse to meet my eyes.

"You didn't," I mutter, walking back toward it. "If you did..." I open the door to Jase then turn around to my brothers. "What did you think this would accomplish?"

"Uh, I'm confused," Jase says.

"Sssh." I bat at him. "Tate? I know it was you."

"For once, no." He shakes his head. "Aidan."

"Aidan!"

"What? I was actually hoping he'd show up ten minutes ago so you wouldn't have to do the cross-examination alone." He pauses, grimacing. "But there we go. My timin' was off."

"Cross-examination?" Jase asks. "What am I... Oh."

"Oh" sounds about right.

I thin my lips and look from him to Tate. Tate's staring at him, his hand covering his mouth. He's rubbing his palm across his lips, and the contemplative look in his eye makes my heart skip a beat—and not in a good way.

"We're just gonna... Yeah. Go." Jessie grabs Chelsey, and they run to the door.

"Yeah, we've gotta do that...thing, Ella. Right?" Sofie asks, getting up.

"Yeah. Yeah—I remember the thing." Ella grabs her purse, and they run after Jessie and Chelsey.

"You're all shit friends!" I yell as they slam the door behind them. And after all the awkward things I've gone through for them.

Now that they're gone, it's gotten decidedly more awkward. Total silence. Nobody even breathing loudly. It's as if we're all holding it in and waiting for someone to break the silence.

I wonder if I can make an escape myself.

Yeah. I've done my time in this—it's Jase's time.

Hey, I might be in love with the guy, but I'll throw him under the bus if I have to. Equality and all that. I've already been ripped a new one.

I make to take a step back, but Tate beats me to it. My heart beats faster as my biggest brother and personal bodyguard rubs his hand on his pants and approaches Jase.

He holds his hand out.

I take a deep breath.

To some people, that might be nothing. But to me? Growing up in the center of my tight-knit, overprotective family he's always spearheaded? It's everything.

Jase puts his hand in Tate's, meeting his eyes, and shakes it.

Tate yanks Jase toward him, his hard gaze moving to me. "I told you the other day she'd give you her heart no matter what I think. And, luckily for you," he says, taking his eyes back to Jase, "you're as close as it gets to being good enough to her. But, if you hurt her, I'll make the devil look like a fucking fluffy bunny."

Jase turns his face to me, his green eyes sparkling. "And I told you I'd never hurt her."

Now, my heart is thumping for a whole other reason. Partially because they spoke about me, but because this idiot told him that he'd never hurt me while knowing it could get his ass kicked.

"You know what? I believe you." Tate lets his hand go and steps back. He smiles slowly, looking between us, but all I can really see is Jase's smiling, green eyes locked on mine. "Oh, fuck me." Tate grabs me, kisses the side of my head, then pushes me into Jase.

Jase locks his arms around me, laughing quietly. I can't help the smile that curves my lips as I curl into him and look at my brothers. They're trying not to smile, but they're all failing to varying degrees—except Aidan.

He looks smug.

"You knew, didn't you?" I ask him. "The Hyde Park pictures."

"Yeah." He smirks. "You're a shit liar. Plus, you grinned like a little bitch the whole time."

I shrug a shoulder. "I'm smart and beautiful. I can't be a good liar too."

"And there's my baby sister," he laughs, running his hand down the side of his face. "You probably want to know how we got the pictures, right?"

"Pictures?" Jase's chest rumbles against my cheek. "What pictures?"

"The pictures of you giving me the Bucket List Book Kiss," I say, moving to the coffee machine.

"Don't drink all the coffee," Tate mutters.

"Don't wake me up next time, fuckhead!"

Jase snorts. "You're in a good mood."

I glare over my shoulder. "Just because we don't have to hide our relationship anymore doesn't mean you have permission to speak with me before coffee, okay? I've done enough of personing before caffeine."

"Personing," Kye muses. "Is that a technical term?"

"It's a shut-the-fuck-up, let-me-get-coffee, and tell-me-why-y'all-have-a-small-photo-album-of-me-making-out-in-the-rain term."

"Someone write that shit down," Conner pipes up. "That's the making of a platinum album there, because I'm pretty sure all our girls have said something similar."

"We'll collab Dirty B. with Jase Masters," Aidan agrees. "Song'll be called 'Real Girl.'"

"Sign me up," Jase replies, and when I turn, he's grinning and he winks at me.

Such a fucker. All the men in my life are fuckers. They're all lucky I love the shit outta them or it wouldn't be a good day for them.

"Spit it out, fuckers."

"We were sold them," Tate says.

I slam my empty mug down. "I'm sorry?"

"By Madison Bentley," he adds, looking at Jase. "She has designs on fuckin' up your career. She already thinks she's winning because you apparently don't have a manager."

Jase stills.

Well, damn. This is awwwwwkward.

"As of yesterday," he says after a moment of them all looking at him. "Truth be told, I thought that's what you wanted to talk about. Can't say I'm unhappy about the real reason, but I'm pissed she spilled it before we could tell you ourselves."

"Water under the bridge." Aidan gets up. "But Madison could pose a problem for you. I think she was hoping to sell these pictures for publication, but our attorney in the US fixed that pretty quickly. These pictures are owned by us, and if she sells them, we get paid." He grins in such a way that tells me they've fucked her.

Hard.

In the ass.

With a porcupine.

Excuse me, but: *Fuck. Yesssssss.*

Ads retrieves the pictures from the trash can, all crumpled from my bitchfit, and uncreases them before he hands them to Jase. "It looks like she had you followed. We actually had Chelsey talk to her and she screwed her seventy ways to Saturday."

"I knew her being a rocker's daughter would come in handy one day, despite her denying it." I sip on my hot coffee. Ahhh. "See? Having an asshole dad worked in our favor pretty well, it seems."

"Yes." Conner slides his eyes toward me. "But that doesn't mean Madison is done. She knew y'all hadn't told us about your relationship, so she was one-upping everybody when she came to us last night."

"I'll one-up my heel up her vagina."

"Eloquent, sis, real eloquent."

I shrug.

"What do you mean she isn't done?" Jase asks—that's the important question. "Do I need to talk to my lawyer?"

"No. You—" Tate pauses when there's a knock at the door.

I open it. "Hi, slutface," I say to Chelsey. "Come to help me now, have you?"

She rolls her eyes and walks past me, into the room, holding her phone up. "Kye texted me. I saw the word Madison and came running. Do I need to run her over or something? I could probably arrange a hitman."

"And that's why I texted her." Kye smiles at her warmly. "What Madison will do next?"

"Oh, boy. That basket of vampire kittens." She looks to the ceiling then at me and Jase.

Jase wraps his arm around my waist.

"Most unlikely: She'll leave you alone. Most likely: She's gonna keep on effectively stalking you until you pay her a ton, she gets a higher bid, or y'all get an injunction against her that means she or anyone who is paid or shares funds with her will get their asses thrown in jail if they keep on."

"What would you do?" I ask her. She's done this a million times with her father—she'll know.

"Pay her twice and then get an injunction." She slides her phone into the back pocket of her jeans. "She ain't smart. She's desperate to get her name back out there and desperate to ruin Jase's because he got the success she believes she deserves. She's one tiny fish in the whole world of the media and she ain't gonna get far. Y'all don't hafta worry about her."

I know that, deep down, but still... "Can we talk for a minute?"

"Sure. Come down to my room. Jessie just ordered enough bacon to feed, well, these guys." She cocks her thumb toward my brothers and goes to the door.

"I'll be right back," I say to Jase, leaning up to kiss his cheek.

He turns his face at the last minute so my lips brush across his, and my cheeks heat when he flattens his hand against my lower back.

"She's still my sister!" Tate growls.

I dart back, smiling, and follow Chelsey out of the room. She grabs my hand the moment I step into the hall and drags me toward her room.

"Well, that wasn't awkward at all." She laughs, letting us inside. "Right. What do you need to talk about?"

I sit on the edge of the sofa, unsurprised to see Jessie munching her way through one crispy rasher of bacon. "How do you deal with it? The media attention?"

Jessie pauses. "You're the sister of the world's biggest boyband and you're asking us that."

"Yeah. Because I don't generally get pictured kissing my brothers."

"Ignore it." Chelsey sits at the table and grabs her own rasher. "Seriously. Remember how badly it got to us at first? Jessie because she wasn't used to it—and forced into it—and me because I know how badly it can destroy you. Now, though, with Kye? It means nothing to me, honestly. Same bullshit, different day. You'll get used to it."

"Plus, it won't be so bad, right?" Jessie adds. "He lives here." She pauses almost before she's finished speaking. "Shit, Lei. You had to go fall for a guy who lives in another country, dintcha?"

I inhale deeply before letting it go. Yeah, I did. What a damn idiot I am—but I don't have control over my heart.

"We can make it work," I say softly, more to reassure myself than anyone else. "We still have a week here together. I have to believe we can make this work."

"A week is enough," Jessie says quietly, meeting my eyes. "Maybe y'all can work something out. I believe in you, Lei. You can do this."

"It's just gonna be hard at first," Chelsey says. "Eventually, his work will bring him to the States, and then you'll see each other more. We could come back for a real vacation, even."

"I like that, but I have to get a job when I go home, remember? I can't live on nothing." Unless...

What if Jase's idea isn't bad? I could write a book, couldn't I? I must have read a million chapters of my stories where I wished it had gone another way or they'd said or done something different. Must have loved a character so much that they needed their own book a thousand times. Wanted this and that to be longer, thicker, sexier.

Why can't I take the book I want to read but can't find and write it?

No reason.

"What are you thinkin'?"

I look up at Chels and then at Jessie. "Yesterday...Jase told me I should write a book."

They share a look.

"It's not a bad idea," Jessie agrees. "But that takes a long time. What about until then?"

"I saved a lot to move out and I haven't really spent lots of money here. I can probably pay Mom and Dad rent for six months and be okay. I think I can write something in that time."

The more I talk about it, the more the idea grows roots and takes hold in my mind. Hard work—I know that, but why not? Why not try?

Jase was right. Do the thing you love.

Words. I love words. I love words and books and romance. I love *love*. I could write love into a book. I know I can.

"Do it," Chelsey whispers. "It's your passion, Lei. Your room has books in every empty spot. Do it."

"I will." I swallow. "Will you read it and help me?"

"Yes."

"No."

The answers came at the same time, and I know who said what.

"Come on, Jessie. Don't be a bitch," I plead.

"Negative. Bitch is in my DNA." She bites off bacon, grinning.

"I'll let you read the really sexy parts."

"Okay, then. Yeah. I'll do it."

I take a deep breath and smile widely.

I can do this.

And Jase and I...

Well. We'll work it out.

We don't work it out.

We spend the next nine days in a whirlwind of concerts and signatures—and not-so-stolen nights at his apartment. In fact, I hauled ass outta the hotel and to his place, where I stayed the whole time we were in London.

Now, I have to say goodbye.

And I've never been more afraid of anything. Not falling for him, not letting him go. Nothing except saying goodbye and knowing that the next time I see his face for real may not be for a couple of months.

I have resolve though. I know we can do this. We've done enough between us in a measly three weeks. We can do this.

It doesn't stop the doubt.

But we can.

Jase opens his car door and gets out. I sit for a moment longer, watching in the rearview mirror as my brothers' cars pull in next to us in the parking lot. This is goodbye. I don't want goodbye. I don't want see-you-later.

I want see-you-in-ten-minutes. Hold-on-let-me-pee. Wait-there-I'm-coming.

"Leila?" Jase asks, leaning in. "Are you getting out?"

I shake my head and look down. I didn't think it'd hurt this badly. I don't want it to hurt this badly. I almost wish I hated him instead of loving him. Then it wouldn't matter.

He slides back into the car, shuts the door behind him, and turns to me. "Baby, you have to go. I'm going to look at management in the US. You know that. I'll be there soon."

"I know." I look over at him. "But I don't want to."

"Hey." He reaches forward and rests his hand at the side of my face. "You think I want you to go? I don't. I'm gonna miss the hell out of you."

"I know. You are sure you can't be here to see us go tomorrow?"

His lips turn downward. "I wish I could. I promised Kian I'd visit his doctor with him."

"That's okay," I reply, turning my face in toward his palm. I know how important it is for him to be with his brother for an appointment like that, since he explained the extent of his injury. "So, we'll talk later, when you're back?"

"Of course. I'm meeting my lawyer in a couple of hours. Then dinner with my parents, so I won't be able to talk for a while, but I promise we'll talk as soon as I'm home."

"Okay." I smile tightly, my eyes dropping again.

"Don't," he says quietly. "We can do this, love. It's not as bad as you think."

"We're only a few thousand miles away, right?" My voice gets thick at the end, and he pulls me across the center console and against him.

"Right. But think of it like this—when you wake up, I'll be having lunch. I promise to send you a goofy, stupid bloody picture every morning so I'm the first thing you see when you wake up." He kisses my hair. "And I'll even reply straight-away."

"Fine... But then I'll send you a goofy, stupid freakin' picture before I go to bed every night so I'm the first thing *you* see when you wake up."

"Waking up and you being the first thing I see sounds good to me, babe." Jase smiles. "You need to check in, and I need to go back into London. We've got this, Leila, love. I promise you."

"I know," I say thickly. "We've got this, slick." I firmly press my lips to his. Then I wrap my arms around his neck and squeeze him as tight as I can. God... He's everything.

The romantic in me is his world.

The realist in me knows I've seen the world, because I get to look into his eyes and feel my heart beat faster.

"Got this," I whisper, letting him go and getting out of the car before the emotion beating the walls of my soul down wins the fight and I give in to its overwhelming power.

I smile weakly as Sofie. She's maybe the only person who knows this pain because she once made the choice to leave too.

Despite the differences, I know we'll find our way back, just like she did.

No goodbyes.

Just see-you-laters.

Bellboys come from the side door with carts and start loading our luggage. I swallow hard as my things are placed on a cart, but my moment is broken by Mila as she pummels past me and into Jase's legs.

"Jase! No! No go!" she yells, hugging his legs hard.

"Hey!" he says, bending down and picking her up. He puts her on his hip and wraps his arms around her while she rests her arms around his neck. "I'll see you soon, pretty girl. Just a little while."

Mila pouts and frowns in a way only a three-year-old can. "You sure?"

"I'm surer than sure could ever be."

"That vey sure," she says. "Otay. You call, yeah?"

He smiles. "Obviously! Look how pretty you are. I have to call you. Just don't tell Anny Lei Lei."

"Ohhh..." Mila turns back and looks at me. "Anny LeiLei, go, go. Ssh. Don' listen," she orders.

I stick my fingers in my ears.

Jase whispers something in her ear, which causes her to giggle, and then kisses her cheek. Mila grabs his face and plants two huge, smacking kisses on each of his. Then she wriggles down and runs to Sofie.

I lean against his car as everyone says goodbye. Sofie hangs back after hugging him then hands Mila to Conner. She meets my eyes, smiling the tiniest amount.

She knows.

When everyone's gone, I meet Jase's eyes. His sad smile tugs at the deepest parts of my soul, but I... I take a deep breath and throw myself at him. My arms wind around his neck, his go around my waist, and I breathe him in.

I'll never get enough.

I'll miss this more than anything. Miss him. Us. Everything we are.

Everything we have been and can be.

"I'll miss you," I whisper into his neck.

"I'll miss you too, beautiful," he whispers right back. "We've got this. Remember that. And remember the Bucket List Book Kiss. I'll give you the Bucket List Book Love one day. I promise."

My throat clogs so hard that I can't reply, and I attempt to swallow the huge lump that's formed.

That's one hell of a promise.

I add a new item to my ultimate bucket list.

Get Jase to clear the bucket list.

I kiss him once more. Drink him in. Breathe him in. Hold him so tight that it feels like I'll be torn in two if I don't hold him for a moment longer. Beat the sick feeling in my stomach down and beg my heart not to break as I force myself to pull away from him.

Don't cry, I tell myself. *Don't let it break free. Don't let him see.*

I'm not sure I could take it if he saw me cry.

I kiss the corner of his mouth, relishing the rough brush of his stubble against my jaw, and pull away from him before I can do anything else—like cling to him for my fucking life.

Sofie's there instantly.

She grabs me, wraps one arm around me, and leans into me.

I don't look back.

I can't.

My heart cracks, shattering further with every step I take from him because it'll be for an indeterminate length of time. Because it'll be weeks and weeks until I feel that kiss or that touch one more time.

But she's there. My best friend. The one person in my universe who understands what I'm feeling.

Goodbye.

See you later.

They both fucking suck.

The second I cross into the hotel, breaking the barrier between outside and in, I give in to the pain, and in the most heartbreaking way I've ever felt, I don't break.

I don't collapse and sob.

I don't live the pain.

I feel it.

With slow, silent teardrops rolling down my cheeks.

I say see you later.

chapter twenty-two

She's crying.

She's fucking crying.

She tried to hide it, but she can't. She's shit at hiding stuff. Bloody awful.

I want to run after her and hold her and whisper in her ear that everything's gonna be okay. That we can do this. That we really have got this.

But...no.

I can't.

"You wanna go after her." Kye stands next to me, watching Sofie comfort Leila as they disappear through the door. "I know. I did it. Not last Christmas, but the one before. We made a dumb choice with how we told them we'd gotten new management locally. I chose to fuck it and go after her. Best choice I ever made."

"I shoulda gone," Aidan jokes. "She didn't speak to me until I brought her glasses of wine for an hour straight and promised to pay for her next tattoo if she could find a flower that meant 'asshole.' She didn't, but I paid anyway."

"Two days," Tate says, coming to the other side of me. He rests his hand on my shoulder. "You land, you go to Trident, you sign, I give you the keys to my old apartment."

"We've got her," Conner reassures me. "Mom and Dad are expectin' you. Give her that fuckin' book love she craves so badly."

"I already have." I swallow hard, staring at the empty doorway she just walked through. "She just doesn't know it."

Tate smirks, squeezing my shoulder. "Yet. She doesn't know it *yet*."

"Thank you," I say, making sure to hold my emotion back as much as I can. It's not enough because it trickles through. Seeing her cry is the worst thing ever.

Tate grabs my other shoulder and turns me to face him. "You're family now, Jase. Did it kinda fucky, not gonna lie, but you're family. We look after our own."

"And when it's Leila..." Conner trails off.

"We do it even better," the twins say.

"Here," Aidan adds, waving to the driver. He pops the boot of his car.

Kye does the same, and another goes up. "Jessie and Chels didn't notice we were suddenly up a few cases." He grins as the cases are pulled out. "Go get your damn flight."

I'm terrified.

I've been in South Carolina for almost twenty-four hours now, waiting for Leila to get here. Her parents have been nothing but accepting and, quite frankly, fucking amazing ever since I arrived yesterday.

But, now, I'm waiting for her to get here.

And I know she's going to bloody kill me.

I'll take it.

I get to see her. Stay with her.

I never told her about the visa. I definitely never told her that I needed to be able to make music, and I never told her how her brothers helped me with their management and arranged the meeting for this morning.

I will forever be indebted to Dirty B., to the Burke brothers themselves, for not only bringing me on their tour, but ensuring my career would live past it and the small buzz of controversy that was drummed up.

I owe them more than they'll ever know.

More than I'll ever know myself.

I don't know how long I've been sitting here. Leila's dad comes out several times to check on me, but I'm always okay, mostly because of the sound of the sea. It's so soothing, sitting at the edge of the Burke property and watching the water creep up to my toes. It's been a long time since I was near the sea and could just breathe.

I'm thankful for this moment. Even if it is excruciatingly long and torturous as I wait to hear the rumble of the cars.

Maybe she'll think I'm crazy. I don't bloody know. She might tell me to fuck off, and I'm mad for thinking it'll be worth it anyway.

Every heartbeat seems like forever. Every damn crash of the wave breaks through my mental silence with a realistic boom.

Until finally... Finally, I hear the cars.

The engines purr over the sound of the waves and even the tires as they crunch over the gravel drive. My stomach churns, my heart clenching, my blood pounding.

Waiting seems like it's impossible.
She's here.
Feet from me. On the other side of the building.
God, I want to go to her.
I want to touch her, hold her, kiss her.
Didn't know I could miss someone this much this quick.
I wait.
Wait.
Wait.
Wait.
Until the back door opens.
Wait.
Wait.

"I want to go to bed." Leila's voice carries across the garden to where I'm sitting where grass meets sand. "I'm freakin' tired, Tate."

"Fresh air will do you good," Tate insists loudly. "Plus, I have a surprise for you."

"If it's another lobster, I'm not interested."

"Not a lobster. Or a snake," he adds, which makes me smile. "Come on, Lei. Please? Trust me?"

"No."

"Lei..." Conner adds. "You trust me, right? I'm not the mean one."

"Fine." She sounds sad, and her voice pulls at my heartstrings.

"Good. Here."

"What! Con! Get the hell off me!"

Ah. He covered her eyes. He said he would.

I look back as he leads her down the steps.

"Trust me," he says. "Ain't a surprise if you can see it."

"Asshole!" she fires off.

"We'll see." Conner smirks, Tate beside him with an identical expression on his face, and removes his hands from her eyes as I turn away.

Waves crash. Birds sing.

My heart thumps.

She gasps.

"Jase Masters," she calls through the fresh, salty sea air. "If you're sittin' there on my dang beach, I'm gonna fuckin' kill you slowly and painfully."

I smile at the ground and stand. I turn and throw my arms out, shrugging. "Does standing take the same punishment, love?"

Her blue eyes are like beacons compelling me to look directly at her. She stares at me for a long moment before she turns and shoves Conner and Tate with her entire body.

"You fuckin' assholes!" she screams, her voice cracking. "You aren't funny! What are y'all up to? Why'd you do this to me?"

"Leila."

She turns to me when I speak, her eyes on fire, her heart roaring in their depths. "What?"

"Come here."

"No!"

"Yes!" I argue. "Bloody hell, love. I know you're stubborn, but hear me out."

"No!" she repeats, folding her arms across her chest. "You're here and you're not supposed to be and I'm damn mad at you!"

"Leila! Damn it, woman!" I yell. "Listen to me!"

Tate grabs her and drags her toward me. He lets her go as she swings for him. Then he runs back up the garden, toward the house, Conner just in front of him. The door slams as they go inside, leaving me and Leila alone on the beach I've spent so much time on today.

"Please?" I add now that we're alone.

She purses her lips, her eyes wet and glistening with emotion, but nods. "You have thirty seconds."

"I got my visa to live and work here. Then I sacked Lawrence. I couldn't tell you because I thought it changed everything."

"You have longer than thirty seconds," she acquiesces, pushing her hair behind her ear.

Always the left ear. The same I always tuck her hair behind.

"My record label didn't change. Then I spoke to your brothers. We talked for a long time, and I chatted with their management company."

Her eyes find mine.

"They wanted to meet me in person. I couldn't go before because of the tour. This morning was the earliest I could see them."

"And?"

"And I was outside their office before they'd opened, ready for my meeting with them."

"No, you tosspiece," she replies, using my own word. "And what? And fuckin' what, Jase?"

I step closer to her, my lips unable to resist turning upward. "And I'm under new management, baby."

"You—you're...what?" she whispers, looking up at me, real emotion filling her eyes this time. "You bastard!" she yells, shoving at my chest. "If you tell me you're stayin' in Shelton Bay, I'm feedin' you to the dang sharks!"

She's feeling violent this evening. I don't blame her.

I take a few steps back, out of her reach. "I'm staying in Shelton Bay."

Leila stares at me with a mix of such anger and love that it's paralyzing. She's visibly fighting with herself, trying to see which will win out, but she doesn't say a word... At all.

Just stands.

Staring.

Trying to work out how she feels.

"I couldn't leave you," I say quietly. It's worth a try. "Tate suggested we talk to Trident and see if they'd be interested. They were. I didn't want to get your hopes up, love. I could have flown here and met with them for them to say no and us not be able to reach an agreement. I didn't want to give us both unfounded hope."

"I cried, Jase. I've never cried for anybody in my life. Except you."

"I know." My voice breaks. "I saw you. Kye told me how he felt when he did this to Chelsey. We made different choices because we have different reasons."

"Tell me," she demands, lifting her chin, flattening her hands against her upper stomach. "What was your reason?"

She's going to kill me, her family, and her best friends for this.

"I didn't want to come to South Carolina and be with you until I knew I could give you everything to chase your dream," I say quietly, making sure not to break eye contact as I pull keys from my pocket. "Tate is renting me his and Ella's old apartment. Take them. Go." I throw them to her, and she catches them. "You'll find the second bedroom is turned into an office, complete with a wall-long bookshelf, desk, and brand-new computer. Super-comfy chair, too. And it's yours. To write your book."

"They told you," she whispers, clutching the keys to her chest. "Why would they tell you?"

"Because they know I'm so in love with you I'd do just about anything for you." I stuff my hands in my pockets and look down for half a second before my eyes find hers again. "Leave the country I was born, my home, my friends, my family... For you."

"Why?" She goes to press her fingers to her mouth and then drops them to her chest. "Why'd you do it, Jase? That's insane."

"Yes. Completely." I close the distance between us and run my hand over her cheek, sighing as she turns her face into my touch. "But, Leila? Three weeks with you made me believe in my dreams over and over again. I'm already there, baby. I'm touching the sky already. But you? Your feet are on the ground, but your mind's in the clouds. I want to give you what you've given me—the confidence to be whoever I want to be. Go write the next great romance novel. I'll massage your shoulders and crack your fingers at the end of every day if it helps. Follow your dreams, love, because you reminded me to grab mine with two hands." I take her face with my other hand as she rests her hands at my sides. "That's why I'm here. I want you grab my dream with me while I help you chase yours. We got this, remember? You and me, babe. We've got this."

"Bucket List Book Love." She chokes on the final word. "You promised."

"I'm trying."

"You did it." She dips her head and pushes her face into my chest. "You ticked them off. Both of them. Damn it, Jase." She wraps her arms around my neck, moving onto her tiptoes.

My arms slide around her waist. "You're the world, Leila. I'll write songs about you and you'll write novels about me. Got it?"

"Pushin' it," she murmurs, her voice thick with emotion. She turns her face and cranes her neck up to look at me. "You're really stayin'? Here?"

I bend my head down so my nose touches her. "Try and get rid of me, beautiful. Go on. I dare you."

"No." She tugs my face the rest of the way so our lips touch.

I pull her against me, smiling against her mouth. "My sassy, Southern girl," I whisper against her sweet lips. "I bloody love you."

"I bloody love you right back, tosspiece," she whispers, laughing through her words.

"Fuckin' right," I say right before I kiss her again.

We got this.

Bucket List Book Love and all.

epilogue
Leila

ONE YEAR LATER

"Do it," Jase whispers behind me. "Push the button."

My mouse hovers over the orange publishing button. I can't push it. Jesus, I'm terrified. What if it goes wrong?

Sure, I have a hot cover, perfect editing, and epic marketing sponsored by my biggest supporters—Dirty B., of course—but this book is a part of my soul. It's a literal piece of me put onto paper that will soon be exposed for the rest of the world to see.

Ten months ago, I finished writing the draft.

Eight months ago, I got lucky and secured an agent.

Six months ago, the book went to auction between two publishers.

Five months ago, I decided I wanted to control my own destiny, and my agent, fully supportive, let me take my own path.

Tomorrow is my release day. Tomorrow, Australia time, that is, since we're in Cairns and ready to leave for the Great Barrier Reef in exactly forty minutes.

Jase Masters, a.k.a. Hot Brit, a.k.a. slick, a.k.a. love of my motherfreakin' life, helped me clear my ultimate bucket list—adding the one thing I didn't know I needed to do.

Write a book.

When I ticked that off, tucked away in the office of the apartment he rented from my brother, the local coffee shop, Mom's kitchen, Aidan's man cave, the beach, and sometimes even Jase's shiny new truck, we added another.

Publish a book.

I'm seconds from it.

"Do it," he whispers, lightly squeezing my shoulders. "You can do it, love. I bloody believe in you."

"I'm scared." I lean back on the chair and take my hand off the mousepad. "What if it's shit, Jase? What if it sells nothing? What if it dive-bombs into oblivion and I've put everything into it and it fails? What if the last year has been for nothing except a whole ton of heartbreak? What if everyone hates it? What if this book is the worst thing I ever have written and ever will write and nobody understands how much of my heart is in it?"

"That won't happen," he says certainly. "You forget those nights we plotted at two in the morning? The breakfasts I cooked while you rambled your plot points and I helped you make sense of them? The six a.m. wake-up calls because you just had to write that scene I knew you'd delete a week later? The red pens and the highlighters and the frustrations? The tears and the hugs and me slamming your computer away so you'd take a break? I know how much of you is in this book, baby. All of you. All you have to give. Press the button."

"Do it, Lei," Conner says, coming up the other side of her.

"Move!" Ella demands, resting one arm over her small bump. "Do it. So help me, Lei! I didn't share my brownies with you when you edited for your benefit."

"Oh, Jesus. Not the brownies," Jase mutters.

Ella turns on him. "You wanna go, Hot Brit? Let's go. Outside. Right now."

"Like I'm gonna fight the woman who holds the title for the cutest pregnant bird ever." Jase smirks. "What if I buy you brownies?"

"Ella!" Tate growls. "You're gonna kill me."

"She's messin'!" she yells, pointing at me, a hint of a Southern accent finally breaking through her New York one. "I'm gonna hormone her ass soon!"

"Dollar!" Mila yells, running into the room, dragging Bunna by her ears. "Aunty Ella! That's a dollar!"

"Can we get ice cream?" Ella asks, looking down at the world's cutest four-year-old. "I'll pay. Lots of ice cream."

I laugh quietly into my hand, leaning against Jase.

"No!" Sofie yells, running in. She points her finger at everybody. "No! She had it for breakfast thanks to the twins. Kye, Aidan!"

"How did we go from your button to brownies?" Jase asks quietly in my ear.

I shrug. I don't know. It makes perfect sense though. That's just my crazy, perfect family. And the addition of a second niece or nephew is even more perfect—even though the idea of Tate as a father is positively terrifying.

I plan to be out of the country when that happens.

"Come on, Sof," Tate says, grabbing her and hugging her. "You're the first of the second generation of Mrs. Burkes. You need to give her a little leeway."

"We eloped for a reason, you know that?" Sofie fires back.

Yeah. The secret Las Vegas wedding went down like ten tons of shit in the middle of summer... Not well.

"I thought it was brilliant," I add, staring at the computer screen.

Boy, that button is both exciting and intimidating.

"Ice keam is good," Mila finally responds. "With sprinkles?"

"Triple sprinkles," Ella replies.

"Ice cream?" Jessie asks, walking in and holding her scarlet hair on top of her head. She's now finished one arm full of flowers, and the faint red lines of her newest tattoo on the other, which she got right before we came here, are on show. "I could go for that."

"With sprinkles!" Mila screeches in her adorable way.

"Can y'all give me a little privacy?" I ask loudly, swiveling my chair. "I need to publish my book and I'm crapping my pants as it is. Help me out here, y'all."

I turn back to the button.

"You're publishing?" the twins ask, walking through the door, their voices echoing through the room.

Some things never change.

"Just missing Chels," Sofie notes.

"Present!" Chelsey shouts, barreling into the back of my chair. "Did you do it? Did I miss it?"

I shake my head. "I'm scared."

"We've got you," Conner says, moving closer to me.

"Scooze me." Mila's voice travels through the room as everyone crowds around my chair, my space, my happy place. Her little, dark head bobs through between Conner and Sofie, and she lays her tiny hand on the mouse, taking care not to touch the buttons. "Aunty Lei Lei," she says quietly. "Why are you scared?"

"Well," I say quietly, stroking my hand over her wild hair. "I wrote a story book, and I love it a lot. I'm afraid no one else will."

She tilts her head to the side. "Why?"

"Because I just am, I guess. I don't want anybody to not like my book. The orange button on the screen is the magic button so people can read it, and that's very scary."

"Can I push too?" Mila's wide, innocent eyes calm me, the gentle touch of her hand on my cheek the ultimate relaxant.

"With Uncle Jase?" I ask, looking at him.

"Ready." Jase holds his hand up, wiggling his fingers.

I lay my hand on the mousepad. Jase puts his over mine, and Mila happily lays hers on top of his. Our fingers intertwine until we all have a touch on the left mouse button.

"Leila?" Tate says, stepping up to me, next to Conner.

The twins stand next to him, my best friends between each of them.

"We love that you finally found what made you happy," Tate continues. "And, even if you think this doesn't work, we'll be here for book two, and all the ones that come after. We're proud of you, sis. More than you know."

I close my eyes, warmth threading through my veins.

Jase kisses my cheek, right by my ear, and whispers, "So proud of you. Doing what you love."

I click the mouse.

And I hit publish on the book I wrote and named after everything my family has been through.

Dirty Secret.

The End

Sign up for Emma Hart's New Release Notifications:
http://bit.ly/EmmaHartNewReleaseNotification

Join Emma Hart's reader group:
http://bit.ly/EmmaHartsHartbreakers

Thank you for reading DIRTY LITTLE RENDEZVOUS! I hope you enjoyed Leila and Jase's story as much as I did. If you're new to the Burke family, the brothers' stories are all available as ebooks only for purchase now, across all online retailers.

Dirty Secret - Conner and Sofie
Dirty Past - Tate and Ella
Dirty Lies - Aidan and Jessie
Dirty Tricks - Kye and Chelsey

about the author

By day, New York Times and USA Today bestselling sexy romance author Emma Hart dons a cape and calls herself Super Mum to two beautiful little monsters. By night, she drops the cape, pours a glass of whatever she fancies - usually wine - and writes books.

Emma is working on Top Secret projects she will share with her readers at every available opportunity. Naturally, all Top Secret projects involve a dashingly hot guy who likes to forget to wear a shirt, a sprinkling (or several) of hold-onto-your-panties hot scenes, and addictive, all-consuming love that will keep you up all night.

She likes to be busy - unless busy involves doing the dishes, but that seems to be when all the ideas come to life. This has recently expanded to including vacuuming, a tedious job made much more exciting by the voices in her head.
Naturally, it also takes twice as long to complete.

You can connect with Emma online at:

Website: www.emmahart.org
Facebook: www.facebook.com/EmmaHartBooks
Instagram: @EmmaHartAuthor
Twitter: @EmmaHartAuthor
Pinterest: www.pinterest.com/authoremmahart

Email: emma@emmahartauthor.com / assistant@emmahartauthor.com
Publicity: Danielle Sanchez at dsanchez@inkslingerpr.com
Representation including subsidary rights: Dan Mandel at dmandel@sjga.com

Printed in Poland
by Amazon Fulfillment
Poland Sp. z o.o., Wrocław